The Venom Of

VENGEANCE

To: Marilyn,

A Clovis Belden Series

Volume Two

May God be glorified in all things!

J. ALLAN SMITH

To my wife who always supports me
and to my brother Jerry who patiently endures.

The Venom Of

VENGEANCE

PROLOGUE

"Wren, Wren!!!" I cried. "Wren, where are you?" There was no reply. Panic began to swell up in my throat, and my heart pounded in my chest. "Wren," I screamed. "Oh Lord, please, please help me find her. Don't let her die. Take me instead if you're going to take someone today. Wren!"

The shouting of my own voice awakened me from my sleep. My t- shirt was saturated with perspiration, and beads of sweat erupted upon my forehead. My lungs heaved fast and heavy, as if I had just run a wind sprint. My eyes, wide open, stared at the ceiling above, but I was unable to ascertain what had happened or where I was. My body trembled and shook. In spite of the drenching sweat that continued to erupt from every pore of my body, cold, icy chills coursed through my veins and every fiber of my muscles, like the bitter cold streams flowing from the snowcapped mountain peaks during the spring run-off. For a long moment I lay in the bed trying to determine what had happened, only to realize that I had once again been haunted by the same reoccurring nightmare that had stolen my rest and my sleep for the past three weeks.

A light tap-tap on the door and the voice of my daughter, Heidi, brought me back into the present reality. "Daddy, are you okay?" She asked as she entered into my bedroom and moved closer to my bedside.

Touching me gently on my arm, our eyes met and she asked,

"Were you dreaming again about Mama?"

I smiled weakly and nodded my head in the affirmative.

"Was it the same dream that you have been having for the last month?"

"Exactly," I stated.

Heidi did not know how to respond except to squeeze my forearm and smile back in return.

"Isn't today the day that you are supposed to go fishing with Uncle Mark and Uncle Will?"

"Yup, I guess I had better get up and put on some coffee. They'll be here after a while."

"No, Daddy, you lay here and rest for a moment longer. I'll get the coffee started, and then I'm going back to bed."

While sipping my coffee of the pre-morning dawn, reading the Billings Gazette Newspaper, I chuckled to myself as I noticed that the book about Clovis Belden and the assassination of Vice President Peterson that I had published only 10 months ago was still on the best- seller list, where it has been for the last four months. The irony of it all is that I searched and searched for a publisher that would be willing to pick it up and make a run for it, but over and over I was bombarded with the same rebuttal. No one was really interested in a story that was thirty years old, especially when most of the facts and details of the events could be read in nearly every history book in the nation.

Columbine Publishing was a small, run-of-the-mill, nearly-bankrupt business that needed something to keep them afloat. Fortunately, for me and for them, they made me an offer, and seeing how no one was beating down my door to offer me anything better, I accepted. It took six months to put the story together in book form and to secure a loan from the local bank to pay for marketing and advertising. It was boom or bust for their company and they knew it, but they believed in me and they believed in the story. When the book was finally released, sales went ballistic. Every Wal-Mart, Kmart, and bookstore across the nation had it displayed near the front door. Nook and Kindle were racking up downloads one after the other. Amazon was receiving multiple reviews daily, most of them ranking in the four and five star category. Not all of the reviews were so glamorous, of course. Some were downright distasteful and mean. However, the royalties I was receiving assured that I would not have to work another day in my life if I didn't want to. Of course, while it may have been an option, I could never quit working. I love hard work.

Glancing up from the paper and taking another sip of coffee, my eyes fell upon the bamboo fly rod standing next to the door. The cherished gift seemed to beg and plead me to pick it up and use it. That was precisely my intention. Mark and Will and I were planning a day fly-fishing on the Yellowstone River. The stonefly hatch was on and we anticipated the action we knew awaited us. The weather promised to be clear and mild and although we knew that we should be in the alfalfa field cutting hay that day, we had long since decided that, as much as possible, we would not allow work to interrupt our time spent together doing what we loved to do the most.

Staring at the bamboo fly rod, my mind in a trance, thoughts returned to Clovis. He had given the rod to me on the day that I married his beautiful daughter, Wren. Both of them were gone now, and yet I doubted there was a day that they didn't cross my mind, especially Wren.

Lost in the thought of the moment, a knock on the door brought me back into the present. I went to the door and opened it.

"Good Morning Brothers. Mark, Will." I greeted

"Good Morning to you, Ross. How are you doing?" Will asked as he gave me a shoulder bump and shook my hand, followed by Mark.

"Fine, just fine. You boys care for a cup of coffee?" I asked.

"You bet." The two said in unison.

Taking a seat at the dining room table while I poured a couple cups of hot, rich, black coffee, Mark noticed a copy of my book lying on the table and picked it up.

"How are book sales, Brother?" He inquired.

"Great." I replied. "I couldn't ask for more."

"Is it still on the best seller list?" Will asked.

"Yup."

"Well, I just finished reading it yesterday." Mark stated.

"Do what?" I asked incredulously. "Do you mean to tell me that you have just gotten around to reading it when it has been out this long?"

"Well, shoot, Ross. It's not like I wasn't there and don't recall what happened and all."

Slightly embarrassed, Will cleared his throat "Ross, I admit that I just finished it last week. In fact, while Mark and I were driving over here, we were wondering why you didn't include the events that transpired after Clovis was exonerated."

"Yeah," Mark cut in, "Why didn't you write about the mess we ran into up in the Missouri Breaks while elk hunting the same year President Watson declared Clovis a free man?"

"Or," Mark added, "how about the float trip we took down the Smith River? Shoot, both of those trips still give me the jitters when I think about them. I still don't know how any of us got out of there alive."

"Well, Brothers," I stated while taking another sip of the coffee and burning my lips, "I really didn't think anyone wanted to hear about the events that took place after we got Clovis back out of the Bob. Especially when I let thirty years go by before I even put the story together."

"Hmmm," Mark grunted, "most of the publishers thought no one would want to read your story either, but look at it now, still on the best sellers list. People are falling in love again with Clovis, Ross. Oh, and one other thing, Will and I have noticed that you keep referring to those events taking place 30 years ago. I think you even stated that in your story. Truthfully, we got Clovis out of the Bob 23 years ago this coming August. Think about it. Heidi is only 22 years old and she was born the following year."

I looked at Mark while evaluating his comment but did not respond for a moment while I chewed and contemplated the

4

years. "It sure seems like it's been a lot longer than that."

Mark and Will both looked at me with understanding eyes. They knew how much grief and heartache I had endured through the years, and it has been my observation, that when troubled waters flood your heart and soul for days and months, even years on end, a person has a way of losing track of time. Coupled with the fact that the effects of the excruciating pain and trauma that my body had endured and the abuse of wear and tear, I was feeling the results sooner than a man of my age normally experiences. It appears to me that time just flies by too quickly for most, but in the latter half of my life, time has trudged along rather slowly.

Mark and Will had a good point concerning Clovis, however. It was ironic to think that a story many believed would never get off the ground, let alone take flight, had proven the extreme opposite.

I contemplated the points Mark and Will were making. "Why do you suppose people have attached themselves to Clovis again the way that they have?" I asked.

Will quickly responded. "That's easy, Brother. There are a lot of people who remember what it was like here in this country years ago. They remember the leadership of President Watson and the uncompromising spirit of Clovis, who in the face of standing to lose everything, still stood for what he believed was right. You just don't find that around here anymore."

"This is the way I see it," Will continued, "When the way things ought to be and the way things are, are not one in the same, people will attach themselves to people who represent how it used to be, even if it's only in their memory."

"Yeah, I guess you're right. I hadn't quite thought of it quite like that." I answered.

"Ross," Mark inquired, "listen Brother, you need to let people know what Clovis endured and lived through after he was acquitted. People need to know that being a national hero isn't as glamorous as it's all cracked up to be. Shoot, you know. We were there on both of those trips, and like Will said earlier, it's a miracle that we are alive here today. Why, we've got enough memories of time spent with that man to fill a whole library full of books. And listen, Brother, you have a God-given talent to remember details of events like they had just happened. Oh, and what about conversations you have had with people? You recall them word for word. No one is better suited to write his story than you are."

"Let me chew on it today while we are fishing, and I'll give you an answer this evening." I promised.

Throughout the day, I considered the request of my brothers. I did not take their requests lightly and I was even more stringent on keeping the promises I made. I had finally written the story of Clovis and how he had single-handedly prevented the assassination of President Watson. When the American people learned the truth, Clovis' reputation metamorphosed from a crazy, killing, lunatic to a deeply loved and admired hero. Deep in my heart, I knew that writing more about Clovis would heavily tax my emotions, yet I also knew that there were other people who wanted to know more about the events that followed the exoneration of Clovis.

After perhaps the finest day of fishing that my brothers and I had ever experienced, we loaded back into the truck, and I told them that I would write of the events that transpired throughout the years. I still tremble when I reflect upon how quickly trouble found its way to Clovis, even though he had been pardoned by President Watson.

I have come to the conclusion that the wake we leave in our passing will often return to haunt us again at another time. The reoccurring dream that has been stealing my nights of rest is a powerful testimony to how sharp and deadly the venom of vengeance can sink its fangs deep into the distant future.

CHAPTER 1

The media news coverage of the excavation of Clovis Belden from the Bob Marshall Wilderness went global. Kyle Sooner with CNN interviewed Clovis and me outside of a barn, live before the world, as we, my father, my brothers and Clovis' wife Judy and daughter Wren, had managed to escape death from the hands of those who had conspired to kill us. As Kyle covered the story, including the evidence Clovis and I had collected, the reason for the assassination of Vice President Peterson became clear to the world for the first time in three years. The public's opinion of Clovis Belden metamorphosed from that of being a brutal, lunatic, violent killer to a praised, honored, glorified, national hero. Thinking back to that moment as I now write this so many years later, I remember how Clovis used to quote from the Bible, "And ye shall know the truth and the truth shall make you free." I could not think of another example where that statement was exemplified any clearer than in his case. It just took a little longer for the truth to be revealed than he had hoped.

Within an hour of the live televised broadcast, the FBI were ordered by Chief Officer Mitchell to question and arrest all who had any suspicious involvement with the conspiracy to assassinate the President, including those with in the Federal Bureau of Investigation who, because of their selfish greed for money, had sold their soul to the devil along with members of AFFA (Alternative Fuel For America), who had conspired and persuaded Vice President Peterson to attempt to take President Watson's life in order to expedite the production of ethanol fuel. It was considered to be the greatest scandal within the Federal Government since Watergate. Mitchell had received direct orders from none other than President Watson himself. Heads were going to roll. In fact, several of the FBI agents who were involved in the scandal, turned their own guns on themselves, knowing that they would receive the death penalty. Fearing what might await them while waiting on death row, they decided that there are worse things to experience than dying.

After the televised broadcast, a crew from Malmstrom Air Force Base airlifted Mark and Will by helicopter, back to the top of the Chinese Wall in the Bob Marshall to retrieve the body of our brother, Little Joe, who was flown back home and prepared for burial. Another crew was sent in to bring back the bodies of the men that we had terminated while defending ourselves. I never did find out if they found them all, and really I didn't care.

Dad and I were flown home to the ranch by the FBI. Agent Jonathan Jones was very empathetic to our situation. Although I had given him a pretty sound beating a week earlier, he held no grudge toward me and in fact, became very instrumental in helping us escape. He really took an immediate liking to my father. Something about their personalities seemed to find a place of common ground.

Up until that time, I had never experienced the level or depth of grief as fully as I did when Little Joe had died in his effort to save my life. Although I avenged his death that very same day by taking the life of Kirby, the man who had killed him, I soon discovered that vengeance can never fill the void of loss. I have determined that while vengeance may bring a feeling of retribution, it is only temporary at best, and nothing can replace a loved one that is gone. I would learn that lesson again in the years to come.

The news of Little Joe's death broke my mama's heart. Her spirit was broken. Mama and Little Joe had shared a special bond that was uniquely their own. The mother I knew, always wearing a smile, always cheerful in all kinds of weather and so full of life would never be so again.

We kept the funeral small and private; however, we did allow a few of Joe's friends from high school to attend, but we really did not want to make it public and exploit the affair any more than necessary. Joe's wife and boys flew into Billings and rented a car to attend the funeral. I had offered to pick them up at the airport, but she had made it perfectly clear that she didn't want anything to do with me and blamed me for the loss of her husband. To this day, she still does. My sister flew in from Texas along with her husband that following evening. It was the first time in years that all of us were together in Montana at the same time. I only wish it had been for a brighter occasion.

We buried Little Joe on a high bank overlooking the Stillwater River directly above his favorite fishing hole. Although the day was bright and sunny and beautiful, it was a day of gloom and darkness for the Tyler family. Grief gripped the hearts of all of us and sadness seemed to squeeze at our throats. Very little was said and only the whimpers and wailing of all who loved Joe could be heard. Even the preacher, who had a history of being 'long-winded', struggled to find the words he desired to say as we stood at Little Joe's graveside. My mind seemed to be caught up in a clouded, foggy haze, and nothing I had ever experienced before had left me feeling as empty and void as the loss of Joe. There were so many things I still wanted to tell him and so many things I desired for us to do together, and yet in an instant, the twinkling of an eye, his life was stolen from us. I felt robbed, raped, and stripped naked of everything I considered valuable to me. Even the vengeance that I had successfully attained by killing Kirby did not alleviate or quash the heavy weight of emptiness that ached within my soul.

I stepped to the edge of the bank of the river and looked down into the crystal clear water. It struck me that nothing had changed. The water still flowed, following the course that the river had carved out of the earth thousands of years before. The trout that hovered along the gravel bottom went about their daily business of eating and surviving and stuffing their stomachs with aquatic insects as they fattened up for the coming winter. The realms of nature continued. The loss of Joe did not even bring a hesitation to the pattern or design created by the Designer.

The thought made me consider the frailty of my own life, allowed for a short time to be such a small part of a much grander picture; life was indeed but a vapor. Joe's time had been cut short, and while Joe enjoyed his life, the last few years had led him into the trap that I myself had fallen into. It was the trap that made you believe that more money brought more happiness, but all it had done for Joe and me was lead us further and further away from the passions we so much enjoyed. Our passion for hunting and fishing and the beautiful wild country of Montana had been forsaken. Opportunities to make more money elsewhere had been placed on our plates, and we had both yielded to the temptation, leaving Montana behind and finding that the new life we had pursued, indeed, provided more money, but the money could never satisfy the longing of our souls to return to the life we had grown to love and know so well. Joe would not be given a second chance, but I decided right then and there as I had so many times during the past two weeks that I would not allow myself to be lured into that snare again. I was home in Montana, and I had no desire to leave for any extended period of time. I would make the most of whatever there was that remained. It was a lesson that was resonating in my heart and soul a little bit more each day.

For a moment, I closed my eyes and I could visualize Little Joe, standing knee deep in the river below, casting his fly upon the surface of the water, hoping that a hungry trout would strike. Little Joe was a master with a fly rod. Every movement of his body seemed in harmony with the fly line that torpedoed through the air almost effortlessly and yet as purposeful as a paintbrush in the hands of an artist. Joe didn't know it, but there were many times when I would stop, perhaps hidden in the brush along the river, and just watch and admire the graceful ease he demonstrated with making his fly rod dance the way he did. Although I handled a rod well and caught plenty of fish, I knew I would never be the master of the art such as Joe.

Picking up a small rock, I tossed it into the water. It landed with a splash and the rings that followed quickly dissipated and disappeared along with the flow of the current. Such is life, I thought, so soon gone, and the mark we leave upon its surface is quickly swallowed up and forgotten. Somehow, I did not believe that the mark Joe's life had made upon me would disappear so quickly. I would carry his memory with me to my own grave.

As I looked intently down into the water a nice size cutthroat trout rose to the surface to snatch a caddis fly that was floating on a rippled wave. The cycle of life had just materialized right in front of me. Death happens so life can continue. I made an oath to myself that I would return to this portion of the river as often as I could to cast my fly upon the surface and visit with the memory of my brother Joe.

Clovis, Judy and Wren also attended the funeral and as I continued to stare into the water's depths, I felt Wren's hand gently entangle her fingers in mine. Our relationship, if you could call it that, was only in its infancy at that time. Still, her soft touch and silent presence brought a sense of solace and consolation. Lord knows, I needed it.

The following day, the four of us flew to Washington D.C. to meet with President Watson. I hated to leave my family at home to grieve, and I expressed my concerns to my father. "Son, we'll be all right." He said. "Staying here is not going to bring Little Joe back to us. You should go and be there for Clovis. Your brothers and I will attend to things around here."

After the President had pardoned Clovis of all accusations made against him, he personally invited Clovis to the White House, along with Judy, Wren and me to publicly extend his gratitude before the entire Nation on television. He invited us to join him and his family for a meal, the likes of which I have never witnessed before or since. The Peterson family was nowhere to be seen and I wondered, knowing the relationship the Watsons and Petersons had held for so many years, just what had happened after finding out that Vice President Peterson had actually planned on killing President Watson? I wondered, but I didn't ask. There are some things that are often best left unsaid.

After supper was over, President Watson invited us into his quarters where he desired to speak to us privately.

Behind closed doors, Watson opened, "I really need to be honest with you, and that's why I have called you in here. Mr. Belden, you saved my life, even though you did it by taking the life of the best friend I ever had, or at least, thought I had. I can never repay you for that."

Clovis just bit his lower lip and slightly nodded, and replied, "I am familiar with the emotion you are experiencing to some degree. We just buried Joe Tyler last week. I never met the man, but he showed up because his brother, Ross, here was trying to help me, and in the process, Joe is gone. I am and forever will be indebted to him."

Watson's eyes never left Clovis as he spoke. I remember thinking that this man is so real and so genuine. His full attention was yours when you were engaged in conversation with him. I glanced up at Judy and Wren; their eyes were wet and glassy. They were moved by the naked honesty of both men, who held nothing back as they expressed the sentiments of their hearts.

Watson stood from his seat and stepped toward Clovis who had also risen out of a reverent respect for the man and the office, and Watson again shook his hand and this time, threw his arms around him and hugged him and expressed what words could not possibly say. Then stepping toward me as I too stood, he shook my hand and stated, "Mr. Tyler, please accept my deepest, heartfelt condolences for the loss of your brother Joe."

I firmly grabbed his hand. Now my eyes were full of tears again, and I couldn't seem to find my voice. I finally managed to simply say, "Thank you."

Wren reached up from her seat and took a hold of my hand, an act or jester of support that I was finding to be so comforting. Nothing was said for a moment and then President Watson broke the silence, "There is something that I need to speak to you about today, and I want to do so in private. That's why I have brought you in here. I do not know if you realize what the future holds for you, but your lives will never be the same again. Are you aware of this?"

We all looked at each other, and we were not sure just exactly what Watson was trying to imply.

"Let me explain." Watson continued as he hit the remote that opened a large curtain. Behind the curtain was a screen with a presentation of slides. Another push of the remote and the lights dimmed. The first slide on the screen was a picture of the gate that led into the Belden ranch, as the driveway proceeded up the canyon to the ranch house and quarters adjoining the Bob Marshall Wilderness. "I am sure that this picture is quite familiar to all of you, especially to the Belden family." Watson stated. "After today, your lives will no longer be safe. There will be those who will desire to seek revenge and although many of them are in prison or behind bars or at least will be for a very long time, many of them have a lot of pull on the outside and a lot of money to make just about anything happen they choose to make. Clovis, are you aware that Kirby has 3 brothers?" Watson asked.

"No, Sir, I was not aware of that." Clovis answered.

"Well, he does. The worst one is in a high security prison in Michigan, but is due to be released in less than a year. The other two are also wanted by the law and are at large, and we have no clue where they are hiding. We do believe that they are state-side, but we don't know that for a fact." Watson paused for a minute to let the information soak into our minds.

"Mr. Tyler," addressing me personally, "we do know that Karl, the one in prison, has already laid claims on you and has ordered everyone to leave you alone. At least that's the word as it has been passed along the line. For the time being, you're probably safe, assuming his two other brothers will honor his claim."

13

"It's only been two weeks since we brought Clovis out of the Bob. How could information like that pass so quickly, and how does someone in your position receive word so fast from the interior of a maximum security prison?" I naïvely asked.

Watson smiled. "First, Clovis saved my life. I am indebted to him forever, the way I see it. I will do everything in my power to make sure his life is safe. Second, and I really shouldn't reveal this information to you, but I am going to, simply because I want all of you to try to develop an understanding of the gravity and seriousness of things I am about to discuss with you. So, to answer your question, let me just say this: We have people doing time in prison for crimes they did not commit. When a heinous crime takes place in this country, and we are unable to capture the arbitrator, we sometimes hire someone to take the fall to appease the nation. I know that must sound down-right deceitful and it is. I don't deny it, and I don't like it much myself. However, by doing so, the true arbitrator often relaxes and does something or says something that implicates himself, and we catch him. We then publicly apologize to the fall guy and graciously award him for the mistake. Of course, this is all agreed upon beforehand. While the fall guy is in prison, we utilize them as informants. They reveal information that the FBI and other agencies follow up on. Much of that information deals with terrorism and homeland security."

My jaw nearly dropped to the floor. Having worked in Chicago, I was familiar with the mob and their distasteful approach to accomplishing nearly anything they desired. I didn't feel much better about our own government using some of the same deceptive strategic tactics. I reasoned that such manipulative action could be only justified in an effort to achieve a greater good.

So far, Judy and Wren had not said a word. I was wondering what must have been going on through their minds. The air seemed thick at the moment, but Watson released the tension when he started back again. "Let's get back to the matter at hand. That's your safety and security." Moving to the next slide, Watson displayed a drawing of the same location, but this time with a high stone wall, iron gates, electronic cameras, laser motion devices, and so on. He explained that these would be installed at the entrance to the ranch to provide maximum security. At the ranch house, all information would be monitored through a screen and alarm system when anyone approached the entrance. No one would be able to enter without being detected and would have to have the proper clearance.

The third slide was a satellite photo of the entire ranch with a red marked border to indicate the boundary lines of Clovis and Judy's property. "Here," Watson stated, "We will have surveillance camouflaged cameras hidden along the border of your property. This system alone will cost nearly 5 million dollars to install, which, of course, we will cover all expenses. These cameras are filtered to pick up heat and ultra-violet light at night and are operable to temperatures down to -75 below zero. They are state-of-the-art and even have built in heaters to assure that ice and snow will not accumulate to the lens."

Again, we just sat there in silence. Perhaps the information was too much for us to swallow all at one time, or we were just dumbfounded to think that this was already in the process of consideration, and we did not know a thing about it. I was more inclined to believe that we were each having an extremely difficult time believing that our lives were really in that much danger again.

Watson paused, "Would any of you care for something to drink?"

"I think I'd like a coke or something if you've got it." I requested. Wren agreed, as did Clovis and Judy. Watson pressed a button to an intercom and stated, "Sam, would you bring in a six-pack of bottled coke and a tub of ice?" In less than a minute, Sam entered the room with a cart of cokes and several other flavors of soft drinks along with cookies, cheese sticks and assortment of other finger foods. We helped ourselves and sat back down to listen once again.

"Before we proceed, do you have any questions at this time?" Watson implored.

Judy asked, "Mr. President, do you really think that our lives are in that much danger? I mean, this seems a little extreme to me?" Wren was shaking her head affirmatively agreeing with her mother. The same question was plaguing my mind.

"I figured you would ask." Watson replied as he hit the remote and advanced to the next slide. "Do you know this woman?"

"Isn't that Mrs. Arnold that works at the post office in Augusta?" Wren asked.

"Yes, it is." Judy answered.

"You're both right." Watson interrupted. "We offered Mrs. Arnold a fine retirement package last week and replaced her with one of our field agents."

"Why did you do that?" I asked

"Anthrax!" Clovis blurted.

Watson turned his eyes quickly to Clovis. "Did you already hear about it?" He asked.

"Hear about what?" Clovis asked in return. "Did something happen?"

"The day before yesterday our agent found an envelope addressed to you and ran it through the scanner as she has been doing to all of your mail. It tested positive, and our specialists are trying to locate prints, evaluate the handwriting, checking the history trail to determine where it might have been sent from and swabbing for anything that might provide a DNA sampling. Nothing has shown up so far, so we know that we are dealing with a professional. Does this eliminate any doubt to the magnitude of your situation?"

I felt myself getting sick. The mere thought of the Belden's living like caged animals, in danger constantly both inside the cage and even more so outside of the cage was nauseating to me.

Clovis stated, "That doesn't sound much like a life if you ask me."

"No, Sir, it does not." Watson reiterated. "There are other options, and I want to share those with you too, but before I do, there is also something that I want you to consider. When you leave here to go back home, if that is what you decide to do, you'll be wanted by every television talk show in the country. This country loves you Clovis. I do too for that matter. You represent so much of the values that this country was founded upon. Your faith in God to lead and direct your life is an inspiration to millions. That includes me. It is my personal opinion that your voice needs to be heard, and it needs to ring throughout every household in every city and every state. People long for someone who has no tolerance for evil and refuses to compromise their principles no matter how demanding or costly the sacrifice. We can make that happen."

"But, Mr. President, you're a man of principle, and everyone knows that you're a God-fearing, Bible-believing, truly wonderful man." Wren strongly suggested. "Can't the nation simply find that in you?"

"Thank you, Wren. I appreciate the compliment. I am very much like your father in that regard, but unlike your father, I am often bound hand and foot to bureaucracy. Your father here doesn't have that albatross around his neck. Besides, I must say, that right now, although the polls are weighing heavy in my favor, I will admit that having a man like your father on my side will pretty much clinch up my opportunity for re-election." We all chuckled and for certain it was needed.

After a brief pause, President Watson advanced to the next slide, which again was another satellite photo of the Belden Ranch. "The three circles you see on the photograph image are the areas of the three highest elevations on your ranch." I noticed Clovis slightly bobbing his head up and down in concurrence with the statement. I also noticed that he kept running his fingers through his long gray beard and rubbing his chin. He was worried. There was more here at stake than his personal life, and the whole situation was bigger than him. I wasn't exactly sure what thoughts he was pondering, but if they were anything like my own, they weren't good.

Watson continued, "On these three points we have our newest radar systems that we can install. They function both laterally and vertically and are capable of detecting anything larger than 50 pounds. What this does is to help us detect anyone who thinks that they might decide to parachute out of the sky to infiltrate your ranch. Clovis, I am sure you are very well aware of how effective that tactic is, considering your assignments in Viet Nam."

Clovis just nodded.

Judy and Wren, I observed, kept moving their eyes from the screen and looking at Clovis. It occurred to me that their thoughts and their opinions, although certainly welcome, would fall in behind whatever Clovis decided to do. They completely trusted his judgment. He was definitely the leader of their household and obviously took the assignment seriously.

"Mr. President, you mentioned other options. I do believe that I've seen enough of this option at least to get a general idea of what it will take to allow us to continue living on our ranch and to try to get our lives back to normal. It seems like an awful waste of the taxpayers' money if you ask me."

Watson cleared his throat. "Ok, I'll show you the next option, but let me make myself perfectly clear. Your lives will never be normal again. It's imperative that you keep that in mind. Even if we provide you with top-of-the-line protection, you'll find that going anywhere will be a chore, and living as reclusive as you possibly can will be the safest and surest means of survival."

Advancing through a few more slides, Watson stopped at Option #2. "This option is the most often chosen by people who, like you, are or have become a high security risk. With this option, we relocate you out of the country to any place in the world you want to go. It's very similar to a witness protection program, but of course, you're not witnesses awaiting a trial to testify. We change your names, your social security numbers, and your financial records and move your money to foreign exchange banks, and if you wish we could cosmetically alter your appearance. We provide you with a fine home to live in and a large income to sustain you for the rest of your lives. The one caveat to this option is that you can never come back to the States, not even to visit. You cannot call or write. Those means of communication are too easy to track and forfeit the entire design of the program. It's not 100% bullet proof, but it's the safest alternative we have."

Studying the nonverbal cues of Clovis again, I could tell that option did not sit well with him, and I had just figured out the reason when he spoke and made it perfectly clear.

Clovis stood up from his seat and articulated the man I have always known him to be. "Mr. President. I am an American citizen. This land is my home. This land wears my sweat, blood and tears and a whole lot of them. This land is the home of my father and his father, and I wear that heritage like a badge of honor. The land I am standing on is the land I fought for overseas. To guard against the grips of communism, I fought to defend a country I wasn't even attached to. And I did so because I am bound by honor as a citizen of this country to protect the liberty and freedoms we enjoy." Pausing for a few seconds he reopened again, "And this land is the land I most recently sacrificed three years of my life for, living in a cave in the wilderness with a million dollar bounty on my head and an endless army of greedy people trying their best to collect it, because I found myself in a situation where the highest office in the country was threatened, and there was no one else at the moment to assure that heinous deed did not transpire. I did that because I love this country, and it takes great leadership to make the kind of nation we are today. Now, not only does leaving this land that I have loved and fought for rub me in all the wrong directions, but it seems a bit hypocritical for me to go off and leave it like some scalded dog with his tail between his legs after I've given so much to protect it."

By the time Clovis had finished, he had worked himself into frenzy. It was, I believe, the first time that I had ever really witnessed Clovis getting riled. There was no doubt in my mind that Clovis stood solid on his principles. The moral fiber that coursed his veins was unbreakable. President Watson's eyes staying glued on Clovis, he approached him and extended his hand, his eyes wet and glassy. "Mr. Belden, God grant it that we had more men like you in this country." They shook hands again. Judy and Wren were smiling, their chests swollen with pride for Clovis. Wren reached over and squeezed my hand again, confirming the confidence she had in her father. Obviously, she was not too acute on the second option either.

"Is there another option?" Judy asked.

President Watson shook his head affirmatively, hesitating to mention it, but finally relented. "There is another option, but it is a long shot at best. Now, I'm not saying that it won't work; I'm just saying that we've never actually really tried it, although Mr. Belden, you used it pretty effectively yourself for a while." I wasn't quite too sure what President Watson was alluding to, but was soon to find out. "However," Watson moved on, "if it does work, it holds the possibility of providing you with the security you desire and an opportunity to go about your business as usual or something like it anyway. As I said, your lives will never me normal again."

"Let's hear it." Wren demanded.

"All right then, but let's take a short break." Watson spoke into the intercom, "Curtis, Jim," is all that he said. Two secret service men entered the door and stood at the entrance. Watson showed us the restrooms and then stepped into another room and disappeared for ten minutes or so. After we had all stretched and taken a nature break, we resumed again.

"The third option goes like this." Watson remotely dimmed the lights and returned to the screen. On the screen was a picture of a wrecked airplane. "Not all of the details have been hammered out, so I am going to do my best to paint a scenario of what I and my advisors suggest within the confinements of this option. This option proposes that Clovis goes on tour for six months. Right now the press is chomping at the bit to get to him." Judy and Wren chuckled and smiled. The fact that the President of the United States would use such back-woods terminology actually elevated their opinion of him. Proceeding, Watson continued, "I do not know if you ladies realize it or not, but we have gone to great extents to try to keep your faces from the cameras. The more we can protect your identity the better. I remembered that I had wondered why Judy and Wren had not been asked to be present with Clovis when he spoke on National Television. I had not given consideration to the fact that the President was doing his best to keep their physical identity obscured in an effort to protect them.

President Watson had paused for a moment to let the idea sink into the minds of the Belden family, but when he received no response, he continued. "Now, back to where I left off. Clovis would have the opportunity to speak to America in his down-to-earth fashion that just fits him for who he is. We of course would provide protection for him, and we would also have our press conference committee prep him to the types of questions he is sure to be bombarded with. During this time, we install the security system to your ranch as was detailed in option #1. Now, here's where things get tricky. Six months into your tour the three of you are tragically killed in an airplane crash. Full media coverage will exploit the catastrophic event, a private memorial will be held in your honor. I, of course will attend, and in a month you will be forgotten. Of course, this still limits the amount of time you can spend away from the ranch, and it calls for a change in personal appearance, such as shaving your beard, Clovis, or a new style to your hair Judy and Wren. It would also mean that somewhere down the road, the deed to your land would have to be sold, which we can make to look legitimate on paper, but carry no legal weight with it whatsoever. As I said, we are just considering this as an option, and have not fully explored all the details and possibilities."

"Mr. President," Clovis stated abruptly, "I do not want to appear rude, but as for tonight, I believe my poor brain has about taken all that it can absorb. If it is all right with you, these are things we would like to have a little time to consider and discuss among ourselves. Right now, I'm doing well just to stay awake."

"Certainly," replied Watson. Perhaps we can discuss these things further tomorrow after you've had time to consider them and get a good night's rest. We have rooms already prepared for you. I do believe that you will find everything to your satisfaction, but if you don't, don't hesitate to say so. We will accommodate you by every means possible."

Watson led us to the door where we were ushered to our private rooms. I was given a room to myself.

While working for the Chicago Tribune, I had been sent to cover stories all over the country on many occasions, although most of my work involved the local news. I was often put up in some very luxurious hotel rooms, but nothing I had ever slept in compared to this. It was spotlessly clean and absolutely enormous. I found it amusing, however, that I was very much ready to return home to Montana and sleep in my normal bed. In fact, a sleeping bag thrown out underneath the stars in that immense Montana sky seemed more appealing to me at the moment. I chuckle to myself as I write this. Even after all these years have passed, I find it amusing that I would still rather toss a sleeping bag on the ground or lean my back up against my old saddle close to a campfire and cover up with a sleeping bag than to crawl in between the finest sheets ever fitted to a hotel bed.

As I lay beneath the slick, cool, satin sheets I was wondering what Clovis and Judy and Wren were thinking. Certainly, they were still up discussing the options that President Watson had presented. I wondered too if I was going to be a part of the picture. Was I going to be included in the grand scheme of things, a part of their plans, or did the seriousness of the situation demand that, for the safety of their own lives, I would no longer be permitted to be a part of their company? Honestly, I wasn't sure just where I stood. Looking back now, it amazes me how much uncertainty clouds the mind of a man. My feelings for Wren were strong, and I was certain hers for me were just as much so, but the situation demanded a decision that would affect all of them collectively and I wasn't sure if there was room for me as well. Nothing had been said that would indicate a feeling either way. On one side, it stood to reason that I was not to be taken as even a serious consideration. Wren and I had spent very little time together and not really enough to be regarded as anything serious. Again, my feelings for her were undeniably strong, but we hadn't even spent enough time together nor had the opportunity to discuss any future plans. We had buried Little Joe just a little more than a week before and had been together during those moments of grief, but as far as really dating and getting to know one another, we had not had the luxury of walking down that trail together yet.

Wrapped in my own thinking, my thoughts were interrupted by a light tapping on the door. Grabbing a bathrobe I put it on as I was only wearing my boxer shorts and quietly opened the door. Wren stepped into the dark room.

"Ross, can I sleep with you tonight?" She asked.

"Uh, well, uh, I guess, sure." I stammered, slightly surprised and a little embarrassed.

"Oh, not like that. I won't do that until we're married." She rebutted, lightly slapping me on the arm. "I just want you to hold me. There are a lot of things on our minds, and I need you to just hold me. These are life changing decisions my family must make, and it's difficult to know what to do."

Well, I guess she answered my question. She had it in her mind that the two of us were going to tie the knot. That meant that whatever the Belden family decided to do would directly involve me. I wondered if she had expressed her feelings to her parents.

Wren crawled into the covers and curled up next to my side, her hand upon my chest. Her clean body and perfume were intoxicating. I felt as if I could never get enough and believed in my heart that I never would.

As I held her close, both of us silent, except for the beating of our hearts, I asked her, "What option do you believe your father will take?" Wren replied, "I believe he'll choose option #4."

"But there wasn't an option #4." I rebutted.

Wren leaned up on her elbow and looked me in the eyes, her long hair falling across my face and gently kissed me on the lips, "Oh, but option #4 existed before the other options were ever discussed."

"Well, what is it?" I asked.

"We do nothing. We go home, and we get back to living and running the ranch. That's option #4, and that's what mom and I figured Dad would choose in the first place. He only listened to President Watson's suggestions to see how serious he was and just how far they were willing to extend themselves for our protection. I do believe Dad is going to request a new gate at the entrance of the property with a remote controlled device for entering and exiting the ranch, but beyond that, he doesn't want anymore."

I considered what Wren had just shared. "Aren't you concerned for your safety and your family's safety?" I asked.

"I'll let dad discuss his reasoning tomorrow when we meet again with President Watson. You'll see why he believes this to actually be the best choice."

"Wren, I'm going to fly back to Montana in a couple of days. I need to get home to Mom and Dad. They do not need to be there alone to suffer through this period of grief over the loss of Little Joe. I spoke with them today on the phone, and they told me that Mark and Will have flown back to Tennessee and are packing up their belongings. They figure to take Dad up on his offer to come back and work the ranch and hope to be up there in a couple of weeks."

"I thought you might say that. Mom and I will be home in a week or so. I'll let you know. Will you come up and see me when I get back?" Wren asked.

"Oh, I'll have to think about it," I jested.

Wren smacked me on the chest as we both chuckled.

Lying there, I could not recall ever feeling so comfortable in the presence of another human being. It was as if the two of us had been created for each other and yet, again, I knew so little about Wren.

"Wren, how old are you?" I asked when it suddenly dawned on me that I did not know.

"How old do you think I am?"

"I'm guessing about thirty." I answered. "Do I look like I'm thirty?"

"No. Your skin and soft complexion make me think you're only about twenty, but you carry yourself in a manner that, well, I don't know, I guess just portrays a greater maturity level than what you would see in a twenty-year old."

"I'm twenty-five." Wren replied.

"It does not bother you that I am ten years older than you?" I implored.

"Not in the least."

Pausing for a moment to contemplate her response, I finally stated, "Wren, it might be a little early to say this, because when you consider things objectively, we've really not spent a whole lot of time together, but I feel more certain about this than anything I've ever known. I love you."

Wren buried her face in the nap of my neck and whispered, "I love you too, Ross Tyler." That was the first of many times I heard Wren say those three words. As I write this, it occurs to me that I never did grow tired of hearing them. One thing is for certain, even after all these years I still love her too.

CHAPTER 2

The next morning after breakfast had been served, we were ushered once again into President Watson's private chambers where he was busy reading the Washington Post. Upon entering the room, he immediately stood and moved to greet each one of us individually. For a man who held the highest position in the world, he was cordial, hospitable and humble. It occurred to me at that moment that every time I was in his presence, it was much like getting a breath of fresh, clean air.

After ascertaining that all of us had found the accommodations suitable and had eaten enough for breakfast, Watson got right to the point. "So, have you given any consideration to the options we discussed last night?" He asked.

Clovis answered, "Yes, sir, we have. I have decided to take option #4."

Watson looked at Clovis in bewilderment, baffled by the response, but did not ask.

Clovis continued, "Sir, this is the way I see it. While you are able to secure the perimeter of my property with the highest level of security you have to offer, that does nothing for my family and me beyond the boundary of my property. Let me explain. When I was in Nam, I took out a colonel at over a thousand yards At that time, there were not a dozen men in this world that could have made that shot. Now, considering the technology we have, and our modern day weaponry, that shot could be made at twice that distance. If someone wanted to sit and wait outside the boundary of our property, your security system is not going to stop a bullet from crossing the border." Watson shook his head affirmatively, understanding very well the point Clovis was making. "Second," Clovis pressed on, "when you leave the entrance of our ranch, there is a mile of gravel road before we even get to the main highway. A sniper could lie in wait there just as easily or for that matter, place a land mine along the road. In other words, this government could spend millions of dollars and still not prevent what might or might not happen anyway. Thirdly, I just can't see myself living like a recluse, scared of my own shadow for the rest of my life. Now, that doesn't mean I won't be keeping my eye looking over my shoulder, but my wife and daughter here both agree; we want to go home and live as much of a normal life as we possibly can."

"Well, you've made a pretty tight case. I worked as a lawyer for years in Atlanta, and I don't think that I could refute this one. You'll have the gate finished before the week is over."

Watson convinced Clovis to speak with the press that same afternoon, and we all decided we would fly back to Montana the following day. I booked a flight to Billings while the Beldens would catch a flight from there to Great Falls. To this day, I will never forget that first time Clovis spoke to the press. Of course, I have it recorded and have listened to it hundreds of times.

Clovis wore his wranglers and a nice plaid, western-cut shirt. His hair was put back in a ponytail and actually tucked in behind the collar of his shirt. His beard was lightly trimmed and groomed. The press committee had tried to convince him to wear a suit and tie, but he wasn't having any part of that. They did manage to get him to wear a sports jacket along with his wranglers and boots. To say the least, he looked pretty sharp.

As Clovis approached the press box, cameras flashed and the lights shined so bright in his eyes I noticed he was squinting. He turned back and politely asked the camera crew if they could dim the lights, which they did so immediately. I wondered if Clovis had ever spoken in front of a large audience. He tapped on the microphone to make sure it was working and stood there silently while the crowd of hungry reporters began to slowly hush their clamoring and then he began.

"Before I answer any questions this evening, I'd like to say a few things first, and then I will try to answer your questions one at a time. Are we all in agreement with that?" He asked. The crowd responded positively.

"First, I'd like to thank my wife Judy for believing in me and not running off with some other guy while I was playing mountain man in the wilderness." The crowd roared with laughter. "I'd like to thank my daughter for all that she did behind the scene to make my evacuation and rescue possible. I'd like to thank Mr. Ross Tyler for believing in me, even though we had never met, and I'd especially like to extend my appreciation and my gratitude to his father and brothers and especially to Mr. Joe Tyler who lost his life in an effort to help bring me to exoneration. Finally, and most importantly, I'd like to thank Jehovah God for not only caring for me, but for my family for all of these years. I am indebted to Him beyond measure."

A moment of calm, tranquility, and peace fell across the audience as Clovis paused. There seemed to be a reverent spirit in the air that could only be expressed in silence and hung there for a few moments. Clovis then began. "I am an American citizen. Native to this country, I have worked my living in the soil of this great land. I have fought to keep us free from the expanding grip of communism during our conflict in Viet Nam. I believe in the fundamental principles upon which this country was built and what our founding forefathers saw fit to establish in our great Constitution. I even pay my taxes and don't try to cheat our government, although we all know they get more than their fair share." Again, the crowd exploded in laughter. "I do these things because I love this country, and I believe we are the greatest nation on the entire face of this planet. I make no apologies for that. Are there things we have done that perhaps we should have done differently? Yes. Are there things for which we ought to be ashamed? Yes. God forbid that we don't ever feel shame and remorse when we make the wrong call or find our leaders supporting unethical conduct. Still, for all that we are and all that we are not, we are human, and as one great spokesman once said, 'to err is human'

"The events of three years ago, when I made the choice to take the life of Vice President Peterson to spoil his opportunity to assassinate President Watson was a choice that I have had to live with every single minute of every single day. Many of you are probably wondering if I regret making that choice and the answer is unequivocally 'yes'. Although I was but a lad and still wet behind the ears, many of you remember and history will prove me out on this, that when our beloved John F. Kennedy was assassinated in Dallas years ago, our nation underwent the greatest emotional and financial upset that we have ever known throughout the history of this great country. At a time when we are finally finding faith in our leadership once more, we were not ready for that kind of upset again. I hate that I killed Mr. Peterson. I regret it with all of my heart, and I will carry that burden with me to the grave, but if I had to do it all over again and once again, I was the only one at the time to foil the plan, I would do it. That's how much I love this country." The crowd came to their feet roaring and applauding. He had touched a nerve, a nerve that had long needed to be touched. Clovis had captivated their hearts. I believe he did so, not just because of what he had to say, but because he was so solid and sure and confident and most of all, he was real. There was no hoopla about him. He didn't pretend to be something that he was not, and deep in the hearts of the crowd was an admiration for the man that could not be denied.

As the crowd settled and returned to their seats, Clovis stated, "I will be happy at this time to try to answer your questions as long as you are nice about it." The crowd immediately began raising their hands. Clovis continued, "But, as I was saying, if you have a question to which I refuse to comment, I will say it one time. If you try to press me further, then all questioning is over and I am done. If we can agree on that, then let us continue."

Clovis pointed to an elderly man who sat quietly, but had his hand risen. "Sir, do you have a question?" Clovis asked.

"Yes sir, Mr. Belden. You mentioned earlier that you regretted taking the life of Mr. Vice President Peterson, although you deemed it necessary to protect President Watson. Can you explain in further detail why you regret taking Mr. Peterson's life?"

Clovis paused for a moment, took a deep breath and slowly exhaled. The crowd was silent, and then Clovis addressed the man eye to eye as if no one else was in the room. "I loved Mr. Peterson. He seemed to be a man of honor and dignity from all appearances, and truthfully, I think he was exactly that kind of man. Mr. Peterson was drawn away by the greed for money and the lust for power, and personally, I don't think anyone of us is immune to that kind of temptation. My deepest regret and sorrow lies in the fact that I made a widow out of his wife and made their children fatherless." There was a crackle in the voice of Clovis. The crowd hung on his words.

"Next question…."

A young attractive lady asked, "Mr. Belden, your military history was made public and portrayed an image of you as being a brutal killer during your term in Viet Nam, yet here today, you do not appear brutal or vicious by any stretch of the imagination, but rather, gentle, confident, humble and compassionate. How do you manage to separate the contrast between the two?"

"I served my country to the best of my ability, engaging the enemy by using tactics that required every ounce of stealth and concealment I could muster. Making a single mistake would be lethal. I have found that a man will do what he has to do and become good at doing it or he will die. I had to develop this mindset all over again as a fugitive of the law these past three years. I do not consider myself a brutal or vicious man. I find no joy in killing. The assignments I completed in Viet Nam were much easier to justify because it was war. Taking the life of Vice President Peterson, the second highest office in this great land, in order to protect the highest office in the land, was much more difficult. Like I said earlier, I still believe that I made the right decision, but I regret that I had to make it."

Mr. Belden," someone spoke up. "It's been rumored that a million dollar bounty was on your head while you remained at large. Did anyone ever try to collect?"

Oh, that was a tough question. It was a question that I had danced around with Clovis while talking to him in the cave while I recovered from my wounds after being tortured. Clovis, however, did not elaborate on the subject and quickly moved to another subject in our discussion. I was curious how he would respond now before the press.

"To answer your question, yes, there was a million dollar bounty on my head, and yes, there were many who tried to collect, but as I stated earlier to the previous question, a man will do what he has to do in order to survive."

"How many tried to collect on that bounty?" Someone from the crowd shouted.

"I refuse to comment." Clovis answered abruptly.

A middle-aged man started to press the subject, but quickly received an elbow as a reminder that Clovis had made it perfectly clear that if he refused to answer or comment, that was it.

"Mr. Belden, Sir. Will we ever know the details of exactly what happened in the Bob Marshall Wilderness and how you were rescued?"

Clovis replied, "I have given Mr. Ross Tyler and him alone the permission to write the story. If and when he chooses to do so, I am sure that all of your questions and concerns will be answered."

"Mr. Belden, can you explain why you choose to hunt animals with weapons of such a primitive nature?"

Clovis chuckled. "I am sure," he stated, "that there are many in this room who do not understand hunting, and I am not going to take the time to tell you why I hunt. If you are a hunter, there's no explanation necessary. Why I choose to hunt with a longbow and arrows that I have crafted myself, is simply because I enjoy the challenge. I will be honest with you; I don't hunt because my family

31

needs the meat, although we do eat everything I bring home. Shoot, I've got nearly a thousand head of prime Black Angus beef that I raise on my ranch. I don't hunt for the meat. I hunt because I love the challenge of meeting a wild creature on his own turf up close and personal. Sometimes I am successful; most of the time I am not. That's why they call it hunting. Along with that, I am completely passionate about the Rocky Mountains, and I am especially partial to the ranges of Montana. It is one thing to drive through them on the highway, as I am sure many of you have before, but it's a completely different world when you step off the asphalt and move into them and experience all the wild grandeur that our Creator has blessed us with." Clovis was on a roll. I could see the sparkle and gleam in his eyes as he shared his passion and obsession for what he loved the most.

"Have you ever heard a ruffed grouse beating its wings during the spring mating season or a turkey gobble on some nearby ridge, or an elk bugle in some deep, dark wooded canyon in mid-September? Have you listened to a campfire crackle and pop deep in the wilderness and heard a wolf howling in the distance as you stared into the flames? Have you ever watched the bighorn sheep or mountain goats scale a cliff that defies all logic or witnessed a sow grizzly playing with her cubs on some grassy meadow filled with wildflowers? These are the things I've grown up with and continue to admire, and truthfully, I haven't even touched the surface. But here's a question for you? Where else in the world can a man have the liberty and freedom to enjoy these kinds of things than right here in America? It's the only life I've ever known. It's the only life I'll ever want to know. It's the life that I would sacrifice my own to keep." Again, the crowd was on its feet.

"Mr. Belden! Mr. Belden! What are your plans for the future?"

The crowd hushed again. Clovis simply looked out across the audience, a glimmer of tear in his eyes, but a smile on his face. "I'm going home. Thank you. God bless America." Clovis waved and turned from the podium and walked out the back door.

CHAPTER 3

I parted ways with Clovis, Judy and Wren at the Billings airport as they flew on to Great Falls where they would then drive on to their ranch outside Augusta. I told Wren that I would come and see her in a week or so because I needed to spend time with my parents. Knowing that grief is often felt and experienced the deepest a week or two after a death, I figured Mom and Dad might appreciate some company.

My sister, Joe's wife and kids had all flown back to Texas. Mark and Will were back in Tennessee trying to pack and get ready to move home to Montana, but I didn't expect them for at least another week, maybe two.

When I arrived home, I realized that my fears had been correct. Dad seemed to be managing all right or as well as could be expected, but Mom was in a bad way. Dad told me that he couldn't get her to eat. He had taken her to see the doctor who had prescribed some medicine to cope with the depression, but he couldn't tell that it was really working. Mom's eyes were sunken and were encompassed with large dark black circles. She had lost weight, more than she needed to.

I tried to comfort her by every means I could. She always seemed like she was cold, and I would bring her a blanket and a hot cup of tea. "Thank you, Ross. I sure do love you. You're a good boy, you know." She looked at me through distant eyes. "I wish Joe would call. I haven't heard from him in a long time."

"Mama, Joe's gone." I told her. "He's gone. He's never

going to call. We just have to keep pressing on, Mama. Joe loved you very much. It would tear his heart out to see you like this."

Mama wept.

There did not appear to be any signs of improvement. I called Wren and told her that it would be another week before I was able to come up and see her, but I guess she decided that was too much time to be apart. She showed up at our ranch the following afternoon. I must admit, I was quite elated to see her.

Right away, Wren jumped in and helped by doing all the things that women seem to do so much better than men. She cleaned the house and washed the dishes and prepared the meals. She dusted and polished and placed vases of wildflowers in the house. She managed to find some Indian Paint Brush that had not wilted in the early autumn frost, still growing on the hillside just out beyond the barn, and she put them on the nightstand beside Mama's bed. They were Mama's favorite.

Wren stayed for a week and had to get back home. Clovis and Judy were flying to Los Angeles where Clovis had a number of speaking engagements with several television talk show hosts, and Wren needed to be home to look after the chores on the ranch. I told her that I would stay and help Dad with his ranch and look after Mama until Mark and Will got back from Tennessee. President Watson's assigned crew was almost finished with the new entrance into the Belden Ranch with all of the security that it could provide, although there had not been a whisper of threat from anyone. The incoming mail was still being sifted and scanned to ensure safety for Clovis and his family. Other than some hate mail from animal activist groups because of their scorn for hunting, most of it was fan mail encouraging Clovis to keep up the good work of standing for the principles on which this country was founded.

Dad and I worked the ranch and made sure the fence was in good shape for winter. It would not be long when we would head for the high country and bring the cows back to the valley where we would feed them and look after them during the long winter months. We had plenty of hay put up, and things were looking good.

One morning, almost a week after Wren had left to go home, Dad asked me to saddle up and go for a ride with him after he had looked after Mama. I knew something was on his mind and he needed to get it off his chest. We rode up to the old homestead where we had almost lost Little Joe when he had broken his leg while checking his traps in a severe winter storm one Christmas Eve. Dad didn't say much on our ride there, but when we reached the old house, he dismounted and pulled some papers out of his saddlebags and invited me to step over and sit beneath the shade of an old cottonwood on a picnic table we had put there years ago.

Spreading the map out on the table, we placed small rocks on the corners of the map to keep the wind from blowing it away. Looking at the map, it was a map of his ranch, and it was divided into three parts with a red marker. I noticed that it had been divided into four parts, but had been altered and reconfigured, now that Little Joe would no longer be a part of the inheritance.

"This section right here where we are standing with this old farmhouse is yours. It is not as large as the two sections that I am giving to Mark and to Will as you see their property is here," indicating with his finger the portions of the ranch that were to be theirs. "However, your grandfather, as you well know, built this house. It has good bones, and it's still solid and could be fixed up real nice. It will be a great place for you and Wren to raise a passel of children." I smiled and lightly chuckled to myself. He slapped me up along the shoulder and asked, "You are going to marry that girl aren't you?"

"Well, Dad, what makes you think she'll have me?" I asked.

Dad laughed mockingly out loud in his own funny way. "Son, a girl don't come down and take care of your mama the way she has all week when she's got work at home she needs to tend to if she didn't love you. Now, I'm not telling you what to do, Son, but if I were you, I'd slide a ring onto that finger as soon as you can. Heaven knows you aren't going to find a better one anywhere, and I may be an 'old man' but I ain't blind. She's as pretty as the morning sunrise."

Dad was right, of course, and I knew it. I knew from the first evening Wren and I spent together in Chicago that I had never met a girl more beautiful and compatible and charming in all my life. So far, everything about her appealed to me in a way I had never experienced before. Yet, I was hesitant. I wasn't sure why I wasn't pursuing a deeper relationship with her more aggressively. At first, I reasoned that perhaps my reluctance was founded in fear. Perhaps I was afraid to fall too fast, thinking if I was too pushy I might run Wren off, but I quickly determined that was really not the reason. I think that I was still mesmerized by the idea that such a beautiful creature could be attracted to the likes of me. Even as I write this after all these years, Wren's perfect smile and gleam in her eyes whenever we were together visits my mind with pleasant memories.

Obviously, caught in a trance, Dad was looking at me right in the eye. "Son," he stated for the second time, although I didn't cognitively acknowledge it the first time.

"Are you all right?"

"Sorry, Dad. I was just thinking about what you were saying."

"Well, you *should* be thinking about it, but I wouldn't allow myself to get stuck in the thinking process for too long if I were you. It's time you lock in the hubs, put it in four-wheel drive and get in gear. A girl like her isn't going to wait around too long." Dad chuckled again, but there was a glint of seriousness in the wisdom he had just shared. He threw his arm around my neck and squeezed me without saying a word and then turned back to the map. "Now, how do you feel about this piece of property?" He asked as he looked down toward the river and waved his arm in a sweep, indicating the piece he was giving to me.

I shook my head, understanding what he was saying and was by no means upset or disappointed by the fact that the section he was giving to me was about 300 acres smaller than my brothers' land.

"The real reason I want you to have this property is because you and Little Joe were the closest, and this part, as you obviously already know, includes his gravesite down on the river. I want you to promise me that you'll bury your mama beside Joe when it comes her time. She has asked me to request that of you. Too, when it comes my time to go, I want you to bury me beside your mama."

Dad looked up at me; his eyes were glass coated with tears. "Son, your mama isn't going to last very long if she can't get past this depressed state that she is in. You need to prepare yourself for that." Dad's lips quivered and his eyes quickly diverted toward the horizon to the west.

"Yes, Sir." I struggled to reply.

After a long silent pause as Dad was trying to grab a hold of his composure, he said, "You know, I put my life on the line, time and time again to rescue and save those wounded boys over there in Nam. It was something that I was willing to die for. I never did get shot down, although I had many close calls, and as you learned from Clovis, I took a bullet for him. After a while, you get to feeling like there isn't anything you can't do. It's almost like you feel indestructible on one hand and capable of accomplishing whatever you wish to accomplish on the other. Now, here I am, and I feel totally helpless concerning your mother. Over the course of time I have concluded that the feeling of helplessness is by far the most despairing emotion a man can experience."

As I write this now, I had no idea just how correct my father's statement would reiterate in my life during the years come. I would learn exactly what he meant years in the future.

"Let's saddle up and ride into the high country." Dad stated.

"You bet." I eagerly responded.

All day long we rode side by side. Dad shared stories of his time in Viet Nam, flying his helicopter in and carrying the wounded back to the mobile army hospitals where they could be treated. His memory was so vivid and clear that when he told the stories, it was almost as if I was at the scene watching the entire episode transformed before my own eyes. I had never heard these stories and knew nothing of his assignment in Viet Nam until just a month earlier. It was then that he promised that he would tell me more about his active role in the war when the time was right. True to his promise, he was doing that very thing at the moment.

As we traveled across the ranch and then into the wilderness area of the Absaroka-Beartooth Mountains, the terrain of the land changed dramatically from rolling hills and plains with deep coulees and ravines to steep, pine covered mountainsides, then to granite peaks that pierced high into the deep ocean-blue Montana sky, some with peaks that still remained covered in snow. It's just one of the many splendid wonders of Montana that I have grown to cherish. The diversity of the terrain is unique, and it can change or transform so abruptly, especially in the western part of the state. A person can navigate through the low desert canyon lands, across the wheat and barley covered farm land, to the ridges and coulees into the high plains and plateaus into the deep pine forested hills and top out in the alpine meadows beneath the jagged, snow-covered cathedral peaks in one good day on horseback. I've never grown tired of it.

"Dad, there's something you need to know." I commented as we had stopped to let the horses blow and catch their breath. "President Watson tells me that Kirby's brother, Karl, is in prison and has vowed to kill me when he gets out. That's still a year out from right now. He has two other brothers though, and according to Watson, they are wanted by the law and are at large. Now, as to whether they will honor Karl's vow or not, I do not know. They may decide to take vengeance into their own hands. I tell you that so if in the event you see someone hanging around, be careful."

Dad reached down from his saddle and pulled a timothy stalk and put it in his mouth and began chewing on it. "I'll be on the watch." He stated. He didn't seem too disturbed. It was then that I wondered if I had ever witnessed fear in my father. Surely, there must have been a moment when he was afraid, but try as I may, I could not recall a single incident. I had seen him worried on several occasions but never afraid. As I looked at him, sitting in the saddle, chewing on the end of the timothy stalk, while he gazed out across the endless ocean of mountains before us, it occurred to me that I really didn't know the man. Oh, I knew that he loved us and knew what he stood for and what he stood against. I was very much aware of his compassion and gentleness and at the same time, I knew his expectations. My backside knew the sting of his belt when I violated his rules of operation within the family, but I also knew the feel of his strong arms around me when he demonstrated his love toward me. Until recently, he had never verbalized his love toward his children, but that had changed following the death of Little Joe.

As I sat there in the saddle, contemplating these thoughts, I realized that this man was a man of strength. It was an inner strength of confidence and assurance. It was unnecessary for him to vocalize it or prove it in any kind of way. It was simply what made him the man he was. I wondered if perhaps I had sold him short by not recognizing this inner quality sooner in my life, or perhaps I was learning of it for the first time because I was finding that real strength and true leadership comes from within a man and not to those who seek it. Perhaps, a man cannot fully appreciate the qualities of manhood, until he himself becomes a man. Whatever the reason, my eyes were opened for the first time on that day, and I discovered a new respect and admiration for the man that I called "Dad". I was proud to be his son.

As we turned our horses back toward home, riding along with the sun setting at our backs and the chill of the evening falling upon us, I contemplated more the attributes of my father. It occurred to me that everything that I had become was fashioned by him and Mama. The skills I had acquired, the passions I enjoyed, even the way I walked and talked, were a direct reflection of their influence.

Dad had taught me how to ride and train a horse, to rope and brand a calf, to swing an axe and sharpen a knife that would shave. He taught me how to tie a fly and cast a fly rod and then how to take it down to the river and catch a trout, clean it and bring it home for supper. He showed me how to shoot a bow and arrow and a gun and how to clean a deer and process it for the freezer. He taught me how to read the tracks of wildlife and how to set a trap and prepare the pelt for the fur market. From building fence to running and operating every piece of farm equipment on our ranch and repairing it when necessary, Dad had, through so many patient years of teaching and instruction, reared me to be, not only capable, but proficient.

For years I had taken that for granted. I just figured that all fathers trained their sons this way. Most of the young boys I attended school with were much like me. These skills and so many more were just common place. I have come to realize that such training and instruction is the exception rather than the rule.

Perhaps the greatest contribution my father made to me was the ability to use solid common sense. Most things were not as complicated as other people made them out to be, and if you used a little common sense, it could be figured out. It wasn't until I moved away from home that I learned that common sense is not so common.

Zipping my jacket up tighter around my chest as we now rode into the darkness and came upon the hill overlooking the ranch house below, I chewed on these thoughts for a while longer.

"Dad, thanks for the day and for the ride and for my section of the ranch. I will take care of it all the days of my life." Choking on the lump that had developed in my throat, I tried hard to suppress the tears that were welling up in my eyes.

"You're welcome, Son. I'm proud that I am able to give it to you."

Pulling gently on the reins of my horse, I brought it to a stop. Dad did likewise. I looked across at him and extended my hand. I could see the glisten of his eyes in the autumn moonlight as his leathered glove reached my face, and he wiped the tear from my cheek with his thumb and gently squeezed my jaw with his fingers.

"Dad, I'm proud to be your son."

"Ah, Son, one of these days you'll have a son of your own.

If he makes you as proud as you have made me, well, then you'll really know what feeling proud is all about." Dad nudged his horse closer to mine and reached over and threw his strong arm around my neck and squeezed. "Come on, I'll race you to the barn."

That night after we got back to the ranch house, we ate supper and reclined in the living room in front of the television to watch a special episode of a talk show that hosted none other than Clovis Belden.

The idea of being politically correct obviously did not mean much to Clovis. Clovis broke all or most of the rules by the accepted norms of our current society. He believed in only one God, and that was Jehovah God and declared that it was the same God that our founding forefathers believed and honored. He believed the Bible is God's word. If God said it, that settled it. The idea, in Clovis' opinion, of removing the Ten Commandments from the public arena along with verses of biblical scripture that had been engraved in stone for more than 200 years by our founding forefathers was absolutely ludicrous. Many of the subjects that Clovis addressed were not nearly as open and visible to the public eye as they are today. I guess in many ways, I would say that in hindsight, Clovis was ahead of his times. His counsel, advice, wisdom and occasional warning, seemed like a bit too much to chew on, but his predictions were based upon the fact that history has a way of repeating itself and now, well, he may have been closer to the raw, honest truth that most of us wanted to accept at the time.

While watching Clovis on television, I could not imagine that there could be any doubt in anybody's mind that he was indeed a man of deep moral character and strong conviction. His idea of right and wrong was black and white in his eyes, and if for some reason it might appear somewhat gray or a little fuzzy, it was only because mankind had tried to mix the two together. As much as I admired the man for his fortitude and courage, I seriously doubted that he would be asked to be a guest on another talk show after that first appearance. Boy was I wrong.

When Clovis had finished speaking, Dad turned to me and

flatly stated, "Son, they broke the mold that Clovis was formed from."

"Dad, I'd say that goes for you as well. They just don't make guys like you two anymore." Dad just smiled without saying a word, but I knew his heart was gleaming with pride. It makes a father proud to know that his sons look up to him, especially after they have become men themselves.

The next morning, Mark and Will and their families pulled up to the ranch in their U-Haul vans and pickup trucks, packed to the brim with everything they owned or so I thought. It turned out that Mark had already unloaded one U-Haul van at a storage unit he had rented in Columbus. Tom Boer, a friend of his from Tennessee, had lost his job and always wanted to visit Montana. He was single and practically broke and had nothing but time on his hand, so Mark asked him if he would like to come along and agreed to pay him for his time. According to Mark, Tom acted like he had just won the lottery.

Although it had been only a month since we had buried Little Joe, and Mark and Will had returned to Tennessee, it had seemed much longer, and I was so happy to see them again. Except for my sister living in Texas, the Tyler's were all back home in Montana. Mark had sold his house, and the man who bought it told him he'd give him an extra 5000 dollars if he could be out in less than a week. Will had a contract on his house and expected to close the deal by the end of September, which was only 10 days away. We unloaded their vans and put their belongings in the barn. We used the hay conveyor to move the boxes up into the loft, which really cut down on time, but still, the process took most of the day. Even Mama came out and helped a little. She seemed to be in better spirits since Mark and Will had arrived.

I announced after we were finished that the following morning, I was driving up to see Wren. Even though Wren and I talked every night on the phone, I was missing her in the worst of ways. Telephones just can't take the place of physical presence.

"Sounds like you've got it bad." Will jested.

"Yup, I ain't denying it. I haven't put a lip-lock on that girl in over a week now, and I'm suffering from withdrawals." Everyone laughed, including me, but even so, down deep in my heart, I knew I had never felt this way before. The spark that Wren had ignited in my heart had turned to a raging fire, burning out of control.

I quietly asked Mark and Will to step outside in the cool of the evening for a few minutes of their time. To the best of my ability, I shared with them Mama's condition. Although she seemed happier at the moment than I had seen her since we had buried Little Joe, I somehow doubted that it would last for long.

"Spend as much time with her as possible and try to find her something to do to keep her occupied and her mind off of her grief," I suggested. Both of them understood.

CHAPTER 4

I had not informed Wren that I was coming. I wanted to surprise her. However, the surprise was somewhat dulled by the fact that when I arrived at the new entrance way into The Belden Ranch, I had not yet learned the security code, and no one answered when I pressed the button on the intercom. I knew that Clovis and Judy were still in L.A., but I wasn't sure if Wren was at the ranch or had gone into town. Perhaps she was attending to chores and away from the phone. I waited another half an hour and tried the intercom several times. I considered walking beyond the gate and cutting through the woods back to the ranch road, but I knew the house was still two miles from the gate.

"Oh well," I thought. "It's better than sitting here doing nothing." I reasoned.

Looking at the cameras I wondered how far I would need to walk down the property boundary before I was out of view. I figured about 300 yards would be fine. Once I reached a place I considered safe, I took a step across the boundary line. Instantly, sirens began blaring for about 30 seconds then a loud voice rang out over a hidden speaker.

"Stop!!! This is the Department of Homeland Security. You are entering a secured area!!! Do not proceed any further or you will be shot!!!"

I stopped immediately. I wasn't sure exactly what to do. Feeling like the kid who got caught with his hand in the cookie jar, I raised my hands and slowly took one step backwards from the

44

boundary line. I was uncertain how I was detected. Perhaps infrared light or laser beams that I had not noticed, but it didn't matter. I was in no mood to get into trouble. I walked back to my truck and decided to go into Augusta and see if I could call Wren from there. No sooner had I put my truck into gear than two black suburban vehicles with dark tinted windows pulled up in front of my truck blocking the road. Immediately, doors swung open and men in camouflaged uniforms and bulletproof vests emptied out, all armed with automatic weapons aimed directly at me. From my driver's seat, I slowly raised my palms above the steering wheel, indicating that I was not armed and was willing to completely submit to their instructions.

"Slowly open your door and remove yourself from your vehicle." The voice rang through the megaphone with a clear east-coast accent. I did as instructed. "Put your arms over your head." The voice reverberated. "Proceed to the front of your truck and lie face down in the road." As soon as I did, several armed men ran to me and pulled my arms behind my back and cuffed my wrists. Searching me, they found my .45 stuffed behind my waist hidden by my shirttail. The commanding officer advanced toward me.

"Do you have a permit to carry that weapon?" He asked.

"Yes, I do." I replied. "It's found in the U.S. Constitution under the second amendment of the Bill of Rights." I responded somewhat haughtily.

"Mr. Tyler, my name is Chief Officer Givens. Thank you for being such a good sport." He chuckled as he nodded his head toward the two men standing directly behind me who took the gesture as a signal to remove the cuffs from my wrists.

I did not completely understand. "What's this all about?" I asked.

Officer Givens proceeded to explain. "We've been out here on a rotating assignment ever since President Watson gave the orders to secure Mr. Belden's property. Other than the local wildlife, along with the Belden family, there has not been a single soul out here. When our cameras picked you up on the road coming out of town, we decided we would wait and see what you would do. We hoped you might try to breech the secured property boundary. Watson decided to have that installed anyway. You did of course, and it worked out perfectly. I hope you are not too upset."

"No, I was a little frightened I will admit, but I'm glad to see that the Belden's are living under tight security and that the perimeter of their property is protected."

"Oh, you would not believe the security they have on this place. Not even any of us are allowed to cross the boundary line unless directly ordered to do so by my superiors. However, we also brought you a little gift for your trouble."

Officer Givens turned back toward the first suburban and whistled. The back door opened and out stepped the most beautiful thing I had laid my eyes upon in over a week. Wren smiled and came running to my arms where I hoisted her high into the air and brought her slowly down to my face as she smiled and giggled lightly. I kissed her ruby red lips that tasted like wild huckleberry wine.

"We got you on that one; didn't we?" She asked chuckling. "When Officer Givens called and let me know that I had company coming, I told them to wait and see what you would do and then arrest you if you stepped across the line. I just knew you would."

"Yup, I'd say you got me good that time."

One of the officers handed me my .45 and didn't say anything about it. Everyone started piling back into their vehicles. Wren punched in the security code on the gate and it opened. Jumping into my truck, she slipped over by my side and gave me a big smack on my cheek.

When we arrived at the ranch house, she had the house clean, and we began fixing supper together.

"How much longer are your parents going to be gone?" I inquired. "They're coming back in two or three days. Dad said he was through with the talk shows. He cancelled his other appointments. He said he couldn't take the city any longer and needed to get back home. Mom could not agree with him more. They're both ready to get back to this ranch and these mountains. I was wondering," she continued, "if you would be able to stay until they get back home? I know that we haven't had any real threats or signs of danger, but I will admit I'm a little uncomfortable out here by myself."

"I'd love to do that." I stated. "I'll call Dad and make sure that Mark and Will and their families are settling in all right and check on mom, and unless I'm really needed back there, I'll be happy to stay. In fact, I'd love to stay." She smiled and turned toward me. Her eyes glistened, and I noticed a little flour on the edges of her hair and reached up to brush it out and kissed her softly on the lips. I was falling hard for this girl, and I found it difficult to concentrate on anything other than her. All was well back home. My brothers had managed to unpack everything and move into the house. The house was not exceptionally large, but they would manage all right. I was deeply happy that they had found their way back to Montana. Like me, they had grown up working hard on the ranch, always believing that there was something better beyond the mountains that blocked our view of the horizon. Like me, they had failed to realize that in spite of all the hard work of their youth, we had lived a life that was rich beyond measure. The clean, fresh air, the absence of humidity, the nearly 300 days of sunshine, the unparalleled hunting and fishing, the mountains, the people, all of it were things that we had taken for granted so long that we failed to see just how good we really had it. Now, after so many years of living severed and separated from the life we had grown to love, they had finally found their way back home. Like me, I knew they would never leave again.

For the next few days, Wren and I spent every possible minute that we could with each other. We rode the horses, checking the fence for breaks where deer or elk might have busted down a wire or a tree may have fallen across. We checked on the cows. Clovis had already moved them down from the high country closer to the ranch. One old cow had managed to get caught up in some barbed wire, and we brought her to the barn and doctored her as well as we could, but for the most part, the work was little, and things were shaping up for the winter.

The rest of our time it seemed we were riding our horses throughout the mountains that made up such a huge part of the Belden Ranch. It was toward the end of the week that Wren told me that she wanted to take me to a special place. We saddled the horses, but we did not have to ride far. Wren led the way to the top of the bluff that overlooked the ranch. We dismounted and tethered our horses to a lodge pole pine that had been tied horizontally between two other pines, specifically for that purpose. I could tell this place had been visited many times. A rock ring fire pit indicated that this was a place she liked to come in the evening and sit.

"This is my favorite place on the whole ranch." She commented, as she looked down and out across the valley. "I used to come up here after school and build a fire and just sit here. Many times I brought my books up here to study. Mom always liked it, because she could step outside the door of the house down there and holler for me when she needed me, and I was always within shouting distance. The real reason this place became even more special for me is because this is where Dad shot an arrow down into the yard when he was on the run from the law. The FBI had surveillance all over the ranch headquarters, but not up here. That's when he wrote on his arrow that he was still alive. We had believed that he was killed by that grizzly, and we had already had his memorial. My life changed that day when Mom told me that he was still alive. That's when I decided I was going to do whatever I needed to do to somehow bring him home." Wren's eyes began to water up, and I pulled her close and held her tight to my chest. Her body was quivering.

I could not find the words to say, so I just continued to hold her. Sometimes, I believe, words just aren't adequate for certain occasions, and it's better to just be quiet than to say anything at all. My presence was simply enough.

We sat down on the edge of the bluff and talked for hours,

48

watching the sun go down as it quickly settled in behind the horizon. We shared the stories of our past. From skinned knees and elbows to near-death experiences to broken hearts and lost loves, we opened up to one another like never before. We learned in depth about our likes and dislikes, our dreams and ambitions as well as our hopes, desires and expectations. I was continually amazed at how much we thought and felt alike and how near perfect our dreams meshed together. On one occasion, I shared with her the love that Little Joe and I held for one another as brothers, and it was then that I couldn't hold back my own tears. I sobbed like a baby as she held me in her arms, and I felt no shame for my display of emotion. In fact, I could not recall a time when I had ever felt so comforted or free to express myself. It was also on this particular afternoon that Wren told me that she loved me for the second time. This time, there was something about it that carried more weight, something genuinely serious. I will remember that day for as long as I live. Something inside of me gave in that afternoon. I am not sure how to describe it exactly. Whatever barrier or reservations I had faced or fear I wrestled against in my heart about marrying Wren vanished. I knew I was going to ask that girl to marry me, and it would be soon. As I held her slender but strong hand in mine, I gently pulled a ring off of her finger and examined it closely. I tried it on my little finger, and it came to the first knuckle, but wouldn't budge any further. Wren told me that the ring had belonged to her grandmother, and she wore it to remind her of her grandmother's memory. Wren did not realize at the moment I was sizing up her finger by measuring her ring on my own. Yep, I was going to marry this girl, and I wanted to do it right, which also meant that I would wait until Clovis and Judy returned home so I could ask Clovis' permission. Although he had already indicated his approval, the formality of the long-standing tradition of asking a father's permission for his daughter's hand in marriage was important to me.

Clovis and Judy made it home the following afternoon. They were elated to be home. Clovis kept talking about the smog in

L.A. and the different kinds of people and how they dressed and exotic hairstyles. He even mimicked how some of the people talked. That produced a big laugh out of all of us. He was glad to be back where his Wranglers and cowboy hat and boots were considered 'normal wear'. He believed the poor air quality had damaged his lungs. Now, he might have been exaggerating a little bit, but probably not by much. Clovis asked me to stay for one more day, and I was happy to do so. This would be my opportunity to ask his permission for Wren's hand in marriage.

After breakfast the following morning, Clovis asked me if I would like to go for a ride. We saddled up a couple horses. I rode the Appaloosa I had been riding all week long with Wren. Clovis rode a bay that stood right at 17 hands. We hadn't ridden far from the ranch house when Clovis opened up the conversation.

"How's your mama doing?" He asked.

"Not so good. Oh, I think she's a little better now that Mark and Will are home, and the house is full of kids. They seem to keep her company, but there's something in her eyes that seems to indicate that the improvement is only temporary."

"I've been praying for her." Clovis replied. I remember thinking to myself that it was interesting how Clovis, with so much on his plate the last few weeks, had not neglected to take the time to pray and spend conversation with his God. The more time I spent with the man, the more I wanted to understand about his deep and solid faith. Wren was much the same as her father. It was a quality that made them who they were and not just one to be admired, but a quality to be desired, and I wanted it to become a part of me.

"Thank you." I answered. "She needs them."

We rode for a few moments without speaking until I broke the silence. "Clovis, I know something is on your mind, but before we discuss it, I have a question I need to ask you."

"Yes." He answered. "Yes what?" I asked.

"Yes, you have my permission to marry my daughter."

"How did you know I was going to ask you to marry your

daughter?" I asked, completely flabbergasted.

"Son, it's all over you like I ain't never seen. It's bout like stink on poo. You walk around like a lovesick hound. No offense of course."

"Hmmm, that obvious huh?"

"That's all right, Son. I'm proud to see it. There's no one in the world I would rather have marry my daughter than you, Ross. Judy feels the same way. You have our deepest blessings. Now, I know it goes without saying, but I'll say it anyway, just because I only have one daughter, and I've always believed that I should say it. I will help you anytime you or Wren need me to, but if you ever hurt her, I will make your death slow and painful."

Beneath his light-hearted humor, there was seriousness in his voice that indicated he meant every word that he had just uttered, and I have no doubt he would have kept his word. Clovis was just that kind of man.

Looking off to the west, I could see a thunder cloud rolling in and hear the distant thunder clapping. I thought about the wrath of God, and somehow I felt certain that the wrath of Clovis would be very similar.

"Yes, Sir, I am certain that you would. That will not happen; on that, I give you my word."

Clovis extended his hand across the pommel of his saddle and shook my hand, looking at me straight in the eye and smiled with a light chuckle and a soft gleam in his eye. "I know it won't, Son. I've always looked forward to the day I would get to say that." He stated as he burst out laughing. Looking toward the west at the darkening thunder clouds, he paused for a moment and then stated, "I'm afraid we've got trouble brewing, Son."

"Yes, Sir, I'd say you're right." I responded as I kept my focus toward the storm.

Clovis looked at me and back to the clouds. "No, you don't understand what I mean. I'm not talking about the storm that's brewing up ahead."

CHAPTER 5

Clovis stepped out of his saddle and tossed his reins up over the neck of his horse. I followed his lead and did the same. Walking over beneath a huge pine tree, we sat down on the bed of needles, in the shade, still facing the oncoming storm ahead, which appeared was starting to move to the north of us.

Quietly I sat there, knowing that Clovis was about to share with me something that he was finding very disturbing. Finally, he broke the silence.

"I have always wondered if my past would one day return to haunt me. I am afraid it just might."

"What exactly are you talking about?" I asked, uncertain.

"I was nearly twenty-one years old when I signed up with Uncle Sam to go fight in Viet Nam. Judy was four months pregnant with Wren. It wasn't long after I got into boot camp that they picked up on a few things that many of us Montana boys consider common place, such as shooting well and prowess in woodsmanship, and with some more intense military training, they turned me into a competent sniper and assassin. I learned more about ballistics and bullet trajectory than I ever thought possible. I learned how to dope the wind and how to estimate and accurately compensate for the wind on different bullet weights and calibers. The military taught me how to use a knife to kill quickly and effectively. Most important of all, I learned how to go in undetected and remain so. I became quite proficient at establishing a good hide with excellent concealment and cover, good observation, a field of fire, and a "backdoor" through which I could disappear after my engagement. Of course, I know you know all of this already, but what I'm getting at is that I was good at doing the job. As I told you once, out of the ten men that I trained with, only two of us survived the war and came back home to the States. Of course, you've killed Kirby, so I'm the only one left."

Clovis paused, squinting as he continued to watch the thunderstorm move across the sky to the north of us, bringing only a few gusts of wind and isolated drops of rain to the area where we sat. "You know, Ross, I must admit that I actually enjoyed it. It wasn't so much that I enjoyed the killing. To me, the killing was more of a means to a greater good and for certain, necessary, but the challenge of completing the assignment by sneaking in and taking out the target without getting caught was a real rush. In many ways, you can compare it to hunting. Don't get me wrong, human life should always be regarded at a higher level than an animal, but like hunting, it's the challenge of meeting your prey in their territory without being detected and yet, without the kill, it's not really hunting."

I continued to listen closely because I knew that Clovis had not expressed his worries or concerns or whatever it was that was weighing so heavy on his mind. Clovis often set the stage with all the preliminary background information before stating what he really desired to say. I had already learned that of him. I had to be patient. Any question I might have while listening was usually answered shortly afterwards anyway without asking it at all. I was learning this of Clovis. He didn't talk a lot, but when he started telling a story or making a point, he often took the long way around to get to it. That being said, I was also discovering that he had a purpose in doing so. Very seldom did I ever have to ask him to repeat something or failed to understand what he was saying and have to acquire more information. I suppose Clovis didn't like to repeat himself, so he made sure to get it right the first time.

As I sat there staring at Clovis, I tried to visualize him as a young man, barely out of school, recently married, half-way around the world, fighting for a cause in what proved to be a no-win situation, in a terrain that was so unlike the Montana where he was born and raised, on assignments that were not only classified, but given to him to complete solely on his own and if captured, knowing there would be no attempt of rescue, all the while knowing that he had a wife at home, expecting their first child. Just the thought made me feel a little ashamed of myself when I reflected back to the many times that I had complained because I had too many irons in the fire. All of my life, I've known only the peace and comfort of living in this great land. I had never, at that time, even been across the border into Canada. While I know what it means to work hard, and I've faced some very difficult situations and known my share of tragedies, in light of the life that Clovis had lived, I considered myself pampered. The truth be known, in retrospect, it's the men like Clovis who have made my pampered life possible. In the back of my mind I pondered these thoughts as I carefully listened.

"Most of my targets," Clovis carried on, "were high-ranking military officers. Of course, the more brass a man wears, the more protected he is as well, which makes getting close an even more complex situation. If I've counted right, I took out 47 officers. That does not include the men I killed going to and from the assigned target."

"Whew, that's a lot of men, Clovis." I stated, not really meaning to verbalize anything.

"I know, Tyler," calling me by my last name again. "Here's the thing. I guess, living back here in Montana, on the other side of the planet and the war being long over, I've never really considered that my past would ever catch up with me."

"What makes you think that it has?" I asked.

"Well, here's what's got me wondering, and it may all be nothing, but I think that is just wishful thinking. Over the past three weeks I've made 18 appearances on televised talk shows. All of them were before a large audience of people. On the third appearance, while sitting on stage talking to the host, I looked out across the audience, and I noticed some Vietnamese men sitting to my left. They were all dressed in suits and sitting together. Several of them looked very familiar, like I might have seen them somewhere before, but it wasn't so much their familiar looks that puzzled me. It was the fact that they seemed emotionless, even at times when the whole crowd was roaring in laughter, they didn't change their expressions. In fact, it's like they just stared at me through the eyes of hateful scorn."

"Maybe they were just visiting America, and they don't understand English." I posed.

"I thought the same thing." Clovis added. "Thing is, they were present at every talk show appearance I made after that. They dressed the same and always sat to my left. No emotion. If a man didn't understand English and did not have an interpreter, don't you think attending as many as they did would seem a little odd?"

"That does sound pretty strange. Who do you suppose they might be?" I implored.

"President Watson has his men looking into it. So far, I've not heard anything. Judy advised me to cancel my other appearances, and I think that was the wise choice, but I'm a little worried. I don't deny it."

Shaking my head in agreement, the thought crossed my mind, that if Clovis believed there was a reason to be worried, that was enough for me.

CHAPTER 6

We never know the impact we make on the lives we touch. Whether good or bad, it seems that one way or the other; things have a way of going full circle. The old saying, "you reap what you sow," surely has proven to be true in my life time and time again. Years had passed since Clovis had served his time in Viet Nam. Over the course of many years, I have learned the details involved in the assignments and missions Clovis was ordered to complete and perhaps one of these days, I will write of those, for they are almost too incredible to believe, but for now, the one particular mission that Clovis had successfully completed, would prove to have an effect on both the Belden and the Tyler families.

General Ho Lee had served for the North Vietnamese Army ever since he was 15 years old. Like his father before him, his life revolved around serving his country in a military fashion and like his father before him, he had proven his worth as a soldier and an officer time and time again on the battlefield. He was an expert in weaponry and martial arts and regularly practiced with his sword. As a military statistician, he had mastered the art of guerilla warfare and was causing havoc in the proverbial backside of the U.S. armed forces. The Viet Cong, especially those who served directly under him, practically worshipped the ground he walked on and would gladly march to their graves in his service. Many of them did.

As dedicated and committed as he was to the military, he was as much so to his family. He had four sons and a daughter and as much as possible, he spent his time with them. He was a strong disciplinarian and yet at the same time, he was fair and gentle. These were the same attributes he demonstrated to the men who served under him. All seemed not only to respect him, but they loved and admired him as well. His reputation preceded him wherever he went. His two eldest sons had moved up in military rank and served as commanding officers and by all appearances, they too would have eventually moved into a high ranking position as their father. Such ambitions were not to come to fruition. Both of them had fallen to well-placed shots from Clovis' sniper rifle.

Clovis knew the reputation of Ho Lee before given the assignment to take him out. He knew that he had already destroyed a third of the family, and he also knew that Ho Lee had put a high monetary bounty on his head. Ho Lee had vowed that he would have the head of the Mongoose mounted and put on display in his guest room. Posters had been placed in windows and on trees stating in Vietnamese "Kill the Mongoose," the name he had been given for his ability to strike and kill so swiftly. Fortunately, no one had managed to get a picture or even a good look at Clovis, so a portrait or drawing was not available to put on the posters. Still, in the mind of Clovis, the thought of killing such a man, especially after killing two of his sons, bothered him terribly. The tremendous grief Ho Lee's wife must have already suffered. How much more could she stand if she lost her husband, the father of her three remaining children?

Clovis had never shirked a mission. War does not dictate, nor is it partial to who lives and who dies, but this was one assignment that he wished he would not have to take. In a private meeting with Colonel Jackson, the solitary commander that called the shots for Clovis, Clovis expressed his reservations. Colonel Jackson understood and later told me in an interview that I had with him that it was the fact that Clovis had managed to somehow maintain compassion in his heart that Jackson admired about him the most. It wasn't just the fact that Clovis was so extremely good at completing his mission, but the fact that Clovis always remained gentle in heart and spirit and concerned himself with the welfare of other peoples' feelings and needs. Most trained assassins grow cold and heartless, but according to Colonel Jackson, Clovis never did.

Clovis told me that day, while sitting there with our horses watching the storm that Colonel Jackson really listened to the things Clovis had to say and chewed on it for a while before giving his reply. According to Clovis, Jackson responded to his concerns, "Son, I appreciate the fact that you haven't lost your heart, even for your enemy. I am sure that both Ho Lee and his wife are grieving tremendously for the loss of their two sons, and I am sure that when you take out Ho Lee, his wife will carry a burden that none of us would want to carry. Consider this, however, those American boys we're sending back in body bags are somebody's sons, and some, like you, have wives back home that will grieve as well. Many of them have died as a result of Ho Lee's leadership and command. How many American lives will be spared if you remove him from the picture?"

That was all it took for Clovis. While in his mind, he could justify that what he was doing was simply the causalities of war, that wasn't enough for him. However, to determine in his heart and mind that the targets he removed would actually spare the lives of his own comrades and would eliminate a lot of grief back in the States, gave him a new drive and resolve to intensify his efforts. The following week, he was dropped out at night in a parachute over North Vietnam with a knife, compass, map, flint, headlight, ammo, .45, and his XM21 sniper rifle. He also carried a pair of soft-leathered, doeskin moccasins that easily rolled up to stuff in his daypack where he carried his supplies. Ho Lee was his target.

The United States Army Intelligence revealed that Ho Lee and his men were on the move once again down the Ho Chi Min Trail. The details of their mission were unclear, but certainly, Ho Lee's army was looking to invade and attack the South Vietnamese again. Before flying out, Colonel Jackson wished Clovis luck and God's speed and reminded him, "If you want to kill a snake, you've got to cut off the head." Clovis understood exactly what that meant.

The night was dark and cloudy as the chopper flew Clovis across the border into North Vietnam. Clovis and the pilot had been given the coordinates to the location where Clovis was to bail out of the chopper. No sooner had he made the jump than .50-caliber gunfire from the ground below opened up on the chopper. Waiting until the last possible second to open his chute, Clovis dropped through the air as quickly as gravity would take him, hoping to avoid catching a bullet on the way down and praying that his body was not visible from below in the darkness of the night. When he opened his chute, his body jerked upward, causing his eyes to see quickly the chopper he had just descended from was ablaze and on fire. In just a few short seconds later it exploded, no doubt killing the pilot in the process.

Clovis was sure that a search party would be sent out into the vicinity to see if the chopper had successfully made a drop, so he knew that he would have to hide his chute and make tracks out of there as quickly as possible to avoid getting caught. He also knew that he would have to avoid the dogs.

Cutting a few short lengths of cord from the chute and stuffing them into the pockets of his army fatigues, he quickly rolled the chute into a tight ball and located a swamp where he stuffed it in the mud. He knew that it would only hide it visually, but the dogs would pick up the scent. Looking at his compass and getting his bearings, he took out in a dead run toward the northeast as fast as he could go. It wasn't long until he heard the yapping and barking of dogs, and he knew the race was on. About half an hour from landing, it began to rain. Clovis considered this a direct blessing from God. Not only would the rain wash out his tracks, but hopefully it would be hard enough to eliminate his scent.

He hated to use his headlight, but the jungle was too thick, and the night was too dark to ascertain where he was going. He reasoned that his light would not be visible to his pursuers through this jungle if he could keep the distance between them far enough to keep from being seen. Running as quickly as his legs would carry him through the wet, tangled forest, he leaped to clear a fallen log and caught his foot on a protruding branch, causing him to crash over, head first to the ground, where his head struck another fallen log and knocked him unconscious. When he came to, he wasn't sure how long he had been there. His clothes were saturated with rain, and his head felt like a football, but he could hear dogs and the voices of men and was able to see their lights not far from his location. They were hot on his trail. Knowing he could not outrun the dogs, he quickly climbed a huge tree, ascending it as high as he could climb, hoping the canopy of the leafy branches beneath him would conceal his presence.

Tying the cord around his waist, to the branches of the tree, afraid that he might either fall asleep or slip on the wet, slick bark of the tree, he sat. He could not see the men or the dogs as they approached the tree he was in. Several lights shined into the tree from below, but evidently, they were unable to locate him as well. Still, the dogs kept sniffing around the tree while the rain began to fall even harder.

Clovis did not understand the Vietnamese language so he could not decipher what was being said below. He could tell that someone was shouting orders, and by the tones in their voices they did not want to be there in the torrential rain any longer. Still, they remained and searched the surrounding area. They never wandered far from the tree where Clovis was hiding. The minutes turned into hours, and the hours were long and miserable. He had nothing to eat and the rain was cold. His teeth clattered so loudly, he feared they would hear him from below. Hour upon hour and finally, the sun began to break in the east, bringing to life a new day, but also bringing with it the increased possibility that he would be visible. The dogs had evidently given-up on his scent. Still, the men remained in the area, making it a total suicide mission if he tried to descend. The rain finally eased to a sprinkle, and he could hear voices on walkie-talkies below. On several occasions he heard the name of Ho Lee in their conversation and concluded that these were Ho Lee's men, the best that North Viet

Nam had to offer.

As the day progressed, Clovis felt his muscles cramping from dehydration. He had tried to catch as much water as possible in his hat, but perhaps he still had not drunk enough. Ever so slowly, he extended his legs and tried to stretch them as much as he could without revealing his location. His butt was nearly numb. The cold night turned into a sweltering heat and the gnats and biting flies plagued his body, many of them biting through his clothing. Motionless, he sat. As the hours leisurely dragged by, his thoughts returned to the night before. How did Ho Lee's men know that a drop was about to occur, and how did they know where it would be? This information was kept secret at the highest of security levels. Someone had to be feeding inside intelligence to the enemy.

With nothing to eat and not enough water to sustain him, Clovis was nearly to the point of delirium. His lips were cracked, and he knew he could not hold out much longer. As the sun set in the west, he thought of Judy back home in Montana and wanted so much to be back in her arms again. He had received a letter and a picture of his baby girl Kelli Wren only two weeks earlier, and she looked so much like her mother, beautiful and petite. As much as he felt like he wanted to die, he had to remain alive for their sake. He did not want to make a widow out of his wife and make his daughter fatherless.

Shortly before the sun sank into the horizon, he heard squawking on the walkie-talkies below, and everyone departed. Clovis felt he needed to remain longer to be certain that everyone below had left, so he made himself more comfortable and remained there until after midnight.

Climbing down the tree proved to be a task in itself. Ascending the tree had been spurred on by adrenaline, but now, his muscles were stiff and sore and practically useless. Slowly and carefully he descended safely. Looking at his watch, he had spent 28 hours in the tree. His first order of business was to locate clean water and find something to eat. With only his small headlight it might prove to be difficult to find, but it was only a few minutes when he happened upon a place that provided everything he needed.

A small outcropping of rocks had formed several pools of water from the rain the night before. In the shade of the heavy timber, it still remained somewhat cool and refreshed his dry lips. Much like a dry sponge, almost immediately he could feel his body begin to absorb the much-needed hydrating effects of the water. He drank until he felt as though he was going to founder. Overturning a few rotting logs, he found plenty of grubs in the dark, rich, jungle soil and gorged himself on them, eating them one after another, not bothering to chew them. Peeling the bark off a stand of nearby willows, he chewed on the bitter taste, knowing that it would have the same effect as aspirin and would help to ease some of the pain in his muscles. Then he reclined in a bed of ferns and fell asleep. Daylight would be coming soon.

The morning sun was already making a day out of it when he awoke. His muscles were still stiff, but the rest, water and nutrition had revived his body. Taking a read on his compass and verifying his coordinates with the map, he figured he was only about three miles from Ho Lee's camp. He would take his time and rest, eat what he could find, and rejuvenate for the day as he progressed forward in that direction.

By nightfall, he had located the camp. Vigilantly slipping through the foliage, he identified the Viet Cong scouts and their posts as they stood on night watch. Clovis had long learned that making the kill was one thing, getting out alive afterwards was another, so as much planning as was involved in making the hit, there was as much in making the retreat, maybe more.

Ho Lee's camp was well guarded, sitting in a steep, little valley that would make attack from an enemy tricky and complicated. Clovis was certain that Ho Lee had picked such a place with that in mind.

That very evening the opportunity to kill Ho Lee became available when Ho Lee stepped out from his tent to relieve himself in the nearby woods. Clovis watched him from 600 yards out through the scope of his rifle and even thumbed the safety a couple of times, but his better judgment told him that a safe escape from his present position would be nearly impossible. Tomorrow would be another day.

That night, a safe distance from Ho Lee's camp, Clovis slept. Around 2 a.m., he woke with a start. He had been dreaming of Judy and his daughter, and he suddenly became lonely for home. Something stirred inside of him, and for an unexplainable reason, he felt invincible. Slinging his rifle over his shoulder and grabbing what little gear he carried, he moved quickly through the dark night toward the camp. The night guardsmen were standing around a fire drinking coffee or tea he presumed. Here he very quietly changed into his moccasins to assure that his footsteps would not be heard. He slipped past their presence undetected, staying low and in the shadows until he reached the tent of Ho Lee. Stepping through the front fly opening, he was immediately confronted with a large Vietnamese man standing guard. The man, due to the darkness inside the tent, was unable to discern Clovis' identity. His hesitation cost him his life as the blade of Clovis' knife quickly and quietly slit his throat from ear to ear. The man crumbled to his knees, holding his throat. Clovis grabbed him by his hair and gently laid him facedown to die on the floor to keep from creating a commotion.

Inside the adjoining room, Ho Lee laid flat on his back on his cot, snoring, in deep sleep. With the stealth of a cougar, Clovis moved to the sleeping general and placed his left hand over his mouth and the blade of his knife to his throat. Ho Lee awakened immediately, his eyes bulging in fear, as he looked straight into the face and the eyes of Clovis. One fast sweep of the blade, and it was over. The life and color of Ho Lee seeped out of his face as his blood spilled on to the floor of the tent.

With as much stealth as he had entered the camp, he also departed. Once back to his army boots, he quickly shed his moccasins and laced on his boots. He glanced at his compass and established his bearings. It was a long distance to the designated landing zone for evacuation, where a chopper was supposed to fly in and pick him up. Nearly a mile from camp, he stopped and turned on his headlamp and read the bearings on his compass once again. He was moving on the right course. Clovis always had a great sense of direction.

Clovis was an accomplished runner. Having earned a scholarship to the College of Great Falls for cross-country running, he was able to run at a steady clip and keep the pace all night long if need be. That's exactly what this situation demanded. Headed almost due south, he knew he had been running for hours, but as he noticed the light pink horizon to the east, he didn't realize that dawn was already breaking. He still had a long way to go, but in the daylight, the possibility of being spotted or noticed increased tremendously which meant he could no longer run along the well-beaten paths that led through the jungle. This would slow down progress more than even trying to travel in the darkness.

About three miles out from his destination, he stumbled on a North Vietnamese woman who was carrying water assumingly back to her home. Putting his finger to his lips and pulling his .45, he indicated not to make a sound. Evidently, either the woman didn't understand or figured that Clovis would not shoot her for fear of the gun blast revealing his presence; she started shouting.

A group of Viet Cong soldiers were camped just a hundred yards away and hearing the commotion, grabbed their rifles and took off at a run toward Clovis. The pursuit was on again, and this time they were right on his heels. Running and scrambling through a stand of thick bamboo, Clovis could sense his enemy gaining ground on him. These men were quick. Bullets sped in his direction, some of them hitting the bamboo cane uncomfortably close.

Finally making it through the thick bamboo, Clovis ran into a greater problem. Open rice patties lay before him with absolutely no cover. He knew he could not make it to the other side without getting shot, but he wasn't about to stand there and be captured either. The only choice he had was to try. Running through the open saturated field and hoping to put as much distance between him and his pursuers before they too broke free from the stand of bamboo would make it more difficult to get shot. Clovis was doing well, but tripped and fell headlong into the standing water. It was hopeless now. All he could do was surrender.

Rising from where he had fallen, he started to raise his arms above his head, when suddenly, from seemingly out of nowhere, a chopper buzzed down and opened up with machine gun fire on the Viet Cong who had just entered the rice field. Many stepped back into the bamboo cane for protection, returning gunfire at the chopper. As the chopper swooped down over Clovis, he grabbed the runner of the chopper and pulled himself inside as the chopper lifted off the field, bullets whipping and zipping all around, many of them hitting the body of the chopper.

CHAPTER 7

Clovis paused as he got to this part of the story and looked at me straight in the eye.

"Son! That was your ole man flying that bird. As I told you once before, I owe my life to your pap. He took a bullet for me that day."

"Clovis," I replied, "Dad and I took a long ride last week, and he told me things I had no clue about. You know, until we came in to try to get you out of the Bob Marshall Wilderness a few months ago, I was clueless to Dad's role in the war. He just never talked about it."

"A lot of us are that way, Ross. There are things that happened over there that we wish we could forget, and bringing them back up doesn't do anything to alleviate the unpleasant memories. It was unlike any war our men had ever fought before. You can't tell the difference between a South Vietnamese and a North Vietnamese. It was often impossible to know the difference between friend and enemy. Sometimes they were both. Then, the lack of support we received from our homeland and their continual protest, not only against the war itself, but against those of us who were over there fighting, didn't help matters a whole lot."

"So, do you think killing Ho Lee years ago has something to do with the Vietnamese men that kept showing up in the audience at these talk shows where you've recently appeared? I asked.

Clovis hesitated for a moment and then explained. "I got a really good look at Ho Lee before I killed him. There is an indisputable resemblance between Ho Lee and a few of those men in that audience. They are not old enough to be his brothers, but I'm thinking they might have been his two younger sons and their friends. President Watson is having his men looking into it."

"If no one ever saw you, how do they know you're the one who killed Ho Lee?"

Clovis chuckled lightly to himself. "I made a mistake, Ross. I was meticulously careful about concealment and not being seen or spotted on every assignment. I could blend in with the foliage and the terrain and make myself invisible. I was anal to every single detail that is, except for one." Clovis let out a big sigh and then continued. "As I mentioned earlier, I always changed into my moccasins when the assignment called for close-up and personal. The tracks my moccasins left behind became the identifying factor for the Viet Cong. They knew that the Mongoose wore moccasins. Obviously, they found my tracks in Ho Lee's camp as well as many of those places where I completed other missions. Now, after all these years, here I am, making guest appearances on television. Showing my face to the world and the fact that Mongoose was the nickname given to me by the North Vietnamese has been made public several times. Well, it wouldn't be hard to put two and two together. I'm thinking Ho Lee's two younger sons have finally put a face on the man that killed their father, and they're here in the States looking for revenge. I'm just speculating, but I have a bad feeling about this one."

"What do you reckon we should do? I asked.

"I don't know. Right now, I'm just waiting to hear from Watson. I'd say we just go about our normal business, but keep your eye looking over your shoulder."

Clovis stood up and stretched and looked toward the storm clouds that had passed.

"You know," he commented, "life is a lot like that storm. Sometimes, we look out ahead of ourselves, and we just know we're going to get nailed hard, but then it misses us all together. Other times, it hits us, and we don't even see it coming. You just never know about a storm." I was certain he wasn't talking about the thunderstorm that had just passed, and I also knew his mind was troubled.

As we rode back toward the ranch, the sun had already set. The night was ebony black. In the distance, we could hear the coyotes yipping and singing. A bull elk bugled, and Clovis pulled his horse to a stop. "You know, there's still a little more than a week left of archery season. Maybe we ought to take a ride up to the Missouri Breaks and see what we can do."

"That sounds like fun. I won't be able to get a license, because I'm still a resident of Illinois, but I'd love to go with you. Maybe Mark and Will could come along too, if you don't mind?" I suggested.

"I'd love to have them. If trouble is coming, I don't think it will be real soon. Of course, I don't know that, but it's just a gut feeling. I wonder if Judy and Wren would like to come along."

"We can ask them. I think all of us could stand a little retreat from all we've been through these past few weeks."

The following morning, I kissed Wren goodbye while she was still asleep in her bed. I drove into Great Falls and located a jewelry store to see if I could find a ring that would be suitable for Wren. After several hours of looking and several different jewelry stores, I was about to give up. Finally, I found the perfect ring. The gold in the ring was mined in Montana as were the six Yogo sapphires that surrounded the diamond. Only the diamond was foreign, and it was mined in Africa. The ring would cost me a small fortune, but only the best was good enough for Wren. I intended to marry only once in my life, and I intended to marry Wren.

Obviously, I didn't have that much cash on hand, so I drove over to The First National Bank and made a cash withdrawal from my account. Arriving back at the jewelry store, I did manage to haggle the jeweler down 500 dollars off the price by offering him cash and showing it to him. My heart was racing as I climbed back into the truck and pointed toward home. Now, I had to determine where, when and how I would pop the question.

Arriving back home at the ranch, it was good to be back with my family again. I had only been gone a few days, but it seemed longer. Through the years I have discovered that just a short time away from those whom we love the most, seems to be much longer than it really is. Everyone appeared to be in good spirits and had managed to get settled in. The house was a little crowded, but I think the human presence of family continued to alleviate much of the depression Mama had been suffering with.

After supper, I asked Mark and Will if they would like to take the few days left of archery season and go help Clovis call in a bull up in the Missouri Breaks. Will was a master of the elk language and he used only his voice. He did not need a diaphragm to make a bugle or talk the language of a cow in heat. Mark and I depended on using calls that we either purchased or made ourselves. We used several different types of calls, including squeeze calls, tubes, internal and external reeds. My favorite cow call was one I had made years ago out of a horn from an old steer we had butchered. The sound it produced was low and raspy and had the appeal of an old lead cow, a sound that I had not found duplicated in other calls. It had proven effective on several occasions.

Mark and Will told me that they would discuss it with their wives. "Well, you need to do so this evening. Clovis and I are heading out tomorrow. I am going to meet him at Eddie's Corner outside of Lewistown, and then we're going to drive up to the Bohemian Corner and on down to the Fred Robertson Bridge. I know you guys know the area downstream from the bridge, because we have all hunted there, but Clovis wants to hunt upstream from the bridge. Let me know what your wives say before we go to bed tonight."

Both of them looked at me a little funny. "Ross, you don't know what it's like to be married now do you?" Will jested. "A little more than two months ago, we left our wives and kids alone, back in Tennessee and flew to Montana and then in a chopper into the Bob Marshall with Dad, risking our lives to help get you and Clovis out of that wilderness. We lost Little Joe in the process and left his wife a widow and his children without a father. Then, right after his funeral, we went back to Tennessee and told our families we were moving to Montana. We sold our houses and made the long, grueling three-day trip to get here. Not one time did our wives object. Oh, they asked questions for better understanding and all, but they never complained or bucked us in any way. I just say all that to say that going to them now and asking if they would mind if we run off on an elk hunting adventure, when we've barely been here a week, might be pushing the envelope of understanding a little too much."

The whole time Will was rattling on, Mark was bobbing his head up and down, affirming and confirming that he agreed with Will.

"So, does that mean that you won't ask?" I asked.

Mark looked at Will and then back at me, "No, now we didn't say that. Just don't be surprised if we tell you that we can't make it. Speaking for myself, if Sally has even the slightest objection, I'll not press the issue. I certainly would understand her reservations."

"The same goes for me. If Abby doesn't want me to go, I'm staying here, even though I would love to go."

"That sounds good to me." I confirmed. What Mark and Will did not know was that I had already discussed the proposition with Sally and Abby and asked them if they could live without their husbands for a few days. I knew I was treading on thin ice by doing so, but both of them agreed that their husbands had been busting their tails for the last six weeks to get back to Montana, and it would be good for them to sleep out under the stars that shined so brightly on the land they called home. After hearing this selfless act, I realized just how fortunate Mark and Will were to have married such fine women. I took the 500 dollars I had saved from the purchase of the ring and told Sally and Abby to go to Billings while we were gone and have a good time and not to mention to Mark or Will that we had this conversation.

Before bedtime, the women were inside the house entertaining the children and Mama. Mark, Will and I were sitting on the front porch listening to the sounds of the night. Occasionally, we would hear the coyotes howl in the distance or a nighthawk scream somewhere above the pastures as it hunted for food. A great-horned owl hooted every now and then in the cottonwoods down near the creek.

It was an evening of splendor as we recalled stories of the past and laughed at some of the misadventures we had shared, growing up on the ranch. Whenever Dad told a story, it was always bigger and better than it was the first time he told it, but he told it like it was the first time we had ever heard it, although all of us would be hard pressed to know how many times he had told it before.

Will finally asked, "Ross, what time are we leaving in the morning?" "Yeah, what time do you want to get on the road?" Mark reiterated. "So, your wives said it was all right for you to go?" I asked.

"Ha. Bribery works pretty well with women, Ross. They told us what you did."

Dad just sat there chuckling. Apparently, I was the only one who hadn't learned that everybody else knew about the little stunt I had pulled.

"Well, shoot, so much for keeping it a secret." I stated.

"Yup. You can tell he's not married." Mark chimed.

"I'll wake you boys up at 4a.m. Have your gear ready to go."

"We already do."

CHAPTER 8

Ecstatic about the trip, the three of us were on the road by 4:30a.m., later pulling into a gas station in Big Timber, just as the sun was cresting the horizon to the east. Filling up the truck with fuel and fueling our bodies with large cups of coffee and a couple sausage biscuits, we didn't tarry long. Crossing over the Yellowstone River just north of town, headed toward Harlowton, we gazed westward at the rugged Crazy Mountains, which carried a light dusting of snow that had fallen the night before.

Those mountains held a very special memory for me. It seemed like a lifetime ago when Mom and Dad had asked me what I wanted for a graduation present from high school. I knew that they didn't have a lot of money to spend, and truthfully, looking back on it now, it seems that everything that money can purchase either wears out or rusts out in time, but a memory, ah, now that's something you can take to the grave. So, I asked if Dad would take me on a fishing trip in the Crazy Mountains as soon as the snow melted. That's exactly what we did. We pitched our tent and camped in those mountains for three days. At times we fished on the creek, catching more brook trout than we could possibly eat, but we certainly ate our fair share. Cooking the trout in bacon grease over an open fire proved to be a delicacy.

During the heat of the day, we would cast our lines into the lake and sit in the lush grass in the glowing sunshine, both of us reading Louis L'Amour novels. It seemed that every time we would become engrossed in the novel, a fish would bite, and we would miss setting the hook because we had our attention diverted toward our books. We managed to hook a few, but what a joyful time and pleasant memory that was and still is for me. We liked the area so well, that in the years to follow, we took the whole family on camping trips there.

Lost in the trance of that precious memory, Mark spoke up.

"Brothers, next summer I am taking my two sons and my wife up there into those mountains to camp for a week, the way Mom and Dad used to do for us when we were young. Every single chance I get, I'm going to show them what Montana has to offer. Maybe they won't be as foolish as I was and think they've got to leave." Nothing was said for a moment. Nothing had to be. What Mark had just stated were the exact sentiments on the hearts of all three of us.

Whew, somebody hit me. I can't believe I've made it back home." Mark stammered.

Will gave Mark a good solid punch on the shoulder. "It's real, Brother. We are here. We are home." Looking out across the plains and the mountains and the coulees and river bottoms, Will stated again, "Look at it. Just look at it. My, my, what a morning!!!"

Will was right. There's just nothing like late September in Montana. The mornings are cool and crisp, the humidity is low, and the aspen and cottonwood trees are finding their leaves turning brilliant yellow, fiery orange and hot red, colors that contrast against a deep ocean blue sky. Although Montana was very much modernized, mostly in agriculture, it remains wild in so many ways. With fewer than a million people in the entire state, and the fourth largest state in the nation, it provided all the elbowroom we could ever ask for. That was one thing we had not considered when we had moved. We had no idea how claustrophobic we would feel, living in a city or apart from sky that seemed like it went on forever.

I continued driving north, we watched the antelope and deer eat and play along the side of the road. Pressing on through Harlowton, we passed through Judith Gap and then Garneil, Buffalo, Straw and were soon at Eddie's Corner, just a couple miles outside of Moore. Clovis was already there waiting. Judy and Wren had decided to stay home. Judy had told Clovis that she was tired of traveling and just wanted to stay at the house. Wren, who wanted to come and be with me, felt it would be better for her to stay at home with her mother and let the men be by themselves for a while.

After eating a huge breakfast at Eddie's corner, we drove into Lewistown and then continued on and stopped at the Bohemian Corner where we filled up the truck and headed toward the Breaks-- as they are known by Montanans. As we topped the hill before dropping down into the Missouri River bottoms, I slowed the truck and just stopped on the highway to admire the view that lay before us.

"Something, isn't it?" Clovis asked from the back seat.

"Yes, it is." Will whispered in an almost sacred tone of voice.

"Elk or no elk, just seeing this again has already made my trip." Mark declared.

"I had forgotten just how huge this area really is, and how beautiful it is in its own way. Would you look at those huge cottonwoods and willows down there in the bottom?"

The leaves were magnificent. Will, recalled the first time we came up here. We made our camp down near the area they call Turkey Joe. Wow, what a trip. We relived the trip in our memories as Will recaptured the scene. Dad, along with Will and me, slept in the bed of the truck that first night in our sleeping bags, lying there in the darkness, looking up at a million stars. We could hear the bulls bugling and the cows chirping all night long, and then the coyotes would join in and bring to the symphony their own kind of music. What a night. What a memory.

"Oh, yeah, I remember that night. I've thought of it many times. I've told my kids about it, and I hope to be able to share with them the same kind of trip Dad shared with us on that hunting adventure. Hey, if I recall, you missed something like 5 shots on that trip, didn't ya?" Will jested and poked.

Laughing out loud, I admitted, "You're never going to let me live that one down are you?"

Will laughed and continued, "Listen to this Clovis. Ross here had practiced with his bow, every evening, for two solid months. At 40 yards, he could put all six arrows in a small paper plate. I mean he was ready. Then, I believe it was that very next day, Ross got down there in the bottom, right in the middle of a whole herd. I'm talking a big herd, with several nice bulls at 20 yards or less and, wow, what I would have given to had a video camera back then." Will was really rubbing it in and continued, "You've heard the saying about the guy who couldn't hit a bull in the butt? Well, ole Ross here, he couldn't hit a bull in the butt, or the foot or anywhere else for that matter. Arrows were flying everywhere, like at Custer's Last Stand, and I don't think he even came close. I've never witnessed buck fever so terrible in all my life. I was standing behind him about another 20 yards and I watched him. When he pulled that bow back, his whole body was shaking like an aspen leaf in a hurricane."

Clovis and Mark got a good laugh out of that. Will always knew how to blow a story clear out of proportion. The truth be known though, he wasn't far off the mark. His story was closer to being accurate than my shooting was that day.

"Ok, guys. I don't deny it. That was a long time ago. Where do we go from here, Clovis?" I asked, changing the subject abruptly.

Suddenly, a bullet crashed through the rear window to the cab of my truck, passing through the top of Clovis' felt hat, then nipping the top of my right ear and exited out the front windshield, leaving a clean, slick hole as if someone had drilled it out with a bit. Slamming the truck into gear, I punched it down the highway toward the Fred Robertson Bridge.

"Do you see anyone? Do you see anyone?" I asked, loudly repeating myself twice.

"No!!!" Everyone stated in unison, as they were constantly turning their heads and looking to see behind them to ascertain from where the shot might have come. With my foot in the floorboard as far as it would go and the needle on the speedometer buried out of sight, I drove to put as much distance between the truck and whoever had taken the shot.

"Oh crap!!!" I shouted. Everyone quickly glanced ahead. Waiting on the bridge, three men stepped to the middle of the road, carrying heavy artillery. I slammed on the brakes.

"What do I do? What do I do?" I asked, expecting to catch a bullet at any moment.

"Stay down Mark and Will. Just stay down." Clovis ordered with a serious, but very strange calmness to his voice.

Mark and Will slipped down to the floorboard. I had come to a complete stop.

Staring down the highway at the men standing there with their weapons in their hands, Clovis pulled himself up to the back of my ear. "Listen to me Ross. They're waiting for someone. That's got to be the reason they haven't started firing on us yet. If you'll look to your left at about 10 o'clock, you'll notice a game trail just on the other side of that barbwire fence. When I say 'go', you punch it across the ditch, ram that fence and stay on that trail until it tops that little rise. From there, just keep the wheels on the ground and put some serious dirt between us. Sooner or later, we're going to run out of drivable terrain. Listen guys, when we get to that point. Be ready to grab your packs and follow me. We're going to run like our life depends on it, because it does. I've hunted this area before. I know it pretty well, but it's rough. I doubt it's changed one bit since Lewis and Clark explored it in 1804."

I remember thinking and wondering to myself how Clovis could be so calm, and why, of all times was he giving us a history lesson, when all I wanted to do was get out of there? In retrospect, it was a simple tactic of communication to ease the tension.

"Are you ready, Ross?" Clovis asked.

"As much as I can be, I suppose." I replied.

"Mark, Will, you men ready?" Clovis asked. "Yes, Sir, let's get out of here." Mark replied. "Go! Go! Go!" Clovis barked.

I had already put the truck into automatic four-wheel drive. I slammed the pedal to the floor, turned sharply to my left, peeling rubber on the asphalt, sped down into the bar ditch and came up the other side, taking with me several strands of barbwire and breaking several posts off at the ground, airborne for a short moment, landing on the game trail.

Bouncing up and down and sideways, I had no time to consider if the rest of the guys were making it all right. I just hoped we could get out of range and danger quickly. As we topped the hill, following the game trail, several slugs hit the truck. Even among all the commotion, we could hear the dull ting of the bullets striking the body of the truck.

Clovis spoke up, "That's heavy caliber. Go right. Drive toward that patch of junipers up there half a mile or so."

Following Clovis' instructions, we dropped down into a coulee that put us out of sight from the men on the bridge. We still did not know who or what was behind us. Rather than going up the other side of the coulee, I turned the truck and drove down the bottom for a few hundred yards and then found another side coulee that merged into the one we were in. Quickly following it up, we headed out on to a sagebrush flat. The sagebrush was old growth, tall, and thick and the only choice I had was to try to drive the truck across it, which made for a very bumpy ride and impossible to see any unforeseen obstacles.

Will, who was sitting in the back seat beside Clovis, had turned and glanced out the back window and said, "We've got company boys."

Clovis turned and looked only to confirm what Will had just said. "Yes, Sir, we sure do. About a half a mile back. I can't tell but it looks like they're in a Hummer. In this truck we don't stand a chance of out running them." I punched the accelerator even harder.

A split-second too late, Mark yelled out, "Watch out, Ross!!!"

We had suddenly dropped out of sagebrush into a steep canyon. The truck slammed into a rock outcropping, the only thing that kept us from spilling over the edge, which certainly would have been the death of all of us. Water and antifreeze spewed forth in steam out of the radiator. We were done.

"Grab your gear, Boys. Let's go!" Clovis yelled, to which all of us opened our doors, reached into the bed of the truck, grabbed our packs, and turned to follow Clovis. With the agility of a mountain goat and the speed of an antelope, Clovis led the way, descending down the near vertical drop and with the Tyler boys' right on his tail. Arriving at the bottom of the canyon, we found a game trail that coursed the bottom, headed directly toward the larger bottoms of the Missouri River.

We had barely run more than a couple hundred yards, when Clovis, eased off the trail and ducked in behind a large juniper tree. Mark, Will and I did the same. I stood there amazed while trying to catch my breath.

Mark and Will were sucking wind as hard as I was; Clovis did not appear to even be breathing hard. Once again, I found it hard to believe that a man, who was much older than I, could run as fast and as far as he did without so much as a hint of labored breathing or increased heart rate.

Clovis whispered, "Listen boys," while cupping his hand to his ear. Sure enough, we could hear the sound of a motor. Looking back toward the direction of my truck, we saw the Hummer pull up and parking to its side. Four men got out and walked to the edge, dressed in camouflage clothing.

Clovis whispered again, "Stay down and stay low. Don't let them see us. Don't even move."

We could tell that a couple of them were looking for us through their binoculars as we noticed the gleam of the sun off of their lens. Tucked back into the shadows as we were would make it very difficult for them to spot us as long as we didn't move too much. Reaching into his pack, Clovis pulled out his small set of binoculars and glanced in their direction. Still whispering, he confirmed, "That's them."

"Who's them?" Will asked. It occurred to me that I had not shared with Mark or with Will Clovis' concern about possible danger from a group of North Vietnamese men. I had only mentioned it to Dad.

Clovis turned to me. "I guess you haven't told them yet?" He asked. "No." I ashamedly admitted. "I didn't think we were going to run into danger out here hunting elk."

"Tell us what?" Will asked again.

"Clovis saw some men in the audiences of the talk shows where he appeared that he thinks might be family to a very high-ranking general he killed back in Viet Nam and also thinks that they may be seeking vengeance. President Watson has some men looking into it, but Clovis hasn't heard anything from him."

Mark just sat there shaking his head back and forth, saying "hmm, hmm, hmm." Will's jaw just sort of dropped, not sure what to say. Clovis was silent. Mark finally broke the silence as we all tried to contemplate the severity of the mess we had just found ourselves so bogged down in. "Well, Ross, you had no way of knowing that trouble would come here. I mean, shoot, here we are in the Breaks. This land isn't even fit for human habitation. No one would think trouble from the other side of the world would find us here."

"Yup, that's right, Ross. No one is blaming you." Will affirmed. "I will say this: life with you has always been an adventure. I was kind of hoping that after getting Clovis out of the Bob Marshall three months ago, that our adventures might be a little less dangerous." Will softly chuckled with a hint of sarcasm in his voice.

"Listen up, Guys. If this is anybody's fault, it is mine. I'm not sure why I thought going elk hunting was such a great idea in the first place when I knew that there might be impending danger coming my way. I just knew that you guys hadn't had an opportunity to enjoy Montana in years and with only a week of hunting season left and winter coming on, I thought it might make for a good trip. To top it off, I'm the only one hunting. You guys just came along for the ride and help me pack out a bull if I got lucky enough to stick one. Looking at it now, I guess it wasn't such a great plan after all."

Will rebutted, "Clovis, we know your intentions were good. There's no way that you knew danger would find us out here. Besides, it doesn't matter that we're not the ones who are actually doing the hunting."

"That's right." Mark agreed.

Glassing with his binoculars at the men back up on the bluff, Clovis stated, "These guys are armed for bear. They appear to be looking at something up the canyon. They haven't spotted us yet, but we're kind of stuck here until they move into a position where they won't be able to see us. Let's look at our gear and shuck everything that we absolutely won't need. Did any of you bring a gun?"

"Not me." I answered. "Me either." Mark and Will stated. "We all know that we didn't want to have a firearm on us while you were hunting elk during archery season. I certainly didn't want to get a citation from a game warden."

We all kind of chuckled. At the present, a citation from a game warden would be welcomed compared to the trouble we were in now.

"Wow!" Clovis exclaimed. "This is going to be interesting." Clovis withdrew his breakdown longbow from his pack and strung it and also a quiver full of arrows. "I got us into this mess; I reckon I'll be the one to get us out." I do believe that all three of the Tyler boys just stared in disbelief. The idea of trying to take on four, heavily armed, trained soldiers with a stick and a string was a bit too much to swallow, in fact, it was about as ludicrous as trying to chew a piece of shoe leather and consuming it for supper. Like shoe leather, it seems the more you chew it, the bigger it becomes.

"Clovis, don't you think that we might stand a better chance of escape by eluding these guys and finding our way back to the law?" I asked.

"Yes, that's exactly what I intend to do. However, if these men are Ho Lee's sons, you can rest assured that they are the best at guerilla warfare, and that's what it's going to be like for us down there in those river bottoms. They know how to track down their enemy. Now, let's look at our gear."

Spreading out our gear on the ground, Clovis started naming off the items we each needed to put in our packs. "Knife, flashlight, matches, rope, compass, poncho, one pair of dry socks, one set of dry clothes, trail mix, water container. Leave the sleeping bags, tent and everything else here. Stash them here at the base of this tree. I'll buy you some new ones when we get out of here."

"You mean, *if* we get out of here, don't ya?" Will implored.

"No, Sir. I mean *when*. There's no '*if*' to it. Always think on the positive side. Success only comes to those who believe they can succeed. Not only do I believe that we will succeed, but I believe that before this is all over, the Lord is going to grant us the opportunity to make sure that these boys don't ever pull another stunt like this again."

There was a tone in Clovis' voice that caused the three of us to look at him. I can't identify exactly what made us ponder his comment. Maybe it was recognition of his tremendous faith or maybe it was the fact, that what Clovis was really saying was he was not going to let there be another opportunity for his past to bring anymore threat to his future, and that included keeping all of us from harm's way. Just how he intended to accomplish such a feat was uncertain.

Glassing the bluff again, Clovis spoke up, "Ok, it looks like they have not been able to locate us so they are picking up our trail and coming down off the side where we ourselves descended. Here in a moment, they are going to be out of our view, which means that we will be out of theirs. When I say '*go*', follow me."

Strapping our very light-weight and compact packs on our back, we waited. Clovis shouldered his pack and then swung his quiver over his head and shoulder. I noticed how it fell right into place. Picking up his bow, he looked back up the canyon toward the bluff again. The four men finally descended far enough down the bluff that they could no longer be seen. At the command of Clovis, we ran farther down the canyon, headed for the river bottom. From there, I had no idea what Clovis had in mind.

CHAPTER 9

Meanwhile, obviously without any of us knowing anything about it, President Watson had called the Belden ranch and tried to talk with Judy and Wren. He was, however, unable to get in touch with them. The FBI had conducted a very thorough investigation to find out more about the men that Clovis had witnessed in the audiences where he had appeared as a talk show guest.

The FBI's communication with the North Vietnamese' embassy conveyed that two of the men were indeed the two youngest sons of Ho Lee, and although they had previously served in the North Vietnamese military, they had made the transition into politics and were here in the States to observe the latest technology in the rice production of Louisiana and southern Texas and were given the opportunity to spend a couple weeks of leisure time traveling in the United States. They were spending most of their time in California-- Los Angeles, more specifically—which, of course, is where Clovis and Judy had appeared before the camera crews. According to the informants of the embassy, the Lee Brothers were fascinated with the charm and the appeal that Clovis seemed to have with the American people. With future political ambitions of their own, they used every opportunity to watch and learn from Clovis anything that they might find to be beneficial for leadership in their own country.

The Lee Brothers and their colleagues had flown back to North Vietnam, confirmed by the airlines, and therefore presented no threat to Clovis or his family. President Watson desperately wanted to share this information with the Beldens because he knew that it would put their mind at ease.

After several attempts, Watson made a call to Chief Officer Givens, who, along with his men, kept watch on the entrance to the Belden Ranch, to see if he or his men knew the location of Judy or Wren. Chief Officer Givens confirmed that neither of the two women had left the ranch. Perhaps they were out doing chores or something of that nature and were not in the house where they could hear the phone ring. Clovis had left very early that morning, he reported, but did not know where he was going.

President Watson decided he would wait until later that evening and try to call again.

As mentioned earlier, we of course had no idea what was going on behind the scene and at the moment all that mattered was trying to survive the present. At a steady pace, we ran the course of the canyon as it led into the river bottom.

The Missouri Breaks, although not mountainous, is a rough, broken terrain. Unfit for human habitation, it remains a vast area very well suited for wildlife. The elk, the whitetail deer and the mule deer thrive here, as do the coyotes, the badger, prairie dogs, pronghorn antelope and thousands of rattlesnakes. The summers are typically hot and dry while the winters are bitter cold. Because of its unsuitable habitat and climate for mankind, very little of it has changed throughout the years. Portions of it were used for recreation, but for the most part, the Breaks received very little human traffic. I suppose elk hunters pursuing one of the many magnificent bulls that live in the area probably make up the majority of visitors. Stretching over a distance of nearly 150 miles long and a third that size in width, it can become a very intimidating piece of real estate to navigate.

Clovis led the way down the trail through the bottom of the canyon, carrying his longbow loosely in his hand. Mark and Will followed right behind, while I pulled up the rear. At a steady clip, we felt confident that we were putting the distance between our pursuers and us. It would not be long until the shadows of evening would be upon us. I hoped Clovis had a plan for the night.

Mark suddenly caught the toe of his boot on a rock and was unable to capture his balance before taking a hard fall onto the dusty, rocky, ground, soaking up an armload of cactus pricks as he rolled to a stop, face down in the dirt.

"Mark, don't move." I yelled.

Mark froze. Prostrate on his belly, he looked up only to find himself staring face to face with a large, coiled rattlesnake only a foot or so from his face. As quickly as it happened, it ended even more quickly. In less than a heartbeat, an arrow shot through the air, impaling the rattlesnake through the head and pinning it to the ground. If I had not witnessed it with my own eyes, I would have never believed it.

Will and I looked over at Clovis and then back at each other, shaking our heads in disbelief. Judy had once told me that Clovis used to practice shooting golf balls out in the yard, but I had never really given that too much thought.

Mark was just starting to rise up from the ground as the three of us were walking over to him.

"Are you all right?" I asked.

"Yup!" Mark answered as he was dusting himself off. I could see that he was scraped up a little.

"Thanks, Clovis!" Mark responded gratefully. "I'm sure glad you didn't miss. That sucker would have nailed me right between the eyes."

The thought crossed my mind. That rattlesnake may have bitten Mark or it might not have. I've had some close calls with rattlesnakes before, and I've had them slither away, when I thought for sure I was going to get bitten, but one thing I felt confident about is that if that arrow had been off by half an inch, that rattlesnake would have struck at Mark for certain.

"That was quite a shot, Clovis." Will praised. "I don't believe I've ever seen anyone shoot like that before."

Clovis suddenly, in cat-like speed, withdrew an arrow from his quiver, laid it across the rest of his bow, drawing quickly and releasing the string just as the fingers of his draw hand touched the corner of his mouth. The arrow zipped through the air about 20 yards down toward Mark and impaled another rattlesnake through the head, right in front of Mark who was still trying to gather his senses as he was climbing back up to the trail.

"Mark, you had better get out of there. I think you've stumbled into a bunch of those ornery critters." Clovis strongly suggested.

At the shout of Clovis, Will spoke up, "Listen. Do you hear that?" All of us stood real still. There was a buzzing sound all around us. We were all very familiar with that sound, but never so loudly. Letting our eyes do the walking, we began to notice that there were rattlesnakes all around us. Most of them were coiled up, while some were slowly slithering across the ground.

"They are denning up." Clovis remarked. "It's what they do each fall as they prepare to hibernate for the winter. Mark, carefully get back up here to the trail, and let's all get out of here. I hate those things."

When Mark made it up to the trail, he immediately went over and shook hands with Clovis and gave him a shoulder bump. "Thanks, Clovis. That was close. That was some mighty fine shooting." If any of us had any doubts about the first shot just being lucky, the second shot eliminated all doubts for sure.

"You're welcome, Mark. Now, we had better make like a cow pie and hit the dusty trail. We can't afford to lose too much time, or those guys will catch up to us." Once again we began running toward the river.

As we dropped out of the hills into the huge Missouri River valley, the terrain changed dramatically. The bottoms were mostly flat. Huge cottonwood trees and willows and alders grew so thick and nearly impossible to penetrate that the going was slow. If it were not for the numerous game trails, made mostly by the repeated passage of elk and deer throughout the years, I doubt a person could traverse across it without a machete or something capable of cutting a path.

The encroaching darkness of evening was even more

magnified as we moved deeper into the thick timber. Finally stopping, Clovis turned to us and suggested in a soft voice that we get off of the game trails and sleep in and among the willow trees. Unfortunately, we would not be able to have a fire as doing so might reveal our presence. We all knew that it would be a cold night, and we didn't have much to keep us warm other than the clothes we were wearing.

Mark interrupted, "I've got at least a dozen hand warmers in my pack. They should help out a little."

"Great." Clovis replied. "If you've got a bandana or a sock that you can put one in and put around your neck, keeping the hand warmer right over your jugular vein, it will warm the blood as it passes throughout your body and to your extremities." We of course were already aware of that trick. We had used hand warmers in such a way many times during the harsh cold months of winter in Montana. Nevertheless, we were all thankful that Mark had thought enough to bring them along. Too, all of us had packed a light jacket which would serve to help a little.

Clovis led the way into the thick willows, well off the beaten trail we had been following. "Okay, Boys. This is where we will rest tonight. We will all need to eat and drink a bite, and then when we get ready to sleep, we'll take turns on watch. I'll be happy to take the first one."

Spending the night on the ground, under the clear, colossal canopy of vividly brilliant, shining stars that lit up the massive Montana sky was nothing new for my brothers and me. Many times, while growing up on the ranch, we would go outside with our sleeping bags and spend the night in the yard at the house, just so we could absorb the beauty of the heavens above, which so often, seemed close enough to reach up and touch. The thought of home stirred within me the desire to be anywhere but where we were. I longed for the safety and security that home always provides.

As the three of us lay down on the ground after moving the fallen debris from our resting place, we tucked our hands into the pockets of our coat and stared up into the sky. Occasionally, the coyotes would howl and sing, and others would join in, making a melody that only they could understand. A night hawk would scream as it searched to find its next meal. Nearby, a bull elk would bugle, and another would answer and then another, sending challenges to one another as they still instinctively pursued the estrous cows during this breeding season, which was soon to come to a close. Of all the voices of nature, I am stirred by the bugling of bulls more than any other. Over the years I have contemplated the reason why I am moved so much by their call. I have finally concluded that it isn't so much the sound, but more about what the sound of their voice represents. The elk I have hunted were usually found in the undefiled, unspoiled wilderness, far and away from the presence of man, the only place that I have ever found solace and tranquility. This, I believe, is why I am so drawn to their call.

Will whispered, "This reminds me of that night we spent with Dad so many years ago."

"Yes, it does." I affirmed. "Only we didn't have somebody chasing us on that trip."

Clovis was somewhere farther back in the woods, keeping watch for impending trouble.

"Ross, what do you think Clovis is going to do tomorrow if we survive this night?"

"I'm going to try to get us out of here and contact the law." Clovis exclaimed. None of us knew that Clovis had moved back into our camp. Looking toward the sound of his voice, Will stated, "Dang, Clovis, you scared me."

"I'm Sorry, Boys. I need you to come and look at something for a minute and tell me what you think."

Getting up from the ground, we followed Clovis through the dark, willow-clustered bottom until we broke out into a small meadow about 30 yards wide.

"Look up there at that hill side that rises up directly from this river bottom about a mile or so." Clovis ordered.

"That looks like a fire, maybe a campfire." Mark stated.

"That's exactly what it is, a rather large one." Clovis declared. "Now, here's what I am thinking. There are several possibilities for building a fire. First is the obvious, that is, they want to stay warm. I wouldn't mind one right now either. Second, they want us to know that they are still following us, and it serves as a method of intimidation. Thirdly, they may have built the fire to use as a bait, hoping that we will see it and decide to take the fight to them while they sit and wait to ambush us, or fourthly, they may have built it hoping we believe that they are camping there for the night, while they do their best to slip in on us in the dark. I'm worried that it may be the latter."

"What do you suggest we do?" I asked.

In the glow of the moon and starlit night, I could see Clovis biting his lip as he contemplated the options. I knew he was worried. It wasn't just his life that depended upon the right decisions being made as it had been in the past. This time, Mark and Will and I were totally depending on the choices Clovis would make. It was not like we were totally incompetent in the woods. In fact, we were quite capable of survival, but this, in its own way, was war, and we were inexperienced. Clovis on the other hand had not only survived his three years in Viet Nam and his three years in the Bob Marshall Wilderness as a fugitive of the law, but had thrived. His ability to remain undetected and concealed, along with his marksmanship and survival skills were like none other I had ever witnessed, and yet, as he was asking these questions aloud to my brothers and me, it became readily apparent that, just as important as his aforementioned skills might be, his ability to anticipate the reason, reaction and response of his enemy was even more so. Truthfully, I had absolutely no problem placing my complete trust in Clovis. Mark and Will told me later that they felt exactly the same way. There was no other man to that date that we believed was more capable of getting us out alive than Clovis Belden. Clovis actually made it easy to trust.

While these thoughts were going through my head, Clovis must have been reading my mind. "Ok, Tyler Boys let me ask you. Have

89

you ever heard the hymnal, *Trust and Obey?*" We all whispered that we had.

"Ok, then. This is what I'm asking of you. I'm not the Lord, but I need you to trust and obey me. These men are extremely dangerous. They are masters of guerilla warfare, and they will know every trick in the book. We are at a tremendous disadvantage right now. Our weapons are inadequate compared to theirs. I'm the only one of us who has any fighting experience at this level, where as I am sure that all of them are trained in military combat.

"So, Clovis, are you saying that you think that they might be trying to find us right now?"

"That's exactly what I am saying. If they have night vision or heat sensing equipment, we are at more of a disadvantage than we would be in the broad daylight. Considering the type of artillery they were using when they fired on us early today, we cannot assume that they do not have other highly advanced technological equipment."

"Just tell us what to do, Clovis. We're ready." Will asserted.

"Let's gather some wood right quick. I know it's dark, but certainly we can find some. Be careful where you reach. We cannot afford for one of us to get snake bitten right now."

In less than ten minutes or so, we all had an armload of dried deadfall from the forest floor and put it in a pile near the edge of the meadow.

"What are we going to do?" I asked.

"We are going to build a fire and let them know where we are." Clovis answered. "However, we are not going to be here. We are going to use it as a decoy to divert their attention. This should buy us a little time so we can get farther away from here."

"That doesn't sound like it will buy us all that much time, because it won't take them long to figure out that they have been duped." Mark suggested.

"You're right, Mark. However, this fire will lead them right to a surprise. We are quickly going to build a couple of snares that should even the odds."

Clovis gave each of us instructions about what we needed to do or what we needed to gather. My brothers and I had built many different kinds of snares and knew some that we never used, simply because they were too dangerous and lethal, and we feared if we ever set one, a human might step into it rather than the animal we desired to catch. Still, having the knowledge of the snare's construction accelerated the process of putting it together. These two snares were often called the 'pig stabber', but instead of attaching sharpened stakes to the heavy sapling we left them bare. In no time at all, we had two snares set and concealed. Mark noticed that the design that Clovis had given us to construct would not be lethal, but would only bring injury.

He commented to Clovis, "These aren't going to kill anyone, Clovis.

At best, they might break a leg."

"That's right, Mark. I don't want to kill anyone. I want to get out of here and let the law take care of these guys. I'm tired of killing. Besides, if your enemy is pursuing you, and you kill one of their comrades, they just leave him behind and keep on coming. If you injure one, well, the rest have to stop and figure out a way of dealing with the injured comrade. That takes time and more time is exactly what we need right now."

Clovis explained that he really did not want to move too far from where we built the fire. While in motion, we would be more likely to be noticed or seen, so it was better to find a hiding place and just wait, which is exactly what we did.

All night long we waited, but nothing happened. All of us were tired from lack of sleep and the after effects of the adrenaline rush we had experienced earlier in the day while being chased and running for our lives. Even as tired and exhausted as we were, we could not sleep. If these men were as dangerous as Clovis believed them to be, and I had a gut feeling that Clovis wasn't telling us everything, perhaps because he feared it would immobilize our ability to think cognitively, then we dared not let our guard down. Remaining constantly vigilant was imperative to our survival.

The temperature had dropped significantly throughout the night. We did not have a thermometer, but we guessed it was hovering around the freezing mark. In Montana, 30 degrees or so doesn't mean much, because the air is dry, and it doesn't sting nearly as bad as it does in places where the climate is much more humid, but that evening, very near the river and trying to remain still and concealed, we shivered. Only Mark's hand warmers brought relief.

I asked Clovis, "What do you make of the fact that we've not seen or heard anything?" It did not appear that the Lee Brothers had even made an attempt to come near the fire that we had built, which was now, nothing more than a very light-red ember of ash, glowing in the dark, predawn ebony night.

"They didn't fall for it." Clovis flatly stated. "I believe they knew it was a trap, just like they were trying to lead us into theirs. I don't know that for sure, but one thing is for certain, they haven't showed up. That means we don't have a clue where they are."

"Clovis, I know that we saw four men. Do you think that is all of them or is it possible there are more?" Mark asked.

Standing only inches away from each other, we all turned to look at Clovis. He replied, "I really don't know. I have tried to contemplate every possible scenario that could happen, and I just don't know what they are trying to do. My gut feeling tells me that there are more of them, and I'm afraid that they are setting up a trap. Perhaps there are more of them that have circled around up the river and are waiting to ambush us. It's just impossible to know for sure. All I know is I want to get out of here and get the law in here as quickly as possible."

I didn't speak my thoughts aloud at the moment, but there was a quiver, perhaps a shake in that deep, low voice of Clovis, and I wondered if he was afraid. I had witnessed nearly every other emotion in the man, but never fear.

What I didn't vocalize, Will did. "Are you afraid, Clovis?" Will asked.

Without hesitation, Clovis answered, "You bet your bottom dollar I'm afraid. Fear can be your friend as well as your enemy.

Fear, as long as it doesn't cloud sound judgment, can empower you do more than you might be able to normally. However, although I fear our enemy, it's the uncertainty that I fear the most. Always staying one step ahead is what has kept me alive for all these years, and that usually comes from careful calculation and consideration of what I believe the enemy will do next, or how they will react. So far, I haven't figured that out."

The horizon to the east was outlined with hot pink that gradually grew wider and turned to red, a sure sign that rain was on the way. As the dark, black night slowly grayed, gunfire suddenly erupted and burst toward the west, upstream, the direction we intended to follow.

"What do you suppose that is all about?" I inquired.

"It sounds like it's about half a mile from here. It was an automatic weapon, that's for sure. No one should have a gun down here during archery season, so I'm thinking it's got to be those guys who are after us." Clovis answered.

"Yeah, but who or what are they shooting at?" Mark asked.

"Let's stay in these willows and work our way in that direction and see if we can find out." Clovis ordered.

CHAPTER 10

As we fought through the tangled mess of the river bottom, jumping deer and elk as we moved along, a light, misty rain began to settle over the valley. Soon the rain began to pour, and we were drenched from head to toe. Stepping into the shade of a huge cottonwood, which was still carrying its leaves, though yellow, and due to fall any day, we huddled up together to let the storm blow over. Wet, cold and shivering, we didn't say much. Will then whispered, "Clovis, watch this."

A large bull elk had just stepped out of the willows and alders and had absolutely no idea that we were there. Will, softly let loose a seductive cow call. The magnificent bull raised his head and looked in our direction, as we stayed hidden behind the trunk of the large cottonwood. Standing there trying to locate the source of the sound, exhaling steam from his nostrils in the cool, wet morning air, he was just absolutely stunning. Will gave a soft chirp and then followed it up with an excited estrous cow call. The bull raised his nostrils toward the sky, tilted his head, his long, heavy, ivory-tipped antlers nearly touching his rump, and bugled loudly, followed by a series of guttural grunts. He began walking in our direction. At 15 yards, he stopped and looked again; still uncertain of where the lovesick cow he was looking for had disappeared. Will turned his voice the other direction to throw his sound further behind us and let go another soft chirp. The bull walked up to within 5 yards of us and just stood there for at least a full minute before realizing that he had been duped. Crashing out of there like a fire was underneath him, he disappeared back into the willows again.

We all chuckled. "Clovis, I do believe you could have killed that bull." Mark scoffed jokingly, recalling that Clovis had just the day before put an arrow in the head of two rattlesnakes at more than three times that distance.

"That was truly impressive," Clovis expressed excitedly. "I think I'll remember that experience for the rest of my life. Even though I didn't draw an arrow, just having one of God's most royal and noble wild creatures like that so close is as good as it gets. As far as I'm concerned, we just accomplished what we came here to do. That was some mighty fine calling Will. I can't believe you can do that with just your voice." Of course, we all knew why Clovis didn't shoot the bull. We had indeed come to hunt elk, but tending to the care of a bull after he had been shot is hard work and we were not in the position to forfeit our time butchering and packing out an elk, and Clovis was not going to kill it just for the sake of killing it either. People who do that sort of thing, are, in my mind, no better than the kind of men who were pursuing us now.

"I'd give just about anything for a dry set of clothes right now." I complained.

"Me, too." Clovis stated as he looked toward the river. "I've got an idea."

Clovis pushed his way through the willows toward the river while the rest of us followed. The rain had caused a heavy fog to sit over the river and the nearby banks. Before Clovis told us what we had in mind, we figured it out, and we liked the idea. We started a fire with the driest wood we could find knowing that the smoke would dissipate in the dense fog, making it impossible for anyone, mainly those who were seeking our skin, to detect our presence. After getting the fire going and standing around it trying to warm ourselves, we stripped off our clothes and strung them on a rope we had stretched between and around the young trees that surrounded our fire so we could hang them up to dry. All of us wore polyester camouflage fatigues for which we were thankful. They dry in about the third of the time as cotton. Fortunately, we all had dry socks in our packs. I hate wet feet, and there is nothing that feels better than putting on a pair of dry socks over cold wet feet.

Will commented, "I sure hope we don't get caught like this. You know, with our pants down." The humor lightened the mood a little and soon we were feeling much better. While standing there drying out, we each tore into a protein bar and some trail mix. We lacked sleep, and we weren't about to get any of it soon, but we needed fuel and nourishment, and it boosted our spirits tremendously.

The rain had lightened to nothing more than a mist. The fire had warmed our clothes, and although they were not totally dry, they felt much better as we put them back on. Will, obviously on a roll, spoke up again. "Clovis, that was a great idea, starting a fire in this fog so we couldn't be seen, but when Ross dropped his pants, I thought for sure those white legs of his would send out a light as bright as a beacon." We all laughed. He was right; I had not worn shorts all summer long and did not get my usual tan.

"Where do we go from here?" I asked.

"We've got to find our way to a town or somebody's ranch so we can make a call to the authorities." Clovis suggested. "The problem is, I've only hunted in this area one time, and I wasn't this far up river. As far as I know, I think Geraldine is the closest town, and I don't know if anyone lives between here and there. I think it's too risky to try to go back the way we came. If we get out on top in the flats, we'll just be sitting ducks. I'm still not sure just how many guys they've got with them."

We stood there for a minute or two, waiting on Clovis to make the call, when a scream from the direction we had come muffled across the valley. "They're on us, Guys." Clovis stated. "Somebody just stepped into one of those snares we set last night. That ought to slow them down a little." Because of the heavy foggy morning and the distance from the snare, the sounds of someone screaming in pain could barely be heard, but it was obviously apparent that they were hurting badly. Suddenly, a shot rang out and the screaming ceased.

"Dang it." Clovis bitterly stated while biting his lower lip. Thinking about it now, that's the only time, I ever heard Clovis say anything remotely close to a curse word. The shot did not have to be explained to any of us. Whoever had stepped into that snare was quickly put out of his misery. Clovis turned to my brothers and me and looked at us very seriously. "Now you men know the kind of animals we are dealing with. We've got to get out of here and be careful and fast about doing it. The ground is wet now, and that means it will be easier for us to leave a track behind and easier for them to stay on our trail, and as you well know, the mud down here on the bottom is the stickiest mud I've ever encountered anywhere. It will slow us down considerably, but it will do the same to our followers. Follow me."

We skirted the edge of the willows along the river bank exposing ourselves more than any of us wanted to, but we were able to make better time without the willows and brush to fight, and running on the gravel bar would leave no tracks to follow. The rain was gone and the clouds had opened up to a beautiful ocean blue sky, allowing the sun to filter down upon our shoulders. The cold shivering rain that had soaked our clothes had been replaced with hot sticky sweat as we kept running along the river.

In an instant, Clovis abruptly came to a halt. Pulling his binoculars to his eyes, he looked toward the distant hills that ascended up from the river bottom. His body language indicated that he was very upset before he said anything to us. Lowering the binoculars, he handed them to me and pointed. "Look over there at about 11 o'clock, half way up that ridge, and tell me what you see."

Looking through the lens as Clovis had instructed, my eyes settled on a group of men, three to be exact, hunters I assumed by the clothes they were wearing, who were being marched up the hill at gun point by the men who had been chasing us. I handed the glasses to Mark and then to Will.

"What do you make of that, Clovis?" I asked.

"I think that they think that they've caught you guys. They've never seen your face, well, maybe yours Ross, but maybe not. They know what I look like, but no matter what, they've got the wrong men. You can bet they're going to do whatever they have to in order to make them give me up. The problem is, they don't know. Those men are clueless that we are even here. My guess is they came here to hunt elk just like we have."

Clovis placed both of his hands over his face and buried his eyes deep into their palms for a moment. When he brought his hands down, tears flooded his eyes and streaked down his face. Turning to us, his heart fell out across his tongue. "Men, I made a promise to God above that I was through with killing. I told him that I did not want a part of taking another man's life, no matter what the reason or how justifiable it may seem. I don't make promises lightly. A man's word is his bond, and if he can't keep it, as far as I'm concerned, he's nothing but a detriment to society and a waste of precious space on this earth." Clovis paused for a moment, shaking his head, and then looked toward the heavens and whispered just loud enough that we were all able to hear it. "Forgive me, oh God, for what I am about to do. I don't see another choice, but if there is one, please make it visible to me soon. I am sorry. Please, shine your grace upon me, and if you see fit, as you have so many times in the past, place your protecting arms around all of us. Please, I beg thee again; forgive me by the blood of your Son, in whom I pray. Amen."

"Just what have you got in mind, Clovis?" I asked, not knowing for sure if I really wanted to know the answer.

Clovis sensed the agitation in my voice. "Ross, those heathens up there are going to kill those men. They're going to spill their innocent blood on the ground and probably do it very slowly. Now, you know a little about what it feels like to be tortured. You endured that for me just a few months ago, not to mention the fact that your brother, Little Joe, gave his life on my account. I am not about to let those hunters suffer on my account, nor am I going to let you guys get hurt. For two days we have been running away, trying to avoid the fight. Well, they've called my hand now, and they probably don't even know it, but I'm going to take the fight to them.'

"Clovis, how do you intend on doing that?" Mark pleaded. "Those men are up there with automatic weapons, and you're down here with nothing but a stick and a string and a dozen arrows or so. Ross, Will and I have nothing but our hunting knives. Besides, we don't even know for sure how many guys are up there. It won't be a fight. It will be a massacre, and we'll be the ones who are massacred." Mark's voice was irritated, and his volume increased as the obvious distressed tone in his voice escalated.

"What did I tell you guys about thinking on the positive side earlier?

In my opinion, we've got the advantage."

That was it. Clovis' comment struck the wrong cord, and Mark was now fuming mad. He no more liked the idea of those men dying than Clovis or the rest of us did, but in his estimation, Clovis was not being realistic. "Listen Clovis, I know you're a very capable man, like no one I have ever seen, but you're not thinking too clearly. The reality is this, those men are going to die, and if we don't get out of here, we are too. Thinking positively about the situation is not going to change the way things are. Shoot, when I was in high school, my coach used to feed us stories about athletes all the time, who, because they aimed high and kept a positive attitude, were able to accomplish all kinds of great things. Do you know what that was, Clovis? It was a pile of crap. The reality is this, no matter how hard I tried, no matter how much I practiced, no matter how much I believed, I would have never turned out to be another Larry Bird or Julius Erving. Now that's just the simple truth."

Mark had a strong case, but Clovis just looked at him and smiled. "Oh, ye of little faith. You might not have ever turned out to be another Bird or Irving, but have you ever heard of Mark Tyler? All you can be, Mark, is who you are and be the best you that you can be."

Mark just shook his head, knowing he wasn't getting anywhere with Clovis. I knew Mark, because he was my brother, and I knew when he got mad, there wasn't any sense in trying to talk reasonably with him. Saliva formed at the corners of his mouth and this too was a sign that Mark's anger was beyond rescue; however, I must admit, he stayed calm enough to try in his best effort to speak rationally. "Listen to me Clovis." He said, "Right now, I'm alive and I kind of like it that way. If we go up there, all I am going to be is dead. I don't much like the sound of that right now, at all. I understand what you are saying, but it's going to take more than a positive attitude to stay alive if we go up there.

Mark just looked at Clovis and then he looked at Will and me. None of us had anything to say. I mean, what could we say? Mark was right and even Clovis knew he was right, but the one single fact remained, and it was so vividly clear that any argument or excuse provided fell short. None of us could walk away from the innocent men who were being marched up the hill where they were sure to be tortured and killed because the men who held them captive believed they had captured the three of us. Living with that on our conscience was, in our opinion, worse than dying.

In reluctance Mark paused for a minute to collect his composure, "Ok, ok. I don't like it, but I'm not about to let those guys die on account of me, and I won't allow you guys to go at this alone either. We Tyler boys stick together, and if we die, we'll do it together, but I sure hope you've got a plan that doesn't just turn into a suicide mission. I've already lost one brother, and I'm not too excited about the possibility of losing another, and I sure as heck am not in the mood to make my wife a widow and leave my boys without a father."

Mark's face grew red with anger, but tears welled up in his eyes as he considered and counted the cost that might be involved in taking such a risk.

"You bet!!!" Clovis assured while throwing his arms around Mark and giving him a big hug. "That's exactly why you'll stay alive. I told your brother, Ross, here a few months back something that we would all do well to remember. If you'll live, fight, and stay alive for those who love you rather than for yourself, you're far more likely to succeed."

CHAPTER 11

President Watson had made several attempts that first evening to contact Judy and Wren and assure them that their concerns about the Vietnamese men that Clovis had repeatedly witnessed in the audience, were of no threat and had flown back home to North Vietnam. Since, by every observation and consideration, there was no reason for Watson to believe that there was any immediate threat of danger, he could not put his finger on the reason why it bothered him that he could not contact Judy or Wren and at the very least provide them with that assurance. Some inner voice kept telling him that doing so was vitally important, but he wasn't sure if it was important for them or important for him. Maybe, he thought, he just needed to hear their voice and confirm that everything was all right. With an entire nation to run, he found it ironic that the Belden family and their safety continued to infiltrate his thoughts as often as they did. Clovis had made an enormous and lasting impression on him, and Watson knew that he would not even be alive if it were not for the fact that Clovis had saved his life with one well-placed arrow to the throat of Vice President Peterson 3 years earlier. While Watson was grateful and would no doubt feel eternally indebted to Clovis, he was equally sure that this was not the reason for his great admiration and respect and high esteem in which he regarded Clovis.

Clovis represented values unto Watson that he himself had been raised and reared to treasure and uphold in his own life. Those values carried over into every decision he made, both personally and politically. Still, while comparing the loyalty and devotion to the values and morals of Clovis, Watson felt like Belshazzar, the Old Testament king of Babylon, who, after having the handwriting on the wall interpreted by the prophet Daniel, realized his inadequacies. The writing, no doubt by the hand of God, stated, "You have been weighed in the balance and found wanting." Compared to Clovis, Watson was confident that his own moral compass fell short. In a later conversation with Watson, he told me that as he lay in bed that night along with his wife, his mind drifted back to that terrible and tragic day on the North Fork of the Blackfoot River in the Bob Marshall Wilderness when his best friend, Peterson, had fallen nearly 300 feet from a steep, sheer cliff to his death, clinging and pulling the outfitter Newsome along with him to the hard and rocky bottom below. The tragic death of Peterson had hit Watson like nothing he had ever experienced. The immediate burst of grief and despair shattered his heart as if a grenade had gone off in his chest. The loss of his parents, who had both passed since that tragic day, did not affect him as much as the loss of Peterson. There were still times when Peterson's memory would surface, and Watson would find himself in tears, recalling the many good times spent together. Peterson had been his one true friend for so long, that he could not imagine ever having another friend like him. In fact, Peterson was to him, in many ways, closer than his own wife. This, he determined, was not so unusual for men, because men understand men better than women ever will, and consequently, the need to explain or better communicate feelings is usually not necessary when one man speaks to another because it is already understood. As time progresses and relationships deepen, it becomes even truer. Peterson was Watson's best friend, and in spite of the fact that Watson learned that Peterson intended to kill him, Watson still missed him, and his heart still grieved. His mind returned again to the scene of three years ago as he stood on the mountain and watched as Peterson's body was being airlifted from the bottom of the canyon. Watson learned that Peterson had not fallen to his death accidently, but had succumbed to an arrow in the throat. As destructive as the grief had been to his emotions and the sorrow and emptiness his death had brought, the anger that formulated in his veins and was soon followed by the desire for vengeance was magnified so much more. Watson found it ironic, that Clovis, the man whom he now admired and practically revered, had been the cause for both the grief and the anger.

The cold hard truth remained. If Clovis had not shot Peterson, Watson would be dead. The thought sent chills down his spine. Instead of his best friend's body hitting the rocks below in that canyon and that terrible, dreaded thud he heard on impact, it would have been his body making that sound. He wondered if the sound would ever fade from his memory. Just the thought of it still sickened him, even after all these years.

For 3 years he had sent the best men the U.S. military had into the wilderness to try to arrest Clovis for the murder of Vice President Peterson. Although, based upon the evidence that had been discovered, most of the world believed that Clovis had been killed by a grizzly, Watson was confident that Clovis still lived, but without hard evidence, it was difficult to ascertain approval from Congress to fund what they called a ghost hunt. Unknown to anyone else, Watson had also hired private mercenaries to infiltrate the Bob Marshall Wilderness to kill or capture Clovis. The cost of doing so had depleted his savings to almost nothing. None of the mercenaries had succeeded, and not a single one of them had returned from the Bob either. When his account declared that he could not afford to hire anymore, he secretly misappropriated funds in the governmental budget. While it was certain that nearly every other president in the past 100 years had done the same thing for their own personal reasons, he knew in his heart that it was wrong. It stirred his conscience and upset him immensely. It wasn't just the fact that if the information was ever discovered and the media got a hold of it, he would be ruined, and with the election only a little more than a month away, he hoped that it would never be found, nor was it the fact that he had committed a wrong, a sin that violated everything he stood for, but it was the fact that he had let his greed for vengeance tempt him to do things that he would not normally, in good conscience, have done. In that way, Watson surmised that there really wasn't a whole lot of difference between Peterson and him. After all, Peterson's greed for money and power had led Peterson to attempt to murder Watson, betraying a friendship that had endured and thrived for years. Watson's greed for vengeance had led him to embezzlement of funds by America's tax- paying citizens. In Watson's mind, there was nothing to differentiate from. Both actions sprouted forth from the roots of greed and both were wrong. That was the cut and dry of it.

Fortunately, for both Clovis and Watson, the attempts to extinguish the life of Clovis from the face of the planet and make him pay for the death of Peterson were never successful. Again, it chilled Watson to the bone to think that his desire for vengeance had caused him to stoop to a relentless pursuit of a man that actually had saved his life. How, he wondered, could he ever have lived with himself, if Clovis had been killed, and then later find out the truth himself?

Watson was scheduled to fly to Camp David that next morning for an international peace conference with the Israel and Palestinian foreign ministers, and he really wanted to put this unrest behind him before he left. He could not sleep. It was nearly midnight, which meant that it would be 10 p.m. in Montana. He quietly slipped out of his room, so not to disturb his sleeping wife, into his private office. He picked up the phone and attempted to call Judy and Wren once more. The phone rang several times, but no one answered. On a whim, he decided to call Chief Officer Givens, who, along with his men, patrolled the area around the entrance to the Belden Ranch. Hitting speed dial on his phone, he was immediately connected to Officer Givens.

"Officer Givens?" "Yes, Sir."

"What is the status of the Belden Ranch?" Watson asked with a sense of urgency in his voice.

"Everything is quiet. No one has gone in, and no one has come out." Givens responded.

"So, you have not seen any of the Belden family?" Watson asked. "No, Sir. As I mentioned the other day, Mr. Belden left early in the morning two days ago. I'm not sure where he went and figured it wasn't any of my business. As requested, I am trying to allow them to live as normally as possible without prying into their private affairs. My men and I stay on patrol out of sight and will only intervene when we deem necessary."

"Of course, that's what I've ordered you to do. Listen to me now, I am a little concerned that I cannot reach Judy or Wren. I have called the house on numerous occasions at all different times of the day and night, and I have not been successful. Maybe they just have the ringer off on their phone. I know that Judy must have been tired from their time spent in California and all the talk show appearances they made, and she just doesn't want to be bothered. I can certainly relate to those feelings. Keep up the good work, Officer Givens, and call me on my private line if you see them leave the entrance of the ranch."

"Yes, Sir. We'll do."

The information shared by Officer Givens eased Watson's mind to some extent. No news is good news, he thought, but still he had an aching discomfort in his heart. His gut feeling kept telling him that something wasn't as it should be, but again, he couldn't quite wrap his arms around it tight enough to bring it to the surface. It was late, and he needed to sleep. Tomorrow would be a big day at Camp David.

CHAPTER 12

Clovis stooped toward the ground, and with a stick he began drawing in the sand along the riverbank a crude map of our location in relation to the men upon the hill and the surrounding terrain. Mark, Will and I squatted down to observe more closely what Clovis was drawing and to listen to the plan he had in mind. I hoped it was a good one.

I remember thinking at that moment, and I am a little ashamed to say this as I write this now, but the thought crossed my mind that so far the time I had spent with Clovis usually ended up leading to danger. It had cost the life of my brother, Little Joe, which brought tremendous sorrow to my mother and father and Mark and Will and me, not to mention Little Joe's wife and boys. So, I wondered if marrying Wren was really a wise choice for me to make. It wasn't that I didn't love her. Mercy me, I was so in love with that girl, and it wasn't so much that I feared for my own well-being, but for the safety and protection of my family. Marrying Wren would, of course, mean that my family and I would be obviously exposed to Clovis more often, and I wondered if there were others, who like the group of men who were causing us so much havoc now, would desire to avenge a loved one who had tried to kill Clovis and ended up on the short end of the deal? While I kicked myself for having that thought, in hindsight now, I am amazed at just how accurate that assessment would turn out to be in the years to come.

"This is us, right here and this is them." He pointed with the same stick that he had been drawing with. "It is my belief that they believe that the men they have captured are you guys. They'll begin torturing them to get them to talk and tell them my location, but of course they don't know, because they are not you, so consequently, they will increase the torture. When they realize that those hunters are not who they think they are, they'll kill em."

"We can't let that happen." Will stated emphatically. "Those men are here in the Breaks simply to hunt elk, like we came to do. They don't deserve to be tortured or killed for that matter."

All of us nodded our heads in agreement. "So Clovis, how do we stop that from happening?" I asked.

"I have considered a couple of options. First, I thought about exposing ourselves and making our presence known to them from some open spot, out of range of their rifles and tempting them to give us chase. The problem with doing that is, I believe that once Lee and his men realize that they have captured the wrong men, they'll just shoot them right there before they come chasing after our skin."

I could tell that Clovis was a statistician. He weighed every angle and tried to perceive each and every possible consequence to different scenarios. It was obviously what made him so excellent at staying alive. It wasn't just his vigilance or prowess, but his ability to think one step ahead of his opponent and to mastermind a plan that kept him in the lead. "If only we had a gun." Mark stated. "At least that would even the odds a little, although, not by much." Mark was still a little pessimistic about the whole thing, and to tell the truth, I wasn't too thrilled about it either, but like Mark, we were not about to let innocent men die and have their blood on our hands without making some kind of effort to prevent it from happening.

Mark and Will had families to concern themselves about. The preservation of their lives meant more than just their own desire for life or fear of death, but others depended upon them as well. Not so much was riding on my life, but I wasn't in the mood to die either—not today.

"As much as possible, I want to leave you guys out of this." Clovis started. "It's my fight, and I think I can even the odds on my own, but when I do, I will need you guys close by and ready to run. You will have to run like never before, and we've got to stick together.

Clovis shared his plan. The idea was to hike up one of the coulee's leading off of the river and see if we could circle in behind the Lee's bunch of hoodlums. The problem that presented the worst dilemma was the fact that we didn't know exactly where they were located. We had watched them march the hunters up the hills, but once they got into the cover of the trees, we were unable to determine where they went from there. The view of the surrounding terrain would look different from above than it did from the valley below, so it was impossible to even make an educated guess. Clovis felt sure that their location would be hidden in the timber, not only for the sake of concealment, but for the shade provided by the trees. It was warming up and getting hot. Clovis also believed that guards would be stationed around their camp to keep watch. Obviously, they knew that Clovis was not with the men they had captured, which meant he was still on the loose. So, Clovis' plan was rather simple in design. First, under the cover of the willows and alders in the river bottom, we would move toward the hills. Once we made it to the hills, we would seek higher ground, trying to remain undetected. Then, we would try to locate Lee's men and identify any guards that might be posted on the outside perimeter of their camp. Clovis believed that if he could slip up and kill one of the guards unnoticed, he could take his automatic weapon and put the odds back into our favor. The margin of error was narrow and the window of opportunity would be very short, but it was the best plan he could come up with, and we couldn't think of anything better.

It took the better part of an hour to move across the valley floor and reach the top of the surrounding hills. The scattered juniper trees and sagebrush made it possible to move about without being noticed. However, they also made it difficult for us to have any measureable distance of visibility. It was going to be difficult to find their location.

Clovis was leading the way as we each slipped through the brush, hunkered down and doing our best to be quiet and alert. Clovis suddenly stopped and signaled for the rest of us to do the same as he raised his hand. "I'm not sure, but that area right over there," he said, pointing with his finger, "looks like a good place for them to hide. I'm going to sneak around downwind and see if I can catch their scent."

"Do what?" Mark asked as if he wasn't sure that he had heard correctly.

"You heard him right Mark. Clovis has a nose like an animal." I commented.

"If they're over there, I'll smell them. Those hunters are probably saturated in cover scent or elk scent, so it won't be hard to catch wind of them. If they are there, I'll come back and we'll make plans from here."

The skepticism was evidently written all over the faces of my brothers and me. We had read stories of mountain men back in the 1800's who had developed and honed their own sense of smell after spending so much time in the wilderness, but I guess we either didn't believe it, or we just didn't give it a whole lot of thought. Now, here we were with Clovis, who had spent three years as a fugitive in the Bob Marshall Wilderness, telling us that if he moved down wind, he'd be able to pick up the scent of our enemies as if he were some kind of bird dog. I could tell my brothers were skeptical to say the least.

"Listen guys, I know that you're having a hard time choking that one down. Trust me on this. If they're over there, my nose will pick them up. It's not as good as it was when I was living in the Bob because I have been exposed to so much of man's pollution over the last few months, but it's still pretty good."

"All right, be careful. How long will it take you?" I asked.

"I should be back in about half an hour." Clovis replied and was gone.

This was the first time that my brothers and I had time to talk among ourselves apart from the presence of Clovis. Mark spoke first as soon as Clovis was out of sight.

"Ross, this is a bunch of crap. I know it and you know it. Those men have been trained in the North Vietnamese army since before they had lost all of their baby teeth. About all we know is how to survive in the woods, shoot straight, and we can take care of ourselves in a pretty good scrap, and there isn't much were afraid of, given a chance, but we don't stand a snow flake's chance in hell in this situation. Now, I'm just being realistic."

"I've got to agree with Mark." Will added. "The odds of pulling this off and living to tell about it look mighty slim to me."

"What do you suggest we do, Brothers? Should we just leave and let Clovis take care of it himself?"

"No." Both Will and Mark answered in unison. "You know, we would never do that. We're not gutless. We're just airing the laundry and hoping that by doing so we might discover another alternative, because this one sure doesn't look very attractive."

"I know. I know." I repeated. They were right. This was serious business and presently, I wasn't too keen on the plan either. My thoughts returned to Wren. Amazingly, I had not given her as much thought as I might have expected. Right now, the situation demanded that I stay focused on doing our best to keep from getting killed, but during our wait for Clovis, my mind immediately went to her. I wondered if I would live through this and actually be able to ask her to marry me. That made me remember that the engagement ring I bought was still in the glove box of my truck. I closed my eyes and let my mind drift to her memory. The smell of her intoxicating skin, the taste of her sweet red lips and the huckleberry lipstick she always wore just for me along with her long brown hair and her deep dark brown eyes, not to mention the contours of her body. I could not think of a single thought or memory that brought to my mind as much pleasure as hers. When I opened my eyes, it occurred to me that nothing in my life mattered as much to me as she did, and one way or another I was going to live long enough to let her know how much I loved her. That is also when it occurred to me that the fallacy of our plan was not in the plan itself, but in the fact that we were not one in mind to see it happen.

"Mark, Will, listen up. It just hit me that the problem we have before us is not the plan we have. Sure, we're up against a tough situation right now, but the real problem is that we haven't committed ourselves to make it work. Now, we have known nothing but hard work all of our lives, and I really can't think of anything that we haven't been able to accomplish when we put our heads and hearts together." I paused for a moment feeling a lump come to my throat as I was about to utter the next sentence. "I know that we lost Joe, and I know that his loss weighs heavy in our thoughts. The idea of losing one of you boys is more than I want to even think about, but rest assured, if we don't commit ourselves to doing this thing together, one or all of us are going to end up dead. Now, let's get our heads out and see if we can not only save those hunters from being killed, but prevent those Vietnamese guys from ever bothering Clovis again."

Mark and Will's heads bobbed up and down, affirmatively agreeing with what I had to say. Although we were all fully grown men, mature and capable, I was still the oldest brother and they still followed my lead. Mark commented, "Ross, you're right. I'm sorry for my pessimism.

We've got some serious butt to kick, and it's not going to happen if we go about it with a half-hearted attitude."

"That's right." Will assured. "It's not going to be easy, but we can do this. We'll only fail if we don't put our heart and soul into it and use the good sense the good Lord has blessed us with. After all, it's not like we don't know anything about putting the sneak on something. We've done it hunting all our lives and for certain, an animal's senses are far better honed than a human's. Of course, these animals have guns and we don't, so we'll have to be extra cautious."

"Brothers, I love ya. Let's make sure we live to tell about this story. We've already buried one brother; let's not have to bury another." I commented wistfully. Inwardly, I smiled to myself. I knew my brothers. They were cautious about biting into things that appeared too big to chew up and digest, at least as much as possible, but once they committed their hearts to it, there was no stopping them. We all got that honest from Dad. That leaf had just turned, however, and I knew then that we might have a chance of not only surviving, but putting an end to this once and for all.

Half an hour passed and Clovis had not returned. We were starting to get a little edgy. We each wondered if something tragic might have happened and by the time another half an hour had passed, we were in a quandary about what to do. Just as we were beginning to consider options, Clovis showed up. Like a ghost from out of nowhere, he came without a sound. Considering the dry and rocky the terrain, it seemed impossible for a man to move so quietly across it, but then, Clovis never ceased to amaze me.

"I found them." He stated. "They're a little farther from here than I thought they would be. I swung down wind and picked up a faint hint of odor that I knew was human and tried to stay with it, but the swirling breeze made it difficult to follow. Fortunately, I happened upon their tracks and that made it easy." Mark just looked at Clovis as if he were crazy. He knew that Clovis wasn't lying, but listening to Clovis actually talk about following the scent trail of a human was a pill that Mark was finding very difficult to swallow.

Waiting to hear what Clovis had planned, we listened. Clovis stooped to the ground again, this time, using the end of his large hunting knife to draw in the dust. "Here we are and there they are. That's 3 ridges over from here. They are located in a thick cluster of junipers, and it's relatively flat on top of that ridge. There is quite a bit of cover from the other side, so I believe we can come in from behind them without being seen or detected. We've got to be quiet and if we talk, especially as we get closer, we must do so only in a whisper. Use hand signals as much as possible."

"What are we going to do once we get there?" Will asked.

"My plan is to slip in behind a guard and take him out and steal his gun. Once I do that, I am going to have you guys cause a distraction. In the confusion, I'm hoping to pick off a couple of them from the side opposite of you. My guess is, they'll take cover and then will try to pursue either you or me. If they pursue me, you guys move in quickly from your side and cut those hunters loose and tell them to run like the devil was after them. They're all tied to a large juniper. If they pursue in your direction, I'll slip in and cut them loose."

"How many of Lee's men are there?" Mark asked.

Clovis bit his lip. It was apparent by the look on his face that he didn't want to say, but did so anyway. "I counted eight of them. There may be a couple more, but I know there are eight for sure."

"What if they decide to pursue all of us by splitting up?" Will asked. "I've considered that, so here's what I suggest. If they decide to do that, I want all of us to have a meeting place. I hate dividing our strength, but if they give chase to us, don't stick together. Split up and make it more difficult to follow us. We will meet on the top of that ridge right over there on top of that rock outcropping." Clovis stated as he pointed to a ridge about half a mile away. "You men ready?" He asked.

"Let's do it." Will resounded. Clovis, with his longbow in hand, led the way.

CHAPTER 13

President Watson considered himself a master at putting aside thoughts and feelings, no matter how pressing they were on his mind, when the demand for his full attention and focus was needed elsewhere. However, while meeting with the foreign ministers of both Israel and Palestine, a nagging, troubling voice kept badgering his thoughts. For three hours, peace treaties were negotiated and discussed, and overall the meeting gave the appearance of being successful, at least for the moment. Israel and Palestine had been fighting since biblical times and Watson seriously doubted that a peace treaty made between the two countries would ever last for long. By the time the meeting was over, he found it difficult to recall what terms had been negotiated. The reason, he surmised, was because of the nagging voice in his mind.

Returning to his room at Camp David, he couldn't take this unidentified fear any longer. Something wasn't right, and he knew it. His gut told him that something was askew. It was almost like that sixth sense he often experienced when he used to hunt whitetails in the Georgia pine forests. It was knowing, or at least feeling, that a deer was near, even when he couldn't see it or hear it. This of course was more than that. This feeling carried with it fear and restlessness, and no matter how hard he tried to subdue it, it would not go away. In fact, it only grew stronger.

Exhausted from the long day, Watson lay on his bed, needing desperately to rest and to sleep, but couldn't do so. He went to the phone and called Chief Officer Givens again.

"Officer Givens speaking."

"Officer Givens, this is President Watson. I haven't been able to get a hold of the Beldens. I am assuming that the news today is the same as it was yesterday?"

"Yes, Sir. No one has come in or gone out. Everything is peaceful and quiet."

"Doesn't that seem odd to you?" Watson asked.

"Truthfully, Sir, we haven't been doing this all that long, so I can't say that I've noticed any development to a particular habit, but yes, I'd think that either Mrs. Belden or her daughter would have come out from the ranch to go to town or do something over the last couple days."

"I've got to be honest with you. I've got a bad feeling that I cannot shake. I want you to disarm the cameras and motion detectors and take your men down to the ranch house and check on Judy and Wren. Go in quietly as if you were expecting trouble. You just might find it, but Lord, I hope not. Call me as soon as you find out."

"Yes, Sir. We'll go right now."

Chief Officer Givens rounded up his men and gave them the same instructions he had received from Watson.

"This is live and this is real, men. We'll go in on foot after I disarm the security system. Stay low and be quiet." Everyone double checked their AR-15's to make sure that the chamber held a live round and their magazines were full.

Officer Givens dismantled the security system in just a short minute. He then issued the orders to move down the canyon toward the ranch house, staying off of the road, and moving only through the cover of the trees.

The distance from the entrance to the Belden ranch house was just a little over a mile. As Givens and his men moved closer, they spread out to surround the house. Although it is impossible to surmise the thoughts of the men, a person would think that upon their first observation, they might have suspected something was amiss. The Belden's dog did not bark, and the horses did not nay or talk. It wasn't until they were right up next to the house that they found out the reason why. The Belden's Border collie lay dead in the driveway and the horses in the corral were dead, riddled with bullet holes. Kneeling down and touching the dog, Givens could tell that it was still warm and limp, indicating that it had not been dead for long. Givens also reasoned that the assailants must have used suppressors since the muzzle blasts had not been heard by him or his men.

"Stay low and under cover." Givens ordered his men through the microphone attached to his shoulder. "They must be in the house. Lord, I hope those ladies are all right." Hunkered down low to the ground the men quickly and quietly approached the house-- two to the back door, two to the front and the other two moving from window to window, peeking just over the window sill to determine if movement or life could be detected. All appeared to be clear. Givens and one of his men stormed the front door while the two at the back door covered any opportunity of escape from inside. After a thorough search of the house, no one was present. The house was unkempt and furniture was scattered, indicating that there had been a struggle. A few drops of blood were found on the living room floor, but it was dry indicating that it was at least a few hours older than the blood he had found on the dog. Still, there was no way of knowing from whom or what it came.

Stepping outside of the house and walking across the driveway, Officer Givens and his men proceeded to move toward the barn. Half way across the driveway, standing completely in the open, gunfire erupted from the upstairs doors of to the hayloft, mowing Givens and his men down to the ground. It was like shooting fish in a barrel. Givens and his men did not stand a fighting chance. Two officers were still alive because most of the slugs had hit their bullet-proof vests, but they were badly injured and incapable of walking. The others lay in the gravel drive, their life blood soaking up the dirt in the gravel driveway. Quan Lee, Ho Lee's youngest son, and two of his followers descended from the loft and approached the two men. Crying and wailing at the pain, their deplorable screaming cut straight to the hearts of Judy and Wren, who could do nothing to assist the two men.

With fear and terror in their eyes, they begged for their lives as they obviously could read the intent of Lee and his men. Lee withdrew his sidearm from the holster on his hip and with no more remorse than he might have felt for killing a snake, he shot them dead. Judy and Wren were forced to watch the whole scene from the loft above where their hands and legs were bound, and their mouths stuffed with a sock and gags tied in place.

Of course, there was no way of knowing that all of this was taking place at the time. Clovis, my brothers and I were doing our best to bring a solution to the problem we were facing and had no reason to believe that the waters of despair were troubled back home.

The murder of Givens and his men, secluded President Watson from the information he needed to hear and kept him from receiving word regarding the current status of Judy and Wren. Watson figured that a couple hours at the most should have been enough time for Officer Givens to look into the situation and return his call, but nearly four hours had passed, and Watson had not received a call, nor had anyone answered when he tried to call Givens. The gut-feeling that something was wrong turned more nauseating, and he was now deeply worried. He would wait for a little while longer and then call again. If he didn't get a reply, he would have to do something else about it.

At the same time that Givens and his men had been slipping upon the ranch house of the Belden's, we were trying our best to slither in undetected on Tinh Lee and his men. Tinh Lee was the older brother of Quan, only by a year, and they were the only surviving male children of Ho Lee and his wife. This information I found out later. At the time, it didn't matter who they were. They had captured three innocent men, believing they were us and would kill them if they were not stopped. As I mentioned earlier, we were practically helpless, with the weapons we carried compared to our enemies. Nonetheless, we did not want to see those men die. We had to try to stop them even if the odds were against us. In hind sight--it is true--we could have ignored it and run away, but we knew our conscience could not have allowed it. Of course, that's not to say the Lee Brothers would not make another attempt to kill Clovis at another time. It was the knowledge of these two facts that reaffirmed our commitment to see this thing through.

As we moved closer to Lee's camp, Clovis slowed his pace down and the rest of us did likewise. Stopping and settling in behind a large clump of sagebrush, we all gathered close to Clovis to listen to his instructions.

"Their camp is just right over there." He indicated. We'll have a really good view in about 40 more yards. Be very quiet and do what I do." In just a few short minutes, we were squatting behind a patch of thick sagebrush, watching and listening to Tinh Lee and his men as they were badgering the three hunters who were tied and bound hand and foot with a long pole running behind their backs and through their arms. It appeared that the torturing had just started.

"Where is the Mongoose? Where is Clovis Belden?" Tinh Lee demanded.

The hunters swore that they had no idea. They told him that they had never met the man, but only watched him on T.V. Tinh Lee did not believe them.

I diverted my eyes to Clovis. He had drawn an arrow from his quiver and placed it on the rest of his bow. "What are you going to do?" I asked. "That's 60 yards from here. Even if you shoot and hit one from here, there's seven more that are armed with automatic weapons. None of us will stand a chance."

Clovis turned to me. "Ross, listen to me. Once again I am putting my life into your hands."

"What do you mean?" I asked. Mark and Will were listening intently.

"I'm turning myself over to those guys." Clovis responded. "I can't let those hunters suffer when I am the one they really want."

"You can't do that, Clovis!" Will pleaded. "No way." Mark

119

added.

"Listen, Boys, Lee and his men think those three hunters are you guys, and they are going to torture them until they give up my location, which of course they can't do because they don't know who I am. Maybe I can make a deal with them and turn myself in for the release of the other three, then, you three can do what you can to rescue me. I don't think Lee will kill me straight out. I think he wants to take his time and have fun doing it."

Clovis raised his binoculars to his eyes. Glassing through them for a moment, he whispered, "They are about to get started." All four of us watched over the top of the sagebrush and through the junipers that stood between us and Lee's camp. Lee was yelling at the men again. Over and over again he kept asking the whereabouts of Clovis. The men swore they did not know. With a simple head nod, Tinh Lee signaled to a couple of his men. Like the echo of a professional baseball player hitting a homeroom, the sound of knuckles against flesh and bone shattered the calm of the hot afternoon. Lee's men repeatedly punched the hunters in the face and abdomen. The three hunters were brutally beaten for a few moments and then given another chance to reveal the presence of Clovis. The scene sickened me. It wasn't so much the sight of the blood and the saliva dripping from their faces and mouths as much as it was the fact that they were taking the punishment that was meant for us. The torturing also brought back the quite recent memories of the torture I had received from the FBI and their men in the Bob Marshall Wilderness, where I would have certainly been killed had it not been for Clovis.

"Where is Clovis Belden?" Tinh Lee asked again.

"We've got to do something?" Mark stated, which was almost ironic, because he was the one who earlier did not want to get involved, but at the same time, his statement came as no surprise, because once Mark decides to commit himself, he's in it for the long haul.

About that time, one of Lee's men reached up with his knife in his right hand and pulled on the ear of one of the hunter's with his left hand and then severed it off. The man screamed at the top of his lungs and in the process of doing so, Lee's thug shoved the ear into the man's mouth and forced it down his throat with the butt of his knife until the man had swallowed his own ear. The whole side of his head was crimson red with blood and even at the distance where we hid we could see well enough the terrible scene as it unfolded before our eyes. The other two hunters, though bound and helpless, screamed defiantly, cursing the man for the hideous act of brutality.

Crouched low and on our bellies, we closed the distance down to nearly forty yards.

Lee stood to the side watching and observing seemingly enjoying every minute of this vicious and ruthless act. I wasn't sure just what Clovis was doing or what he had in mind. I noticed then, that he was trying to get a clear shot with his bow and arrow at Tinh Lee, but Lee's position was partially obscured by the trees in front of us.

Lee kept asking the same question over and over in a very heavy Asian accent, "Where is Clovis Belden? Where is Clovis Belden?" When he did not receive the answer he was looking for, he snapped his fingers at the man who severed off the ear of the hunter. This time, the same man grabbed the hunter with one ear and held the long knife to the man's throat.

"Tell me where to find Clovis Belden or your friend will die."

We watched as we could see the fear in the eyes of all the hunters. Pleading, begging and crying not to hurt or kill their friend, the terror and panic they were feeling was as intense as any I had ever witnessed before.

The feeling of helplessness for Mark and Will and me weighed heavy on our shoulders. It was a burden of sorrow and grief and despair all wrapped up into one. The powerless agony of defeat and failure and the recognition of both before they fully transpired only worsened the depth of our vulnerability. The sight of blood was nothing new, but not a single one of us liked to see anything suffer, especially a human, and even more disturbing was to witness someone enduring the suffering that was actually meant to be for us.

Clovis turned his head slightly toward us without taking his eyes off of the scene before him and whispered, "You men stay here, and don't let yourself be seen or caught."

Before we could ask him to explain what he had in mind, he slowly raised up from his squatting position, knees still slightly bent, just high enough that he could see over the top of the sage brush in front of him. In one fluid motion, his left arm came to bear with his longbow in hand, his right hand drawing the string on the bow and as soon as the tips of his finger found the corner of his mouth, he let his arrow fly.

All three of us watched it happen and even to this day, it is still hard to believe. I can close my eyes and still see the whole scene as if it happened only yesterday. The memory seems to always play itself out in slow motion in my mind. The arrow slightly arched upward in the air and then descended toward the head of the man holding the knife. There are times, whether shooting an arrow or watching someone else shoot an arrow, that a person can tell that the arrow will fly true to the mark at the release, even before it gets there. This was one of those moments.

The arrow appeared to hang in the air, suspended for a moment as though it did not want to come down, but come down it did and buried itself into the man's skull, just above his ear, dropping him as if he had been shot by a bullet. Upon impact, Lee and his men were astonished and caught off guard. They were uncertain of from where the arrow had come or even what had just happened. The uncertainty led to hesitation and in a split second, that hesitation cost the life of another man as another arrow from Clovis' bow zipped quickly through his chest. The impact of the arrow striking flesh and bone produced a solid, thud-like sound, followed by a guttural grunt as the man crumbled to his knees, both hands holding on to the shaft that protruded from his chest as blood and froth gurgled from his lips down the side of his jaw. The rest of the men scrambled for cover, most of them ducking in behind the sagebrush, not wanting to be the next to fall prey to the deadly arrows of Clovis.

Clovis picked up a rock and threw it in the brush on the opposite side of the men. One of Lee's men evidently believed the sound of the rock in the brush was Clovis and stood up and started blasting his automatic weapon in that direction. Clovis quickly drew another arrow and sent it on the way. The arrow struck the man in the lower back, appearing to be in the kidney area. He screamed in agony as he fell to the ground. Tihn Lee gave an order in Vietnamese. We assumed that it meant for someone to silence the man who was in such agony, because a gunshot erupted and the screaming ceased.

It was difficult to believe that single-handedly, Clovis, with a bow and arrow had already taken out three of the 8 men in camp who were bent on seeing him suffer a slow and torturous death.

Clovis had moved about 20 yards to our right so that in the event, gunfire should erupt and spray in his direction, we would not be hit. In the chaos and confusion, Tihn Lee yelled aloud, "Clovis Belden, come in now, or I will shoot your friends."

Clovis quickly shuffled his way back to us. "Listen guys, I am going to turn myself over to them. I cannot let those men suffer anymore because of me, and I certainly don't want their blood on my conscience."

"Isn't there another way?" Mark pleaded.

"Clovis, they'll kill you for sure if you go in there." I commented.

Will simply nodded. He agreed with what I said, and I could tell he was not happy about the situation. In fact, knowing him as well as I did, I could see the anger raging up in his face, and I knew I better make an effort to squelch it before he did something stupid. Will was always slow to become angry, but once he crossed that line, like Mark, it was nearly impossible to talk any kind of sense to him.

"Will, listen Brother. This is not a time to lose your head. You can't go getting all mad like you're doing. You'll get killed for sure."

"That's right, Will." Clovis affirmed. "I need you boys to stay hidden, but I'm counting on you to get me out of this mess, too. They still think those three guys they've got tied up are you boys, so they will not be expecting trouble. That means the element of surprise is on our side."

"But just how do we go about saving and rescuing you when we don't even have a gun?" I asked.

Clovis handed me his bow and his quiver. "Here, you can use this." "Come on, Clovis. I'm not that good. I've never seen anyone shoot a longbow like you do. I'm not sure Howard Hill could do any better."

"Ok then, I'll keep it. Listen Ross, I know you'll find a way to get me out of this jam. If you don't, please tell Judy and Wren that I love them and make them understand that I did what I had to do. They won't like it, but they'll understand. They know that I never compromise on principle."

CHAPTER 14

There was no way for us to know that while we were at war with Tihn Lee and his men, President Watson was warring against an aching, agonizing, gut feeling that something was out of kilter concerning the safety and security of the Belden family at their home in Montana. Watson found it peculiar that his worry and concern were causing him so much physical unrest and discomfort. He was nauseated and light- headed and in desperate need of sleep, yet, try as he may, he could not rest. He wondered if he was coming down with something, but his daily physical evaluation administered by his personal physician showed no fever or infection, although his blood pressure was elevated to some extent, which could have been the result of half a dozen things, including everything from the trip to Camp David, to the peace conferences he was about to attend, to lack of rest he so desperately needed.

Watson had not expressed his concerns to anyone other than officer Givens. He really had no evidence solid enough to validate his worries. Looking at his watch, he realized he would have to put his concerns aside for the moment. It was time for him to meet with the Israeli and Palestinian leaders, hopefully to come to some sort of peace agreement. Watson chuckled to himself. He knew his Bible history well and these folks had been fighting since before the days of Moses. They were not likely to quit now. Still, if some sort of truce could be established, it might ease the tension within the United Nations for a while, not to mention the fact that any and everything he could accomplish in a positive manner would only enhance the upcoming election.

In the middle of the negotiations, one of President Watson's secret service men received a call from headquarters and was directed to inform the President immediately to return the call to Chuck Mitchell, the Director for the FBI. Watson excused himself from the meeting, stating that his attention to an emergency situation was needed for a few minutes. The Israeli and Palestinian ministers were cordial and understanding and actually seemed to welcome a break to the negotiations as Watson returned to his private room to return the call. A quick call to the Pentagon and Watson was on the line with Mitchell.

"This better be good, Mitchell." Watson stated emphatically.

"Yes, Sir. I hesitated to call, knowing you were in your meeting, but I figured you could kick me in the butt now for the interruption, or you'd have my head later if I didn't make the call, so I'm calling."

"Get to the point, Mitchell." Watson ordered.

"Yes, Sir. First, I have not been able to contact Officer Givens, nor has he been in contact with me. Normally, he calls this office twice a day, and I have not heard from him since 1800 hour yesterday."

"I sent him and the men in to check on Mrs. Belden and her daughter. I am not sure where Clovis is at this time." Watson answered.

"How long ago did you speak with Givens?" Mitchell asked. About 5 hours ago." Watson replied.

"So, he should have reported back to you by now?" Mitchell asked. "Yes, he should have, but I've been in this meeting for the last several hours and figured that was the reason I had not received word from him. Something isn't right, Mitchell. I've been feeling it for two days now."

"Mr. President, what would you like for me to do?" Mitchell inquired.

"Run our eye in the sky over the Belden Ranch and see if it picks up anything out of place. Too, Clovis was worried about the

Lee brothers from North Vietnam. I know they flew home, but double check all of that too. Probably just a waste of time, but do it anyway. Give Ross Tyler a call, and see if he knows where Clovis might be. Let me know something ASAP. We're going to wrap up this peace conference real soon."

"Yes, Sir." Mitchell answered.

Walking back toward the room where the peace conference was taking place, Watson had a better feeling about the situation. His questions were not answered, and his worries had not been eliminated, but the fact that something was being done about them put his mind at a greater ease. He had no sooner taken a seat to continue the meeting when a secret service agent approached him again and whispered in his ear.

Excusing himself once more, Watson hurried to the phone line.

Mitchell was on the other end. "What is it?" Watson asked.

"Mr. President, I am sending live video footage of the Belden Ranch via satellite to your personal screen right now. Are you there?"

"Hold on, I'm walking into the other room right now." Watson answered as he was signaling with his hands to his men to turn on the monitoring screen for viewing the satellite imagery.

"Yes, I'm standing in front of it now." Watson confirmed. "Are you alone?' Mitchell asked

"Yes, I am alone." Watson answered. "Why is that important?"
"You are about to see why." Mitchell responded.

Watson watched the screen as live satellite coverage zoomed in over the Belden Ranch. A cluster of bodies lay dead in the gravel driveway. As the lens zoomed even closer, it became obviously apparent that the dead bodies were Agent Givens and his men. This was not good. The gruesome video was a solid affirmation to the feelings he had combated for the last several days. Something had been amiss after all.

Watson was stunned by the graphic scene he was watching. It was apparent that these men were mowed down in cold blood. His shock had caused him to pause for a moment, long enough that Agent Mitchell on the other line was unsure if he had lost connection.

"Mr. President, are you still there?"

"Yes. I am here." Exhaling with a weary, frustrated sigh, he continued. "It appears that all of them are dead."

"Yes, Sir. I believe you are right." Mitchell confirmed.

"Has the satellite picked up any additional movement?" Watson inquired.

"No, Sir, nothing."

"Do we have any idea who might have done this or how they were able to bypass our security system around the Belden Ranch?" Watson propped.

"We are not sure. We are just starting to investigate every possible angle we can imagine at this moment. As you well know, Clovis has made a lot of enemies over the course of his adult life. We know a few of them who have publicly declared their intent to avenge the friends and families that Clovis has killed. There are others I am sure."

Watson was kicking himself for not pressing Clovis a little harder to take his family and leave the country. It would have been safer for all of them. However, the love Clovis harbored deep in his heart for the United States resonated with Watson, and Watson respected Clovis for it. He knew that Clovis would never leave this great country, and Watson understood exactly why. He harbored those same feelings himself.

"I'm assuming we have no information on the whereabouts of the Belden's either?" Watson asked.

"We do have a general idea of Clovis' location. We spoke with Mr. Tyler, and he told us that Clovis and his three sons were hunting elk in the Missouri Breaks, but he was not sure of the exact location. As far as Judy and Wren, we have no idea. I have a task force ready and waiting to fly into the Belden ranch to investigate the area, bring back the bodies, and see if they can discover a clue to what this is all about and maybe who is behind it all. Just give me the word, and I'll send them in."

"Do it, Mitchell. I owe my life to Clovis. I promised I would take care of him and his family and here we are, only a month out since I gave them my word, and I've already dropped the ball. If I can't protect one small family and keep them from harm and danger while sitting in the highest office of the land, how am I supposed to provide for the protection of an entire nation? Maybe somebody else needs to hold this office." Watson seethed in his personal frustration and self- disappointment.

Mitchell was stunned. He held the highest respect and admiration for President Watson. No one in his lifetime had served as the leader of this great nation better than he. No other President had demonstrated more integrity and honesty than Watson, and Watson took the job of protecting the security of this nation seriously, from the entire country down to the individual citizen. Watson had worked relentlessly at putting tougher punishment on criminals by appointing hard-nosed judges back into the Federal Courts. Although he knew he could never create a perfect world, he made it clear that it was his desire for the streets and avenues of America to become safe to travel once more.

"Mr. President. With all honor and respect, there is not another man in this country more fitted for the Oval Office than you are. I will, with everything in my power, get to the bottom of this as soon as possible."

"Thank You, Mr. Mitchell. Call me as soon as you've got something. One other thing, Mitchell: dead enemies do not become repeat offenders."

"Yes, Sir. I understand."

Watson, once again returned to the peace conference. His mind, however, was as far from Israel and Palestine as it could possibly be. He was worried for Clovis and Judy and Wren and nearly equally upset and disappointed in himself. He had given his word to provide for the safety, security and welfare of the Belden family, and he had failed and in his estimation; he had failed miserably. Throughout the years, Watson had met and come to know thousands of people, but not a single person, not even his former roommate and best friend, Vice President Peterson had moved his heart like Clovis. Clovis represented so much of everything that Watson ever desired to be.

Obviously, as I write this story, much of what I have learned and come to know is post-facto, and while it is impossible to know the exact thoughts of the people who were directly involved, later visits and conversations have allowed me to develop an idea of what they were thinking at the time, giving me an indication of why and how things transpired the way they did. Watson did share with me later that he found his mind dwelling heavily on the character of Clovis time and time again and doing so made Watson feel that there was indeed a lot of room for improvement in his own life. He told me that although he believed that he was a God-fearing, bible-reading, church-going family man, who strived diligently to practice the principals and statutes of God's divine Word as well as he could, when he considered the incredible faith of Clovis, by comparison, he felt his own faith to be weak. Clovis was a man who not only talked the talk, but walked the walk, and Watson was humbled by the depth and sincerity of Clovis' spiritual conviction. This thought had crossed his mind several times over the last few days, and Watson contemplated the reoccurrence. Watson also considered the history of Clovis' life and the troubles and difficulties Clovis had experienced, and Watson believed it incredible that a man who had endured so much and had encountered so many difficult situations could not only survive but also hold fast to his faith that God would deliver him from evil and harm's way. As President of the United States, the magnitude of the problems and difficulties that continued to pile upon his plate were enormous, and yet compared to the burdens that Clovis had been called to bear, Watson considered his problems to be minor inconveniences.

Another aspect of Clovis' character that Watson admired and envied was his true patriotic spirit. Clovis truly and undoubtedly loved this country. Having fought in Vietnam, serving as a soldier and doing so in a way that really exceeded his call to duty, his allegiance and loyalty was immeasurable. Then, years later, risking his life to completely shut down an assassination attempt on Watson, by killing Vice President Peterson with an arrow, a split second before Peterson would have sent Watson to his death over the side of a cliff in the Bob Marshall Wilderness, Clovis managed to escape and live as a fugitive of the law with a bounty of a million dollars on his head. There was no way of knowing how many blood-thirsty, greedy men had tried to collect on that bounty and came up short. Clovis underwent all of that because, first, it was the right thing in his mind to do and second, because he loved America and what it stood for. The consequence of such a risky and daring endeavor was the only reason that Watson was still alive. Who could not be humbled by such a feat? Who could forget that another man had paid such a great price to keep you from paying the ultimate price? Watson knew unequivocally he was indebted to Clovis.

While these two attributes were qualities to be admired by Watson, there was another quality found in the life of Clovis that Watson not only admired but envied. Clovis was a man who loved life and found joy in the journey, no matter how difficult the road or path he traveled. Clovis worked on his ranch, and he worked hard, and he loved that kind of work. Watson later reported to me in a conversation I had with him as he chuckled to himself, "How many men do you know that really love their jobs?" Still, even though Clovis valued the hard work of ranching, Clovis knew how to lay it down and take time to enjoy and pursue other passions. Over the course of time, I personally came to know this truth about Clovis as much or more than anyone else and learned to apply this same attribute to my own life style. Clovis loved to hunt with his longbow and fish with his fly rod, and in spite of all the work that his ranch required of him, Clovis always made the time to enjoy these two activities, more often than not, with his wife Judy and his daughter Wren who shared the same kind of appetite for these activities. No other man that Watson knew so fully relished life like

Clovis. Watson wondered if Clovis' seemingly unshakeable positive attitude was because the life he lived was so good, or was it because Clovis could find the good in the life he lived. Watson already knew the answer. Right now, all that mattered to Watson was finishing up with this peace conference and getting back to the capital. He hoped and prayed that Judy and Wren were safe, but he somehow doubted it. Before stepping back into the room to reconvene with the peace conference, he said a prayer of his own. "Oh, Lord. If ever there was a time when I needed you-- and there have been plenty of them-- I need you now more than ever. Please, I beg thee, shower your grace upon the Beldens, and protect them with your powerful hand against the evil that men do."

Watson proceeded to the peace conference and fortunately a cease- fire agreement was reached and signed between the two foreign leaders. Watson wondered how long the treaty would remain in effect before it was broken, but for now, he didn't really care. All he wanted was to assure the safety of the Beldens. It had been more than two hours since he had spoken with FBI Chief Mitchell. The uncertainty was unbearably agonizing. He had just stepped inside the helicopter that would fly him back to the capital when a call came to him from Headquarters.

"Mr. President, this is Chief Mitchell. We have a problem. Actually, we have several problems. Mitchell declared in an urgent and worried tone of voice.

"Talk to me, Mitchell."

"Sir, I sent in our task force to the Belden Ranch. I had them fly the choppers in and land about two miles outside of the main entrance and told them to proceed quietly on foot so as not to give away our presence. No one was there at the ranch house or barn, no one except the bodies of Officer Givens and his men. As we suspected, they were all dead. There were signs of struggle in the house, but no one present. Upstairs in the loft of the barn, we found empty cartridges, which indicate that this is where the assailants fired upon Givens and his men. We still remain uncertain if Mrs. Belden and her daughter are with the assailants or not. We believe so, as we found smaller boot prints in the dust outside of the barn."

"You mention assailants, as in a plurality. What evidence do you have to support that there are more than one?" Watson asked.

"The proximity of the spent cartridges lying in the loft indicates that there were at least three shooters, but we have found nothing that depicts a clue as to Mrs. Belden and her daughter or their location or their well- being."

Watson sighed deeply, trying to get his arms around the situation as it played out in his mind. "Have you determined who might be responsible for this yet?" Watson asked.

"Yes, Sir or at least we have a very strong suspicion. I have several groups checking out every possible angle available. One of our new cadets noticed something on a clip from a video at the airport. She zoomed in and noticed that the Lee Brothers who flew back to North Vietnam last week were not the Lee Brothers at all. They were look- a- likes. Obviously, they used fake passports and no one noticed. That means that the Lee Brothers are still here in the country. We are assuming they are involved. It really appears that they have master- minded an incredible deceptive plan to make it appear that they have returned home to North Vietnam. I called the North Vietnamese Embassy, and they told me that they were unaware of any such action. I swear they are lying." Mitchell exclaimed.

Watson was furious, and yet it came as no surprise. His gut instinct had kept telling him that something was amiss, and he had learned long ago to trust it, even when he wasn't completely sure what it was trying to say.

"Mitchell, I am assuming your men are still looking for evidence to secure some kind of idea to what has happened to the Belden ladies?" Watson asked.

"Yes, Sir. I will keep you informed if anything is found, right down to the smallest detail."

"Good. Have you learned anything about the locality of Clovis and the Tyler Boys?" Watson asked.

"No, Sir. As I told you earlier, Mr. Tyler said that his boys were with Clovis in the Missouri Breaks, but he did not know exactly what part. It is a huge area to cover, even with our satellites, but also, there has been substantial cloud cover which is making it even more difficult. We will keep looking." Mitchell assured.

"So what are your men doing on the ground at the Belden Ranch?" Watson probed.

"Well, Sir, we know that if indeed it was the Lee Brothers that killed Givens and his men, they did not access the ranch by vehicle. They must have moved in on foot, but we still don't know how they did that without detection. If they came in on foot, we can assume that they have left on foot as well, but we are looking at every possible angle we can." There was a brief interruption. "Just a minute, I'm getting a call from the Belden Ranch right now. Do you mind if I take it and get back to you?" Watson asked.

"No, I don't mind. Call me back if you find out something." Watson commanded.

With his phone at his side awaiting the return call from Mitchell, Watson twirled his finger around and around his head to signal the pilot of the helicopter that he was ready to get off the ground and back to the White House.

CHAPTER 15

Clovis yelled out, "Lee, I'm coming in, but only if you let my three friends go."

"No deal!!!" Lee hollered back. "You come in, or I will kill them one at a time."

Clovis bit his lip. He knew that Lee meant what he was saying, but he desperately desired to get a little further with negotiating. "Can't do it, Lee. If you so much as lay a finger on one of them again, I will kill you."

Lee laughed aloud. "I doubt that, Belden. You're out-numbered and out gunned."

I watched Clovis as he continued to advance a little closer. I knew the enemy was close, but we couldn't see them. Clovis peeked through a small opening in the sage brush and snatched another arrow from his quiver. One of Lee's men was lying on his belly and his boot stuck out beyond the sage brush into the open. Clovis slowly raised his bow while drawing the string to the corner of his mouth, all in one fluid motion, releasing as soon as the arrow nock touched the corner of his mouth. A split-second later, the horrendous scream of pain and agony indicated that Clovis' arrow had once again found its mark.

That was it for Tihn Lee. He began screaming obscenities at Clovis. The vulgar words in English I recognized. I'm sure the ones in Vietnamese probably meant the same, but I don't feel comfortable writing them in either language. Lee was as mad as a wet hornet. Two gun shots, about 3 seconds apart split the afternoon air. The screaming man with the arrow in his foot hushed, but the wailing and cursing from two of the white hunters took his place. We could not see what had happened, but we felt pretty confident that we knew. Lee had killed his own man with the arrow in his foot and then shot and killed one of the hunters as he said he would.

Our suspicions were confirmed when Lee bellowed out again, "Belden, I've just killed one of your friends. Which one do you want to die next?"

Clovis turned and looked at Will and Mark and me and raised his eyebrows with a look that suggested he had no other alternative but to give himself up. Squatted low, he moved over to the three of us and whispered, "OK, boys, this is it. I don't want to die, but I can't live knowing the blood of those men is on my head. It sounds like they've already killed one. Once again, I'm hoping you guys can get me out of this mess."

Clovis had made that point already once, but this time, I knew would be the last time. He was really going to give himself over to Tihn Lee. He did not know the names of the men whom Lee had taken captive, and I suppose to Clovis, it did not matter. What did matter is that innocent men were being tortured because Tihn Lee believed they were somehow connected to Clovis.

Clovis tried one more time to negotiate. Yelling out loud he stated, "Tihn Lee, let one man go, and I'll come to you peacefully."

"Mr. Belden, I will not let any of your friends go. One is dead, and the other two will be shortly." Tihn Lee hollered back from his hiding place.

I tried to get a bearing on where he was hiding and noticed that Clovis was doing the same thing, but we could not get a visual. Mark and Will and I were all scrunched in close to each other and Clovis was just a few feet to our right. Several times I watched as Clovis ran his hand over his long peppered-gray beard. Contemplating options in his mind, it was apparent that there was no other way than to just surrender himself. His reluctance was not only noticeable, but also understandable.

Clovis answered, "Lee, if I come in, you're going to kill all of us anyway. I just can't see how surrendering is to my benefit at all."

"It's not, Mongoose, unless you consider this. Please, listen closely."

There was a pause, and then voices came over the speaker of Tihn Lee's satellite phone.

"Daddy, Mr. Quan Lee has got Mom and me, and they're going to kill us if you don't turn yourself over to his brother Tihn.

The sound of Wren's voice sent shivers up and down my spine. I started to leap forward and run right toward those sorry, worthless fiends. Will and Mark caught me by the arms before I ran off to what would have certainly been a suicidal mission. Fear and fury pricked every emotional fiber in my heart and mind. Suddenly, this whole situation became very personal. I was ticked. No one was going to hurt Wren.

In hind sight, I realize that I was actually more in love with Wren at the time than I realized. Yes, she was the woman I wanted to marry and spend the rest of my life with. Yes, she was the woman that I wanted not only to be my wife, but also to be the mother of my children. Yes, she was the woman who had captured my heart, stolen my soul, and wrapped both of them in her lovely arms where I would always want to be and never in the arms of anyone else, but not until that moment did I realize that all of what she was to me stood to be lost. For certain, I would do what I could to make sure that it did not happen. Wren and her mother, Judy, had endured enough already. Just exactly how much those ladies could stand I wasn't sure. This was the second time in less than a year that the two of them had been taken hostage on account of Clovis. Both of them were tough and strong-willed, but everyone has a breaking point. Clovis turned to me; his eyes were welled up with tears. He knew he had no choice. The intense anger I was feeling must have been written all over my face. He said nothing. He didn't have to. His eyes locked on mine, and I noticed his lower lip quivering beneath his beard as his clinched teeth indicated the anger and worry that sped through the course of his veins. Clovis was worried, not for his own life, but for the lives of his wife and daughter. He knew that the thread upon which their lives hung was thin and fragile, and keeping it from being severed was totally reliant upon his course of action. His stare held mine for a long moment, and then his eyes went to all three of us as he spoke.

"Men, do what you've got to do. Not only does my life depend upon it, but so does Judy's and my baby girl. Good luck." Clovis stated. For a brief moment, Clovis bowed his head and mumbled a prayer. I could not hear it well enough to understand what he prayed for. He laid his bow and quiver full of arrows down on the ground in front of us and stood up where the upper part of his torso was visible above the sagebrush.

As I write this, I realize that this was probably the first time that Clovis ever had to surrender to anyone. Always before, whether looking back at his assignments during the war in Vietnam or his three year stay in the Bob Marshall Wilderness as a fugitive of the law, he had been able to stay one step ahead of his enemies. His ability to speculate and anticipate his enemy's next move had always proved advantageous to his survival. Now, surrendering was the only move left to make. There were no other options. It would be up to my brothers and me to find a way to rescue him, Judy and my lovely wife-to-be, Wren.

A lump came to my throat as I watched Clovis put his arms high into the air and began walking toward Lee and his men. A million thoughts ran through my mind. Would this be the last time that I would see Clovis alive? Where did they have Judy and Wren? It was rather obvious that they held them somewhere else other than here. It also meant that it made us totally helpless. Anything we did here could mean the death of Judy and Wren, wherever they were. The feeling of helplessness, I have determined, is by far the greatest taxation of spirit and emotion that I have ever felt. I didn't know it at the time, but I would learn later in the years to follow, even more fully just how detrimental the feeling of helplessness could be to a man's life.

"Lee, I'm coming in. Don't shoot." Clovis yelled out loud enough for everyone to hear. Hidden behind the sagebrush, Mark and Will and I watched while keeping out of sight. The whole time, I was praying that they wouldn't just mow down Clovis as he approached them unarmed and defenseless.

Slowly, Tihn Lee and his men stood up from behind the brush that they had been hiding behind, pointing their weapons at Clovis, as Clovis casually, and what appeared confidently, approached them. Clovis walked right up to them. Tihn Lee walked straight over to him and spit in his face and then slapped him hard across his jaw. At forty yards or so where Mark and Will and I remained hidden, it still sounded like the crack of gun. I winced at the sound. I knew it had to hurt. Grabbing Clovis by the arms, Lee's men pushed Clovis closer toward the middle of their camp. Clovis did not resist. At our point of observation, we could no longer see the other two hunters that were being held captive.

"What are we going to do, Ross?" Mark asked as he and Will closed the distance between us even tighter.

"I'm thinking, Brothers. First, I'm thinking that Clovis would want us to concentrate our efforts on his wife and daughter first, but of course, we don't know where they are located. A second choice is to see if we can get to Clovis, but of course if we do that, whoever has Judy and Wren will kill them. So, it seems to me that we need to capture Tihn Lee. He's the only bargaining power we have."

Mark and Will just shook their heads. Without a gun, the whole idea just seemed hopeless. Even armed, we might be able to rescue Clovis, but again, that did little for the safety and security of Judy and Wren. We had to have some bargaining power and that would only come if we could somehow capture Tihn Lee and make a trade with his brother for Judy and Wren.

Will, who was always looking at things from different angles, spoke up. "Brothers, the first thing we need to do is to cut the distance we have between us and them to as close as we can get without getting noticed. Maybe that way we can hear something that might reveal what they've got planned. It appears to me that they want to torture Clovis, because if they just wanted to kill him, they would have already done so."

Will had a good point. If the death of Clovis was all they wanted, they could have done that already. Stripping my pack from my shoulders, I pulled out some camouflage paint.

"Here." I directed. "Let's make sure our skin doesn't shine in this bright sun. Put it on your face and hands, and we'll see if we can sneak in a little closer and find out what they are planning on doing." The three of us were already wearing sagebrush camouflage clothing, the kind we like to hunt in while hunting this kind of terrain. As quickly as possible we smeared the paint on each other.

"You know," Mark suggested, "what we really need is some kind of distraction that will force or cause these guys to leave this area, at least long enough for us to slip in and grab a couple guns."

"If we do something, it needs to be something that won't arouse suspicion. I mean, it's like it needs to be something kind of natural that won't direct anybody's attention to us." Will stated.

"I say we sneak in close and see what we can learn first. Then, we might be able to decide what to do from there."

Mark and Will agreed. "Lead the way, Brother."

Keeping low to the ground we made a semi-circle toward Lee's camp moving meticulously slowly and as quiet as possible. On one occasion, my foot crushed a small twig and it popped lightly. We stopped moving abruptly, but apparently, no one in the camp had heard it. With a sigh of relief, we pressed in even closer, crawling on our bellies until we were within 10 yards of the camp.

Low to the ground, underneath the leaves and branches of the sagebrush, we could see the men in the camp. If we tried to look above the branches, we stood the risk of exposing ourselves, and obviously we didn't have clear visibility looking through the middle of it, but underneath, we could see clearly.

The dead men that Clovis had killed with his bow and arrow still lay where they had fallen. No one had moved them. Their weapons were still on the ground close to them, but of course, not where we could get our hands on one of them. The hunter whom Tihn Lee had killed was also lying on the dusty, dirty ground. His body was the closest to us. I looked at his head, which was caked with dried blood, and dirt that had pasted itself to it. The blood from his missing ear had coagulated in a pool that had filled up the auditory passage way and was drying. The truth is, the whole scene of the man's face was hideous and nauseating, and yet I kept staring into his eyes, which remained wide-open. Something wasn't quite right. My subconscious mind could read it, but I wasn't sure what I was seeing that wouldn't let me pull my eyes off of his as they appeared to be staring right at me. Then his eyelids blinked. The man was still alive and was doing his best to remain perfectly still, only breathing in and out very slightly so as not to give himself away. I nudged Mark, who was squatted to my right, lightly with my elbow and whispered to both him and Will who was directly beside Mark, "That man is still alive. Watch his eyes." Mark and Will both stared for a moment and then they saw the man blink. Without saying a word, they nodded in the affirmative.

"What are we going to do?" Mark asked again.

I wondered how many times we had asked that question in the last 24 hours. So far, almost everything we had done up to this point was a spur- of-the-moment, spontaneous, play-by-ear reaction to the situation as it unfolded and presented itself. In my opinion, it was not going so well. While we had somehow managed to remain alive, and Clovis had single- handily reduced the enemy force by half of what it was, now Clovis was their captive, and somewhere Tihn Lee's brother held Judy and Wren as hostages. Somehow, some way, we had to prevent harm coming to any of them.

Our attention was redirected toward Clovis and Tihn Lee as we heard Tihn Lee speaking on the phone. He spoke in Vietnamese, so not a single one of us understood what he was saying, but it didn't take us long to find out what the conversation was all about.

Tihn Lee turned toward Clovis. "Do you know what that's all about?" He sadistically teased.

Clovis did not answer. He knew Lee would tell him.

"My Brother is on his way here with your wife and daughter. When they get here, I'm going to carve on them a little while you watch, and then I'm going to cut them up in pieces right here in front of you before I kill you.

"How is your brother going to find his way here out in the middle of nowhere?" Clovis inquired.

Holding the satellite phone up, Tihn Lee replied, "Do you see this little blinking red light? It sends off a signal that will lead him right here. They just passed through the town of Stanford. I suppose you know where that is?"

Clovis nodded his head in the affirmative.

"So, it won't be all that long before they arrive. That's when we can get this party started. Maybe then, you'll know how my family felt when you killed our father."

My blood boiled in rage as I knew that Tihn Lee would do exactly what he said he would do.

"That was war!!!" Clovis rebutted.

"This is war!!!" Lee replied sharply. "And you will soon be a casualty of war as my father was."

"What about all the men your father was responsible for killing?" Clovis asked.

"They deserved to die!" Lee screamed out in frustration.

"How do you figure that?" Clovis asked again without changing the tone or volume of his voice.

"Because they were Americans, and all of you Americans deserve to die. You think you can walk over anyone you want. Your arrogance disgusts me!!!" Lee responded and then spit in Clovis' face again.

"Tie him up!" Lee ordered.

The man closest to Clovis, slung the sling of his rifle over his shoulder and moved in to grab Clovis by the arm so he could bind his arms behind Clovis' back. If I had not been watching so closely, I probably would have missed what happened next. With lightning speed, Clovis' hand shot upward, palm flat, the edge of his hand crashing into the esophagus of the man, completely removing any possibility of the man receiving oxygen to his lungs. The man crumbled to the ground with his hands holding his throat, meanwhile his face was turning a deep, purplish blue, while his eyeballs rolled upward and back into their sockets, as his life quickly left him. It was a move our father had taught us years ago as boys when we were growing up but had always warned us that we were never to use it unless it was a life or death situation. The reason had just been made perfectly and vividly clear right before our eyes.

Tihn Lee screamed in anger at his three remaining men. "Tie him up now. Right here between these two trees." Cussing and screaming, I could see a pool of saliva in the corner of his mouth and the veins bulging on his forehead beneath his hot red skin. He was ticked and understandably so. Clovis had single-handily cut Lee's force down to three men.

Lee's men grabbed Clovis, pushing and shoving him until they had him standing between the two trees that Lee had indicated. Spread eagle, they secured an arm and leg to one tree and the other arm and a leg to another. Lee's anger had not subsided, but rather, from all appearances, amplified in a fiery rage that looked to be out of control. Pulling his knife from its sheath, Lee approached Clovis, standing nose-to-nose and eye-to-eye with him. My brothers and I held our breath. There was nothing we could do to prevent harm coming to Clovis without possibly bringing harm to Judy and Wren. We grit our teeth, bit our lip, watched and waited.

As best that I could tell, Clovis never tipped his head nor blinked an eye. He stood helpless before Tihn Lee and yet showed no fear. Suddenly, Lee reached up and grabbed Clovis by his gray-speckled beard and jerked his head upward and back. Exposing his neck, Lee raised the knife blade to Clovis' throat.

"Now, maybe you know how my father must have felt the instant before you slit his throat." Lee Barked. I thought for sure this would be the end of Clovis.

Tihn Lee posed for a long moment with the blade against his

throat and then withdrew. "I will kill you, but I will wait for my Brother." He snarled as he removed the knife from Clovis' throat. Then quickly, in one swift swipe, he cut the front of Clovis shirt, and with his other arm, ripped it from his body, exposing the gray-haired chest of Clovis. Dragging the razor-sharp blade from the top of Clovis' left shoulder down across and over his heart to his lower right hip, Lee sliced through the skin.

Clovis never even whimpered, but we could see him gritting his teeth, and the beads of sweat perspiring profusely from his forehead and face as the hair on his chest was quickly saturated in crimson red-hot blood. The pain had to have been excruciating.

Mark cursed and then vowed lowly beneath his breath, "I'll kill that sucker if it's the last thing I do."

"We've got to do something!" Will desperately repeated again. He, like Mark and me, was feeling extremely helpless and none of us liked it. "Ross, look over there on that rock." Will commented as he slowly pointed his finger beyond the place where Tihn Lee and Clovis stood.

Mark and I followed the direction of his finger and noticed the satellite phone.

"What are you thinking, Will?" I asked as I looked at the phone.

"Brothers, you heard Lee say that phone puts off a signal that will lead his brother here to him. I'm thinking if we could get our hands on that phone, we could lead his brother to some other location where we could intercept him and perhaps get Judy and Wren out of harm's way and possibly catch him and use him to negotiate for Clovis." Will always had a way of finding a possible solution when there seemed nothing to be found. In fact, we always said, "Where there's a Will, there's a way."

Mark whispered, "That's a great idea, but how do we get that phone?

It's too close to Lee and his men. They'll spot us for sure."

We pondered the question for a moment and then Mark replied again, "Ross, remember in the Bob when you called Kyle Sooner from up on the Chinese Wall?"

"Yes, I remember."

"Do you still have FBI Agent Jonathan Jones card in your wallet?" Mark asked again.

"Yes, I do." I stated as I was getting the picture.

"Think about this. If we can get that phone, you could call him. He could contact the FBI headquarters that would know whom to contact to send help here on its way. They could pick up the signal from the satellite and be here in a heartbeat."

"The question still remains. How do we get our hands on that phone?"

CHAPTER 16

The flight was short from Camp David back to the White House. Watson was tired and weary and as soon he was safe on the ground, he called in his personal physician to give him his daily checkup. The doctor told him that his blood pressure was elevated, his body was running a mild fever, and he was dehydrated. He advised the President to go to bed and get some rest; Watson took the advice. The First Lady was in Boston speaking for a charity event and would not be home for a couple of days.

Watson gave specific orders not to be disturbed, except for only one exception. If FBI Director Mitchell called, put him through to his private line in his bedroom.

Watson had just got undressed and was about to climb into the shower when the phone buzzed by his bed. Stepping from the bathroom back into the bedroom with only a towel around his waist, he picked up the phone.

"Mr. President. This is Director Mitchell." "What have you got?" Watson implored.

"One of my men in Communications got to thinking that there is a possibility that the Lee Brothers may not be acting entirely on their own, and if they are not, then they might be communicating with a third party. If that were the case, they would have to be using something other than a landline. Our guess would be a satellite phone."

"So, what are you telling me, Director?"

"We decided to see if our satellites picked up anything?"

Mitchell answered.

"And...?" Watson inquired impatiently.

"Well, Intel says we've actually got several signals, but one of them is in the Missouri Breaks which causes us to think that maybe something is going on up there. I mean, it just seems a little out of place for someone to be using a satellite phone and coupled with the fact that Clovis and the Tyler boys are up there somewhere hunting seems a little too coincidental to me."

Watson considered that for a moment. Perhaps someone had taken one with them while hunting or camping. It wasn't like everyone and their dog owned one, but people did manage to get their hands on them and in an emergency situation they could be the difference between life and death.

"You may be right, Mitchell. Where did the other signals come from?" Watson asked.

"There was one we picked up down near the town of Dillon which is in the southwest part of the state and another over near Missoula. The one that has aroused our curiosity is located east of Great Falls and it's mobile. I mean, the signal is picked up moving eastward along the highway and was last recorded near the town of Stanford. This one could be moving toward the signal we have picked up in the Breaks, but we have not been able to ascertain a connection between the two yet."

Watson was doing his best to decipher the new acquired information and formulate the possibilities.

"What thoughts do you have about what is going on?" Watson asked Mitchell.

"We have several possible scenarios, Sir. Assuming that these signals are somehow related to the Lee Brothers, our best speculation-- and that is all it is at this time--is that the Lee Brothers divided their forces. One group moved in on the Belden Ranch and seized Mrs. Belden and her daughter and the other group somehow knew where Clovis and the Tyler Boys were going hunting."

"How would they know that?" Watson asked.

"That's what the phone call was about that I had to take when you were just leaving Camp David. My men found a wiretap on the phone line. It was rigged so that all in-coming calls would be blocked and just sound as if it were ringing to the listener. That's why all the calls you made to the Belden Ranch never went through. It was also rigged so that only outgoing calls could be made. Clovis obviously called the Tyler ranch to discuss the hunt with Ross and his brothers before they left, and that call was intercepted. We feel quite confident of that." Mitchell proclaimed.

"So, let me see if I understand this correctly. You're saying that not only does it appear that Judy and Wren Belden are now captive to the Lee Brothers, but Clovis and perhaps even the Tyler Boys are as well, and currently they are in two different locations?" Watson asked angrily.

"Yes, Sir. That is what we believe." Mitchell replied.

Watson ran his fingers through his hair. He was tired and exhausted and not feeling well, and trying to maintain clarity of mind and thoughts was extremely difficult. This was a situation he did not want to foil. First and most importantly to Watson were the lives of the Belden's and second of all, an unsuccessful attempt at rescue would certainly draw public attention. Failure to protect American citizens against foreign threats on our Nation's own soil would certainly not assist his campaign for reelection, which was only six weeks out. He had to make the right call and do so the first time.

"Do you think they're using each other as leverage against the other?" Watson asked Mitchell.

"That's what we are afraid of. If the two are connected--and I believe they are--and then we try to stop one, they'll kill the other immediately. For example, Mr. President, if Mrs. Belden and her daughter are with one of the Lee Brothers in the car heading east, and the other Lee Brother has Clovis and the Tyler Brothers captive, then we can assume that if we put a stop to the car with the Belden ladies inside, Clovis will end up dead or vice versa."

"That kind of puts us between a rock and a hard spot,

Mitchell." Watson pronounced.

"Yes, Sir, it does. If we attempt to make a rescue attempt on Mrs. Belden and her daughter, there is still no assurance that we can do it without anyone getting hurt, and we can feel pretty confident Clovis will die. I do not see how we can possibly rescue all of them. It's simply a matter of who lives and who dies. I am going to leave that call up to you, Sir."

"Thanks a lot, Mitchell. How much time have we got until the two join up together, assuming your assumption is correct?"

"Judging by their speed and looking at the distance, I calculate about two hours and 25 minutes. Then, they've got to walk about 4 miles from the highway to get to Clovis, assuming again, that the other signal belongs to them. The problem with that is it will be dark by the time they start walking, so we can assume their travel will be much slower. The cloud cover is not only hindering our satellite visibility, but it will mean a very dark night for them to traverse that kind of country. If we only knew for sure that the signals belonged to the Lee Brothers, it would make it easier for decisive action."

"That sure is a lot of assuming, Mitchell, and you know what assuming can do to a person?" Watson asked. Watson struggled with assumptions. He desired to make the correct decision and his constant resolve to do the right thing, especially when the lives of others were at stake, made it difficult to determine his next course of action. In this case, he did not have much of a choice.

"Yes, Sir, but we do believe that our speculation is the closest and most accurate thing we've got to the truth." Mitchell responded.

"Ok, then let's run it as if we knew for certain. What will be the procedure?" Watson asked.

Mitchell just started to speak when he abruptly paused and then responded back to President Watson. "Mr. President, Intel just notified me that they have picked up transmission from the eastbound mobile unit to the phone in the Missouri Breaks. They are obviously connected. Give me five minutes to think this through, and I'll call you with our plan."

"Make it good, Mitchell. We don't have a lot of time."

CHAPTER 17

Again, our course of action was determined by the fact that we were clueless to anything transpiring beyond what we could only know in the immediate present. My brothers and I had no way of knowing that President Watson was aware of anything that was going on. We believed we needed to get to that phone and make something happen. At the very least, even if they did know, we would be able to describe in detail, the information that they could never acquire any other way.

"Ross!" Will whispered. "I've got an idea." "Shoot, Brother. I'm all ears."

"I am thinking about sneaking around to the other side of that phone. You and Mark make some kind of noise or cause some kind of distraction that will lure these guys your way for a few seconds, and while that is going on, I'll slip in there and steal that phone."

"If we do that, you realize that will reveal to them that we are here, and they'll torture Clovis or those other hunters to draw us in. I can't do that. It has to be a distraction that won't give us away."

Mark poked at my elbow. "Look Ross, that guy on the ground there is trying to communicate something."

I looked over at him and made eye contact. I whispered real low, "Can you hear us?

If you can, blink twice." The man blinked twice.

"Are you able to run?" I asked. The man stared for a moment, apparently taking time to consider and weigh the question and then blinked twice.

"What are you thinking about doing?" Mark asked.

"What if, Will slipped around to the other side of that phone, and this man were to jump up and take off running in the opposite direction, causing enough stir that Will might be able to grab that phone undetected."

"That might just work, Brother." Will commented. "I think I can pull that off."

"Did you hear that?" I asked the fallen hunter. He blinked twice. "Are you willing to do that? I asked again. He blinked twice.

"You know that you could get shot?" I asked as I held his stare for a long moment. He blinked twice. "Don't stop running. Stay low and get out of here. We'll take care of your brothers. You're in no condition to help and will only get in the way if you stay." I instructed. He blinked twice once more.

"Ok, Will, you sneak around to the other side and don't get yourself killed. I'll wait until you're in position before I send this guy off running."

Will started to slip out to make a circle to the far side of Lee's camp where he might get lucky enough to steal the satellite phone.

"Will," I stated, "I love ya, Brother."

"Yup, I love you too, Ross." I'll be all right."

As swift as a deer and as quiet as a mouse, Will disappeared into the sagebrush. Mark and I waited keeping our eyes focused to the juniper trees and sagebrush just beyond the rock where Tihn Lee had placed the satellite phone waiting hopefully to acknowledge that Will was ready to nab the phone when the proper time came and hoping that his presence would not be noticed by Lee and his men.

Tihn Lee and his men were growing restless. It was apparent by the fact that they were tired and getting bored. Clovis still stood stretched out between the two junipers, the blood on his chest had oozed and streaked down his torso toward his waist and dried. The two hunters were still tied together sitting on the ground. Occasionally, they became uncomfortable and moved a little, but usually not without painful repercussions.

Clovis spoke up, "You know that it will be dark before they even find a place to park along the highway, and your brother and whoever is with him will have to find their way here in the dark?"

"I'm sure they'll do just fine." Lee answered, waving him off as if Clovis' comment meant nothing.

"You realize with this cloud cover that it will be fairly warm this evening?" Clovis asked again.

I was trying to figure just where he was going with this line of questioning. I would later find out that he had spotted Will in the brush and was drawing attention away from him by keeping Lee engaged in conversation.

"What is your point?" Tihn Lee asked.

"The point is that this is the time of year that the rattlesnakes begin moving to their dens where they will hibernate for the winter. There will be places in this area that will be crawling with those nasty snakes and even more so after dark." Clovis warned.

"I'm not worried about a few snakes." Lee apathetically commented.

"So, you're not concerned about your Brother getting snake bitten, because I'm definitely concerned about my wife and daughter?"

I didn't listen to Tihn Lee's response, but, after noticing that Will had moved into a position that was as close as he was likely to get to the phone without being noticed, I turned and whispered to the earless hunter lying just several feet in front of me.

"Are you ready?" I asked. He blinked twice.

"OK. When I say go, get up and run as fast as you can. Like I said, don't stop. We'll get your brothers. You're in no condition to fight." He blinked twice again. Looking up at Tihn Lee and his men and then at Clovis and then at this man's two brothers who remained tied, the thought occurred to me that the thread upon which life hangs is so thin that in a blinking of an eye or just a heartbeat, that thread can be severed. In just a moment, the possibility of that happening could easily transpire and for more than just one of us.

I felt certain that the Lee Brothers would not allow anyone to survive for fear that they might be identified. The odds of successfully pulling this off without someone getting killed were so incredible that I did not even want to consider it. I really didn't care if anyone of Lee's group died, but it unnerved me to consider who might die among the rest of us.

I looked back at the man lying there on the ground, ready and waiting for me to give the signal, and I realized that his chances of making it would be very slim. He was going to jump to his feet and take off running, knowing that by doing so, he would bring gunfire down upon himself, but hopefully, Lee's men would move toward his direction just enough that Will could slip in and grab the satellite phone without being noticed. What he was doing took incredible courage, and I believed it was because of the love he must have had for his other two brothers who were still captive. I could certainly understand and relate to that kind of brotherly love. Yet even if Will was able to nab the phone, there was still no guarantee that we could prevent the inevitable bloodshed that I feared would transpire. Still, as slim as it appeared to be, it was our only hope.

I felt Mark's breathing on the back of my neck as he inched up closer to me. "What are you waiting for?

"Will is in position and ready." Mark replied.

"Ok." I answered. Raising my hand so the injured hunter could see it, I used my fingers to count to three, one at a time. One, two, three...

Immediately, the man jumped to his feet and took off running through the sagebrush. Chaos and confusion erupted among Lee's men as they ran in his direction firing at the fleeing man with their automatic weapons. Tihn Lee had also advanced forward with his pistol and fired a couple rounds in the hunter's direction.

My eyes never left the phone. I was worried for Will, but the plan had worked perfectly. Will slipped in quickly and quietly, grabbed the phone off of the rock, and disappeared back into the sagebrush and juniper trees. I glanced at Clovis and met him eye to eye. It dawned on me that he knew exactly where Mark and I were hiding, but he had purposefully avoided looking in our direction so as not to arouse suspicion. Mark and I quietly slipped out of our position and swung around in a wide loop to intercept Will.

"Psst." Will whispered through his lips as Mark and I practically walked right by him.

"Got it." Will stated assuredly.

"Good job." Mark and I uttered in unison.

"Let's get farther away from here and make that call. Time is wasting." I suggested.

Leading the way upward over a little rise, but staying low in the sagebrush, we found a position where we could still watch the camp and yet remain hidden and our voices could not be heard. Opening my wallet, I sorted through the business cards that I always find a way of collecting and found the one given to me by FBI Agent Jonathan Jones. Looking at the number, I punched it into the phone. It rang four times before it was answered.

"Agent Jones, speaking."

"Agent Jones, this is Ross Tyler. I need your help." I stated by passing all the cordial greetings.

"Mr. Tyler, what can I help you with?" Jones asked.

"Are you able to put me through to your Director in D.C.?" I asked desperately.

"Does this involve Mr. Belden?" Jones asked. "Yes, it does."

"Ok. I'm doing so now. Wait until I clear it."

Waiting for just a moment, I heard Agent Jones speaking with Director Mitchell.

"Director, I've got Ross Tyler on the line. Can you speak with..?"

Mitchell cut Agent Jones off short, "Yes, by all means." This is Director Mitchell. Is this Ross Tyler?"

"Yes, it is. We've got a problem, Sir." "I'd say you do." Mitchell replied.

"Sir?" I asked, not knowing how he knew.

"Mr. Tyler, we've picked up satellite signals. We believe that Tihn Lee's younger brother is in transit with Mrs. Belden and her daughter, and they are trying to make their way to your location, and we are assuming that Tihn Lee is there now."

"That is correct." I stated. "He and his men have two hunters and Clovis as captives right now. According to the conversation we were able to hear on the phone, they are waiting for Tihn Lee's brother to arrive so they can kill the entire Belden family in front of each other."

"That's sick!" Mitchell responded.

"Yes, Sir. I think so too. Here's my worry Sir. Somehow, we need to stop Tihn Lee's little brother, but it has to be done in such a way that Judy and Wren are not harmed. We've managed to steal Tihn Lee's satellite phone which transmits the signal for his brother to follow. I am afraid that if one or the other grows suspicious, they'll just kill the Beldens and abort what other plans of torture they've got in mind."

"I see." Mitchell stated. "What happens if Tihn Lee doesn't find his phone? I mean, that is the only line of communication they have with one another isn't it?"

While I was in conversation with Director Mitchell, Mark was watching the camp below through his binoculars, but at the same time, overhearing the conversation. "They do not appear to notice that it is missing at the moment." Mark commented.

"Did you catch that?" I asked Mitchell.

"Affirmative." Mitchell replied. "Who are the other hunters?" Mitchell inquired.

"I don't know them by name, but Tihn Lee believes that they are my brothers and I."

"Hmmm. We need to see if we can use that to our advantage. Let me think about it." Mitchell responded. I didn't know at the time that our conversation was being shared with practically all of the Intelligence Division and also by President Watson who was connected into the conversation at the White House.

There was a pause for a few moments as I was put on hold, and then Director Mitchell returned to our conversation. "Tyler, we are of the opinion that you need to get that phone back to Tihn Lee."

"Do what?" I asked flabbergasted.

"Listen Tyler, without that phone we would not understand the situation as it now stands, so you did right, but if Tihn Lee can't find it, he's likely to kill everyone and just abort the whole plan. I'm telling you, he's more dangerous than a half-cocked pistol with a hair-trigger, and he might just go off at any time."

"Sir, we went to great lengths to acquire that phone. One of the hunters risked his life and may have even sacrificed it in order for us to get our hands on it and now you're telling us that we need to take it back?"

"Yes, Tyler. It's the only way, but listen to me. Turn the phone over so you are looking at the back side." I handed it to Mark and reiterated the instructions as Director Mitchell gave them to me.

"Locate the small transmitter. Remove it. Now cross the white wire with the pink stripe over and attach it to the red." Mitchell instructed.

Mark, always good with electronics, handed his binoculars to Will and then followed the instructions.

"What does this do?" I asked.

"Look and see if the red light is still flashing on the top side of the phone." Mitchell ordered.

"It is."

"What this does, Tyler, is it makes it appear that the phone is still sending off a signal, but it is not. The phone is still operable for calling, but the signal is not transmitting. However, take a look now at the transmitter. You'll see two wires. One is black and the other is blue and green. The blue and green has two small wires wrapped together. Leave one attached as it is and cut the other leaving enough length to cross it with the black one. This will still permit a signal to be picked up by the satellite." Mark again quickly followed the instructions.

"Ok, we've got it. Now what?" I asked.

"Tyler, one of you has got to slip that phone back into Lee's camp and put it somewhere that it might appear it could have been missed or overlooked. Then that transmitter needs to be taken to a place where an ambush can be made to intercept his younger brother, who will use his phone to follow the signal your transmitter gives off."

As I glanced toward the west, the sun was beginning to sink into the horizon. The sky was still partly cloudy, but had cleared up considerably since earlier that morning. The pink and yellow and red hues of the sunset were quickly fading, as was the light of day. Darkness would soon be upon us. The use of a flashlight would be out of the question, as we knew that the light beams would give away our presence. How were we going to set up an ambush for Tihn Lee's brother in the dark and somehow manage to lead them into it? I expressed my concerns to Mitchell.

"Chief Mitchell, let me explain our situation. We are unarmed with the exception of a bow and a few arrows. Even if we were armed, the risk of Judy or Wren getting hurt or worse is too great. Too, if Tihn Lee hears shooting, he'll just kill Clovis and run. We need reinforcement."

"We're sending men right now as we speak." Mitchell responded. "How are they going to get here in time? Certainly you are not sending them in by air. That will be too noisy and achieve the same tragic results." I stated desperately.

"Tyler, we have a truck of heavily armed men about two miles behind Lee and the Belden women. You will need to get that transmitter stationed in position soon. This will give my men as well as Lee a location. We are going to try to get ahead of Tihn Lee's brother and be in position when they come. We are thinking we can out-pace Tihn Lee's little brother, especially since he will have Judy and Wren with them."

The idea was good in theory, but I still had my concerns. "Sir, that still leaves Clovis back at Tihn Lee's camp. Lee will kill him as soon as your men start firing. There's no way that he and his men will not hear the gunfire unless they are armed with suppressors."

President Watson cut in. I had no idea at the time that he had been listening to the entire conversation between Mitchell and me. "Ross, you do not have to worry about Clovis. We've got that covered."

"Would it be too presumptuous of me to ask just how you're going to pull that off?" I asked skeptically.

"I'll let Director Mitchell explain." Watson replied.

"Tyler, once our men are in position and Tihn Lee's little brother are advancing upon the signal broadcasted by that transmitter, we are going to call Tihn Lee's satellite phone. When he answers it, we will launch a non-explosive missile from RQ-1 Predator."

"What is a RQ-1 Predator?" I asked.

"To make things short, Ross, it is a medium altitude, unmanned aircraft used for surveillance and reconnaissance. We can also launch a missile from this craft." Mitchell answered.

"Ok, how will you manage to fire a missile on Lee without hurting Clovis or the other two guys?" I asked.

"That missile will hone in on that satellite phone and take Tihn Lee out of the picture. It will hit him with such force that his body will crumble to pieces. There will be no collateral damage to Clovis or any of the other hostages. We have it hovering at an altitude right now that will allow us to drop the missile right on Lee without the interference of the trees."

"How long will it take from time of launch until impact?" I asked. "From its present hovering position, about 7.2 seconds." Mitchell answered. "Now, go place that transmitter somewhere that will make for a good ambush and get that phone back into Tihn Lee's camp. From the satellite image, it appears you have about 10 minutes of dusk left. You're on your own from here."

"I'll take the phone back." Will volunteered.

I looked at Will, eye-to-eye, and held his stare for a long moment. "I will and... I know." Will answered.

My stare simply stated the words on my heart although they were not verbalized. He knew that I was saying, "be careful and I love you". He grabbed the phone and started to proceed when I stopped him short. "Hey, Brother, take this bow and arrow. I

159

know it's not much, but you can shoot better than I can, and at least it's something of a weapon. I hope you don't need it."

Handing Will the bow and quiver of arrows, Will again melted and disappeared into the landscape on his way back to Tihn Lee's camp. My heart sank a little as I considered the danger he was facing, but at the same time, I also knew that he, more than Mark or I, would be likely to succeed. Will was smaller framed, flexible and incredibly patient. His vigilance is what had made him such a tremendous and successful hunter. Still, he was my brother, and I worried for him.

Mark and I looked at one another. "Any ideas?" I asked.

"I was looking around while you were on the phone. I think that coulee right over there is the best place I can see. The highway is east of here about 3 miles, I'm guessing, and I figure they'll stop along the way and advance on foot from there. I sure hate the idea of Judy and Wren being forced across this country in the dark, especially with all the rattlesnakes moving to their dens this time of year. I'm just glad we've got these snake-proof boots to wear."

"I hear you, Brother. Let's go."

Mark led the way and I followed in behind him. It was dark by the time we made it to the coulee, but the clouds had passed, and the moon was full and illuminating the light colored gray sagebrush well enough for us to see where we were going without the use of a light.

In the coulee, Tihn Lee's camp was not visible. This gave me an idea that we should build a campfire. Certainly, Tihn Lee's brother would be expecting a campfire. After all, he did have one in his own camp. I shared the idea with Mark, and we both began gathering firewood and had a nice blazing fire going in no time. We placed the transmitter a short distance from the fire, hanging it on a tree branch. This place looked quite suitable for an ambush. There was plenty of cover for Mitchell's armed unit to hide in position and wait for Tihn Lee's brother to show up, assuming they could make it here before the others.

Mark and I moved back into the shadows, away from the fire

and waited. Sitting with our backs to a juniper tree, slightly upon the hill, overlooking the campfire below, we waited. It was our first time since Mark and his family had moved back to Montana that the two of us had actually had some time to spend in private conversation. For a moment or two, we just sat there in a peaceful meditation without saying a word. I finally asked, "What are you thinking, Brother?"

"I'm thinking I don't like this situation at all." Mark answered emphatically.

"Me either." I replied. "What's got you troubled?" I asked.

"I feel helpless." Mark quickly identified the same feelings I was having. "I don't like the idea of depending on someone else to take care of my problems. I mean, shoot, I didn't ask for this, but it's on my plate regardless, and it appears that there's nothing I can do about it. Mom and Dad are probably worried sick, and so are Sally and the kids. You did say that Director Mitchell had called the house and talked with Dad to find out where we were, didn't you?"

"Yes, I did." I answered.

"Ross, I've got to tell you. I sold everything I had and quit a good paying job back in Tennessee to make this move back to Montana. I want to give to my boys the kind of life we had growing up and there's no place on earth like Montana. We have before us an opportunity to develop the land that Dad has given us into a very productive cattle business, and I am so ready to get started doing that very thing. Sally quit her job to help me make this dream come true, and I believe she wants it as much as I do. Will and Abby are just as passionate about the idea as we are."

Mark paused for a moment. He was always careful with his words and usually didn't say a whole lot, but when he did, you could bet the ranch he had given it a lot of thought. I could tell that he wasn't finished, so I just waited for him to continue.

"What I'm saying, Ross is I just hope we live long enough to see it happen. I mean, please don't take this wrong, because I think the world of Clovis, and I think it's kind of neat to be a personal friend with such a widely recognized national hero, but so far, my connection with him and yours too, has brought unbelievable danger to our family and death to our brother Joe, which has brought a lot of grief to all of us, especially to mama, and I'm not sure that I want to expose my family or myself to anymore of that."

I understood exactly what Mark was trying to say. It wasn't fear that prompted him to say what he needed to say, but it was his love for his family and the recognition of the fact that he had a responsibility as a father and a husband not only to provide for his family, but to protect them as well. Getting killed would not allow him to do either.

"I know, Brother. I've given that same thought some very serious consideration as well. I love Wren, and I plan on asking her to marry me, but I've also considered the consequences of doing so. Think about this, I don't know how many enemies Clovis has made throughout the course of his life and especially over the three year period he spent in the Bob Marshall Wilderness, and I don't know who might want to seek revenge. I hear rumors that whoever put the million dollar bounty on his head has evidently not been arrested with all the others who were in on the conspiracy to kill President Watson and has not lifted that bounty, and if that is true, that means none of us are safe as long as we are around Clovis. Then, when you throw in the fact that Kirby's brother has sworn an oath to kill me when he gets out of prison, doesn't make for a bright looking future."

Mark just shook his head for a few moments and said, "No, Brother, it appears rather dim when you look at it from that perspective." We both sat in silence again for a moment, letting the thought we had just brought to the surface sink in a little deeper. It was indeed a gloomy one to consider, but the moment at hand was more pressing. It did not make much sense to consider what the future might hold in store when the ever present danger we were facing at the time was something we were not even sure we would live to tell about.

"I wonder if Will was able to make it down to Lee's camp and sneak that phone in there all right. I'd figured he'd be back by now." I commented, breaking the silence.

"Me too." Mark whispered worriedly. "Brother, I sure don't like sitting here on my butt, waiting for Director Mitchell's task force to show up, assuming they can get here before his brother shows up with the women."

I just nodded my head in agreement. Mark and I stared down at the small little transmitter hanging from a tree branch, only the intermittent red light flashing on and off and it occurred to me that so many lives depended upon the invisible signal that small devise was putting out. All that Mark and I could do was sit there and wait, and waiting was something we didn't favor doing very well.

In the light of the bright yellow moon and glimmering stars, we sat in silence, listening to the coyotes howl through the river bottom and the bugles and chuckles of the bull elk as they voiced their testosterone-filled challenges to one another in their attempt to procreate their species. A screech owl whistled to another somewhere close. It was a splendorous night. The temperature was not too cold, and we were actually quite comfortable. Surrounded by the peace and solitude of the evening, it was difficult to believe that so much turmoil, disturbance and danger existed within. Blood would be shed tonight. Lives would be lost. The most we could hope for was that it would not be ours.

"Did you hear that?" Mark whispered, bringing me out of my stupor of thought.

"No. What was it?" "Listen." Mark whispered

Bending our ears and listening real close, we could here light footsteps very much near us. We both knew that they were footsteps of a man and not of an animal as the footfall of every creature is different.

"Maybe it's Will." I suggested.

"It's not." Mark stated. "The step is too heavy. I've hunted with Will down in Tennessee many times. He can walk through a forest of dry, fallen oak leaves and barely make a sound. He mastered that skill when he left Montana."

"If it's not him, then maybe we better find out who it is." I suggested.

We both stood and slipped in behind a juniper tree and listened as the footsteps drew nearer. The sounds of the steps appeared to be leading to a small opening through the brush and the trees. Mark and I quietly slipped to each side of the opening, waiting with our knives drawn. As soon as the figure of the man stepped through the opening, Mark and I had him to the ground with our knives at his throat.

"Don't kill me. I need help." He pleaded, lying on the ground, flat on his back, with his arms raised, palms forward in a position of submission.

There was no question about the identity of the man. He was the hunter who had lost his ear and had managed to escape earlier. We were soon to find out, that he had taken a hit through his shoulder from a bullet while he was trying to escape.

Mark looked at the wound. He poured a little water over it to cleanse it, which was about all that he could do. We determined the fresh air was probably the best thing for it at the time until he could see a doctor.

"Listen guys, we've got to get my brothers out of there and that other guy." He commented desperately.

"That other guy is Clovis Belden." I answered. "You mean that guy on television?" He asked. "That's him." Mark and I said in unison.

"Wow, that's incredible. I thought he looked familiar. Well, my name is Russ. Ronnie and Roy are my brothers, and I've got to save them." Russ repeated.

Mark and I described the plan and suggested that Russ was not in a condition to fight.

"How did you find us?" I asked. It had suddenly hit me that he could not have just stumbled upon our location.

"Your brother, Will, told me where to look. He told me what

the plan is with the FBI and President Watson. I mean, is that really true?" Russ asked.

"Yes, it's true." I answered.

"So what do we do now?" He asked.

"Unfortunately, all we can do is sit here and wait for the task force to show up."

"Man, I don't like that. Sitting around while my brothers are down there just doesn't sit well with me." Russ commented. I could relate to his feelings quite readily.

"I understand, Russ. Clovis is down there at the camp with Tihn Lee, and his little brother is coming this way with Judy and Wren. We are definitely out muscled and out gunned, so we don't have much of a choice. The part I hate the most is sitting here, not knowing if things are shaking down the way they are supposed to."

"How far was Will from Lee's camp when you found him?" Mark asked.

"Oh, maybe a hundred yards. He found me. He was shooting that bow and arrow. He said that he had to see how it shot in case he needed to use it, and he heard me coming and snuck up on me and then told me where to find you guys. He didn't have time to fill me in on the details and told me that you guys would take care of that. I must admit, I don't like the plan very much, but considering the situation, it's about all we've got."

"Yup. We'll just sit here and watch that transmitter from up here on the hill. I sure hope they get here soon."

CHAPTER 18

Little did I know that while the three of us sat upon the hillside in the dark, watching and waiting for Mitchell's men to arrive, praying that they would show up before Lee and his men, the situation was transpiring and unfolding rather quickly. Watson had ordered Mitchell to put his best men on the task force, and they had followed Tihn Lee's little brother, whom I also later learned was Quan Lee. In their armored vehicle, they were able to stay behind Quan Lee and his men along with Judy and Wren at a distance of a mile or two, keeping track of Lee's vehicle by the signal of his satellite phone. Although they could have passed Quan Lee's vehicle and got ahead of the game, they feared that their army vehicle might arouse suspicion

When darkness finally fell upon the vast empty landscape, the task force used night vision optical lenses mounted to their heads to drive without the use of headlights, but still maintaining a safe distance from Quan Lee. Quan Lee finally pulled over to the side of the road, and along with four of his men, they escorted Judy and Wren at gunpoint toward the signal of the transmitter that the three of us were watching.

The task force also stopped along the road simultaneously with Quan Lee and immediately tore off running across the sagebrush flats and the rolling hills toward our transmitter. With the use of night vision head gear and being physically fit they believed they could circle around Quan Lee and arrive at the transmitter before Lee could. Coupled with the fact that they did not have to contend with trying to push a couple of hostages along, it made reasonable sense that they could accomplish it with no problems.

For more than an hour we waited. Nervous, completely unsure of how things were shaking down, we were quickly becoming irritated, frustrated and impatient. I must admit the uncertainty was getting the best of me. I was ready for something to happen, one way or another. Still, we waited and we waited.

When Russ noticed movement down by the transmitter, we realized that the task force had been successful. I flashed my headlight at them a couple of times to reveal our location. Quickly they moved up the hill to our location.

"Which one of you is Ross Tyler?" One man asked. "I am. Who are you?"

"I am Colonel Alex Weaver. I am in charge here. These men and I are going to get into position. We ask that you stay put up here on the hill and let us take care of things from here on out." Weaver ordered more than suggested.

"Do you have any idea how long before Lee arrives?" Mark asked.

One soldier had some kind of tracking device and pulled it from his pocket and looked at the screen. It obviously was tracking the satellite signal of Quan Lee as they progressed forward. "They appear to be just a little over a kilometer." He stated.

"How far is that?" Russ asked, apparently not knowing the metric system.

"That's a little less than a mile." Colonel Weaver responded. "I need you to give me your word that you will stay put. We cannot foil this mission. It has to be quick, quiet and over. Do you men understand?"

"Yes, Sir." We all answered. "What will you do with them once you have apprehended them?" Russ asked.

Colonel Weaver looked Russ directly in the eye and emphatically stated, "There will be no apprehension." We all knew what that meant.

"Colonel Weaver, I have a question. It is my understanding

that as soon as Quan Lee and his men are detained, Director Mitchell will make a call to Tihn Lee's satellite phone. A missile will be launched immediately and will hone in on the signal put off by his phone. In approximately seven seconds or so, the missile will make impact with Tihn Lee killing him instantly. Is that correct?"

"Yes, Sir. That is correct." Weaver confirmed.

"Well Colonel, it just occurred to me, I don't believe we have a plan for Tihn Lee's other three men. My brother is down there trying to return the phone without being noticed, and Russ's brothers along with Clovis are down there as well. Taking out Tihn Lee doesn't completely eliminate the threat. Those other three men are armed with automatic weapons. What's going to stop them from opening fire and killing all of them?"

Even in the darkness I could see the concern in Colonel Weaver's eyes as well as his men. Somehow, this threat had not been considered, and it was, beyond a shadow of a doubt, a legitimate concern. The threat and possibility of injury or death still coming to Clovis, Ronnie, Roy and my brother was real. It was an oversight that could prove to be deadly.

Colonel Weaver pulled his own satellite phone from its case and immediately put a call into Director Mitchell explaining the newly discovered problem. Mitchell ordered Colonel Weaver to send three of his men toward Tihn Lee's camp and be prepared to dismantle any retaliation that might occur after Tihn Lee had been taken out.

"That is too risky." I proclaimed. "Lee's camp is positioned in such a place that it will be very difficult to advance upon them without being noticed."

"Well, just what do you propose we should do?" Colonel Weaver asked.

"I don't know." I stated. "I just don't know. Maybe move your men in as close as they can, but far enough back that they don't arouse suspicion and have them ready to advance as soon as the missile is launched. A lot of ground can be covered in seven seconds. At least 40 yards or so."

Overhearing the conversation, Mark commented, "Whew, we are talking about splitting hairs here. The timing of all of this has to be perfect." Mark was right. Again, it was imperative that both Tihn Lee and Quan Lee were taken out simultaneously or as close to it as possible for fear that if one or the other suspected foul play, they may just kill everyone and make a run for it. Once again, I considered the frailty of life. The thread upon which it hangs was appearing to be even thinner than I had originally believed it to be.

Colonel Weaver called out the name of three men and gave them instructions to try to position themselves in such a place that they might get a clear shot at Tihn Lee's men without the possibility of striking one of the civilians nor betraying their position. The term 'civilian' didn't sit well with me. It just seemed so impersonal. Those 'civilians' included my brother and my soon to be father-in-law. The three men quickly and almost silently disappeared into the shadows of the night. Colonel Weaver looked at the progress on his monitor of Quan Lee and his men who were leading Judy and Wren toward the transmitter. They were closing the distance and were now less than half a mile away. He quickly barked out orders to his men to position themselves, ready to ambush Quan Lee and hopefully rescue Judy and Wren without any harm coming to them. Meanwhile, Russ, Mark and I, waited upon the hill impatiently.

As we sat there it became quite apparent that none of us liked the idea of doing nothing. Although Colonel Weaver and his men were superbly trained for this kind of mission and their skills far exceeded our own, we were men of action. Sitting idly by, twiddling our thumbs, especially when the lives of those whom we loved were at stake, only added to the helpless feeling we had been fighting ever since the whole situation had started.

Colonel Weaver had given us a pair of night vision binoculars so we could observe the scene below from our position. Mark had been doing most of the observing. Through the binoculars, we could see most of Weaver's men and where they had positioned themselves. Somewhere, across the vast landscape of sagebrush and junipers, in the darkness of the night, save the moon and the stars and their glow that permeated the huge Montana sky and filtered itself upon the vast and uninhabitable and open countryside, Quan Lee and his men were moving Judy and Wren toward the signal given off by that transmitter.

It occurred to me that my destiny would be determined on this night. The events that would transpire before the morning sun pierced into the eastern horizon would, one way or another, make an impact on my life that would forever leave its mark on the road that I was yet to travel. No matter how long or how much of that road remained, tonight would very likely influence the course.

I have found it interesting how so many thoughts can go through a man's mind in such a short period of time. As I sat there in the company of Mark and Russ, my eyes focused on the flashing red light of the transmitter in the coulee below. Looking, but not really seeing, my mind was in a whole other world.

I continually found myself entertaining the thought of asking Wren to marry me. I knew exactly how and where I wanted to propose to her. The very thought of it somehow caused my heart to step up its pace and shortness of breath to deprive my lungs. Her face shone vividly in my mind. I could see her long, brunette hair fallen over her shoulders, shining brilliantly as it brushed against the tan, slender curve of her neck, and I envisioned the sparkle in her eyes and the flash of pearly white teeth coursing the contour of her lips. I could see the charming twinkle of delight in her eyes. She was by far the most attractive young woman I had ever dated, and I was still baffled over the reason she was attracted to the likes of me, but she was, and that was all that mattered. As I pondered our relationship, I realized that it had grown deeply, and my love had developed to a point where I had never known love before. Astonishingly, I had only met Wren a little more than three months before when she helped me escape from Chicago where death, unbeknown to me, awaited me for certain. I owed my life to her, but Wren did more than save my life from getting killed, she saved my life by helping me escape the lifestyle I had been living for almost three years, by helping me return to Montana, the land of my youth and the vessel of my passions.

I found myself asking my heart if this could actually be real. Can a man actually find love at this level in such a short period of time? Maybe this was simply an overblown infatuation with the woman. Maybe, because she was so physically beautiful and because her personality so matched my own, I was merely in a mesmerized state that wouldn't allow me to think logically and reasonably, consequently my normal, good, sound, judgment was being betrayed. I chewed on that for a moment and concluded that was not the case at all. In fact, I had never been more certain of anything in my life, and all I wanted was to get out of this present mess and get back to my truck, grab the ring I had purchased out of the glove box and slide it on her finger as soon as I could. "Lord," I whispered to myself, "I've got it bad." I have to admit, I felt out of control when it came to Wren. Not only did I constantly find myself in a stupor of mysticism when I was in her physical presence, but just the thought of her put me in a daze that set me in a whole dimension of oblivion that had a way of practically making me totally unaware of anything and everything else that was happening. It was not a desirable condition to be in considering my present situation, but of course, because I was in it, I didn't think about that at the time.

As I mentioned earlier, it amazes me how many thoughts can literally rush through a man's brain in only a very brief moment in time. I'm not sure how long I had pondered over these thoughts of Wren, but I was suddenly brought out of my mind-wandering travels to the danger of our present situation when Mark flatly stated, "Brother, we've got problems."

Mark and Russ were sitting on the hill, just a few steps behind where I was sitting. Mark had been observing the landscape with the night vision binoculars. I looked back at him as he leaned forward and handed me the binoculars.

"Look about eleven o'clock perhaps 200 yards beyond Weaver and his men." Mark ordered.

Grabbing the binoculars and adjusting them to my own vision, I looked in the direction he had ordered. My eyes caught the glisten of moonlight striking against metal, perhaps shining off of a gun, and immediately I could identify the problem that Mark had just mentioned. Quan Lee's men were on higher ground than Weaver and his men who waited near the transmitter, expecting Lee's men to follow the signal of the transmitter down into the coulee. As I peered through the binoculars it became quite apparent that Lee and his men were also wearing night vision equipment. This was another oversight. No one expected them to have it as well. Spread out in a semi-circled fashion, they were slowly encroaching upon Weaver and his men, and it was obvious that Weaver and his men knew nothing about it.

"How did Lee and his men know that Weaver and his men were down there?" I asked aloud.

"You've got me." Mark answered.

"Maybe they're just extra cautious." Russ exclaimed.

"I don't know, but this isn't good." I stated as I continued looking through the binoculars.

After a few moments my eyes found Judy accompanied by a large Vietnamese man who held her at gunpoint as they progressed forward. "Where is Wren?" I asked aloud, more to myself than to anyone else.

"What's up Brother?" Mark asked.

"I can see Judy, but I don't see Wren." I explained.

A large lump was growing in my throat. Wren could be somewhere else, held prisoner by someone else, and I was not able to see, but an inner voice inside of me nagged at my soul, and I could feel panic begin to swell up in my chest. "Lord, where is she?" I asked as I continued glassing the hillside straining my eyes all the harder to find her.

Mark must have noticed the quiver in my voice. "Calm down, Ross. There's a lot of country out there. Maybe she's just not where you can see her right now. Let me see those glasses."

Reluctantly, I handed the binoculars to Mark. Mark could no more know for certain if Wren was all right any more than I could, but his voice of confidence helped to sooth my fears. It seemed like the Tyler Brothers were always able to do that for one another. We knew each other better than anyone, and throughout the years we could practically read each other's thoughts.

Mark continued to glass the hill side. There was no way that we could warn Weaver and his men of the encroaching danger. If Quan Lee's men were trained in military combat as well as we believed they were, Weaver and his men would be sitting ducks. The element of surprise would be to the advantage of Lee and his men, and that might be the greatest advantage they had in their arsenal and the most important as well.

A sudden chill ran through the course of my body. Up until this time, I had not been cold. The night weather had actually been quite pleasant which was unusual for this time of year. Fear of the unknown or maybe the adrenaline coursing through my veins had caused it, but I began to shiver.

"We've got another problem, Brother." Mark stated to me emphatically.

"What?" I asked, not sure that I really wanted to know.

"I see a suppressor on a rifle. I don't recall seeing any on Weaver's rifle or his men." Mark answered.

Pausing for a moment to process the meaning, I realized that Quan Lee could open fire on Weaver and his task force and the report of the rifles would not be heard by his brother Tihn Lee, or Clovis, or Russ's brothers or the three men that Weaver had sent in that direction, meaning that Quan Lee would soon join forces with his brother Tihn and for certain kill everyone just as they had planned from the beginning. To add insult to injury, it occurred to me that Weaver was the one who was going to make the call to Mitchell at just the right time, so Mitchell could order the release of the missile that was going to take out Tihn Lee. What if Weaver was killed before he could make the call?

Mark spoke out to me without removing his eyes from his binoculars, "Stinks to high heaven, doesn't it Brother?" Obviously, he could see that this rescue mission was designed to fail before it even got started. All the hypothetical scenarios had not been considered and consequently good people were going to die. My mind began to wonder if Mitchell and his men really knew what they were doing. For a flashing moment, the thought crossed my mind about their loyalty and integrity. Although many men had been captured and imprisoned for their part in the conspiracy to kill Watson, we all knew that there were others who still remained at large. Could Mitchell be one of them? Could he be trying to appear as though he was giving his best to prevent harm and injury from coming to us while subtly overlooking what might seem to be less important details all the while knowing that these small details could make the difference between success and failure? I wasn't sure, but one thing remained certain, I was not impressed by their efforts. Russ sat there shaking his head and then asked a question that demonstrated even more vividly how ludicrous this attempt was playing out. "How come Weaver didn't leave us a walkie-talkie or something like that where we could communicate with him? Shoot, we could at least warn him right now!"

"Russ, I think they were more concerned about us staying out of the way and making sure we didn't interfere." I commented.

Mark pulled the binoculars from his eyes and handed them to me. In the reflection of the moonlight on his face, I could see the worry in his eyes. "I can't locate Wren."

I took the glasses and began searching again. Through the binoculars, I found the large Vietnamese man holding Judy. They hadn't moved, but there was no sight of Wren. Slowly and progressively, Quan Lee and his men moved into position. From our vantage point, we could see them, but felt certain that Weaver and his men could not. Our position was like sitting in a spectator box at a pro football game. Our view of the impending danger allowed us to see and anticipate how the battle would play out. It was not looking favorable for Weaver and his men. They were in the bottom of the coulee and would have to look up the hill to see Lee and his men, but doing so was impossible because the sagebrush and junipers were too thick in the bottom to see beyond. This was going to be a massacre, and without weapons of our own there was nothing we could do to prevent it.

I handed the binoculars to Russ. He hadn't asked to look through them, but I knew he wanted to see with his own eyes what was happening. After just a short glance he expressed, "My God, Weaver and his men are about to die, and they don't even know it. Isn't there something we can do?"

"Nope, there isn't Russ." Mark emphatically stated. "It is highly unlikely that Weaver can see us from his position even though we can see him. We're hidden from Quan Lee and his men at the moment, but it's probably only 400 yards across this coulee from here to their position. That's certainly in range of their rifles. We can't bring attention to ourselves. They'll fire on us for sure, and we have nothing to fire back."

"So, we're just going to sit here and watch the slaughter?" Russ asked frustrated.

"I know; I don't like it either." I stated. "This whole thing makes me angry enough to just spit. Judy is a hostage right over there." I said as I emphatically pointed toward her direction. "I have no clue where Wren is at the moment. Will is down toward Tihn Lee's camp, and I'm assuming he's still alive. Clovis is strung up by a man who plans to disembowel him with his knife along with your brothers. Weaver and his task force of men will be crossing over into the Promised Land in the next ten minutes or less and here we are doing nothing. Let me ask you men, are you going to be able to look at yourself in the mirror tomorrow morning knowing that you didn't make any effort at all to end this situation?" I couldn't keep my voice from elevating in a volume a little. I was fuming mad. Not at Mark or Russ, but at the whole stinkin' mess. I was frustrated beyond what my feeble words could so meagerly express. I tried to calm my nerves, but then the fact that I was unable to locate Wren put me into a state of panic. I was about to lose it.

Mark spoke up as I knew he would. "Calm down, Ross. I've been waiting for you to do or say something. The only reason I've held back is because you stand to lose more in this mess than I do, but we have got to keep our heads clear and not let our emotion overrule our sound judgment." I knew he was referring to Wren.

"Brother, as far as I know, she may already be gone." My voice crackled at the mere thought of that present reality, and I could feel the lump swell up in my voice and the tears immediately begin to well up in my eyes. "My God, Mark, we've got to do something. I can't stand it, Brother. I don't want to lose her. I don't want to lose you!!!" That was it. The inner emotion that I was trying to restrain could be held no longer. My weeping burst into sobbing. Mark scooted closer to me and put his arm around my shoulder and pulled my head to his.

"Listen Ross, you need to let the death of Little Joe go. It was not your fault, Brother. It was not your fault." Mark spoke to an inner guilt that he knew I carried deep in my heart, guilt that I still do, even after all these years. Joe had sacrificed his life in an effort to save mine and although I had avenged his death when I so brutally killed his murderer, the fact remained, Joe was still gone. Still, it was the guilt I carried at the innermost core of my soul that crippled me at the moment. I did not want the death of another loved one nor their blood upon my conscience. Russ, who was still looking through the night vision binoculars, stated, "Guys, I'd say we have about 10 minutes before Quan Lee and his men are all in position. If we're going to do something, we need to do it right now.

Now, my two brothers' lives are depending on Weaver contacting Mitchell to make that call to launch the missile that will take out Tihn Lee. Clovis' life and perhaps your Brother Will's life also depend on that call. I'm going to try to quickly slip down there to Weaver and warn him and tell him that he needs to make that call. I can't sit here any longer."

Russ started to rise, but the loss of blood from his injuries made it almost impossible. He was weak and stiff and was in no condition to do anything. "I don't think you're going anywhere, Russ." Mark commented. "You're in no condition to do anything but sit here. I'll go."

It was a statement Mark made that demonstrated the true character of the man he was inside. It was a death wish. Russ knew it. I knew it and Mark knew it. The odds of getting to the bottom of the coulee and warning Weaver of the impending danger that was about to descend upon him and his men were slim. The odds of living to tell about it were even slimmer.

"Ross. Why don't you top this little ridge and run like a mad man? See if you can circle around to Judy? I don't know what you can do, but maybe you can somehow rescue her and find Wren." Mark knew the odds of rescuing Judy and not getting killed were not any better than the odds he was shouldering for him. He also knew that he would rather die trying than to sit idly by and do nothing. My feelings were the same.

Our eyes met in the glow of the moonlight. It has been said that the eyes are the window of the soul, revealing at times the depth of a man's inner most being. That revelation was made perfectly clear as we held each other's stare. There was not a trace of fear to be noticed, but the look of pure, unadulterated determination to accomplish what both of us knew in our heart was impossible and yet refused to believe that it could not be done.

"I'll see you on the other side." Mark stated. I knew his statement had a double meaning.

"I'll be waiting." I replied. "Be careful." Mark disappeared into the darkness, staying low in the sage brush, moving quickly down the hill toward Weaver and his men, doing his best not to be spotted by Quan Lee and his men.

"Russ, you sit here and wait. Here's my pack. It has some food and water in it. We'll do our best to get your brothers back to you." I took two steps and moved into a run as fast I could go, my legs carrying me effortlessly as I dodged through the high sagebrush and junipers, making a circle around toward the man who held Judy at gunpoint. I didn't have much time.

CHAPTER 19

My feet were light and swift as though they seemed to glide just a few inches off of the dusty, rocky soil as I darted through the brush. At one point, I felt my foot step on a large squirmy rattlesnake, but I barely took notice, and if it struck at me, I don't recall. My mission would not be interrupted.

The distance I ran to circle around to Judy could not have been more than half a mile, and I was there in less than five minutes. I slowed my pace to a quiet steady walk as I neared the point that I believed she was being held captive. Inching my way in behind the cover of a large juniper tree, I peered into the moonlit landscape to locate her. In only a few seconds, I saw her standing with her captor. They were only 30 yards or so from my position, staring down into the coulee, waiting for the rest of Quan Lee's men to take care of the business at hand.

Quietly, I shortened the distance by another ten yards. At this point, I could see the reflection of the moon on Judy's face. Tears had streaked down her face and matted in dust. She had been crying, but was no longer. I feared the tears were the result of something that had happened to Wren, but I refused to allow my mind to go there. It was then that I noticed that her captor also wore a night-vision headset. It occurred to me that the advantage that he had over me of being able to see more clearly in the night, might well be the advantage that would put him at a disadvantage.

Tip-toeing ever so cautiously, I advanced in behind the two of them, cutting the distance to about 3 quick steps. Withdrawing my hunting knife from the sheath crouched low and as ready as a mountain lion about to pounce on a mule deer buck, I took a deep breath and quickly assessed the situation again.

The man's AK-47 was suspended by the sling from around his neck, holding the rifle in front of his mid-waist, ready to use. The muzzle was pointed to his left, pointed directly at Judy. One squeeze of the trigger could send her into the Promised Land. Peering through his night-vision goggles, I knew that I would have the advantage in close and personal confrontation for a few seconds anyway.

I can't remember exactly what prompted me to make my move when I did. I have learned that there are situations when your instincts read the moment at hand for what it is, and you must react according to how your instincts interpret.

The man never knew what happened. In one quick movement, I threw my left arm around his head, pulling his body to my right, plunging the knife blade to the hilt into his kidneys and then quickly bringing it back up and slicing across his throat, dropping him to the ground like a sack of potatoes as his life's blood seeped quickly from his body soaking up the dust in the ground where he lay.

"Are you alright?" I asked Judy.

"Yes." Judy answered as she threw both arms around my neck and began to weep again.

"Where's Wren?" I asked as I consoled her weeping.

"I don't know, Ross. I'm afraid she's dead by now." Judy stated as her voice quivered. Somehow, she had managed to say the words, but I could tell that she did not really believe them. There was a fragment of hope, and at this moment even a fragment was enough to keep me going.

"What do you mean? What happened?" I inquired frantically.
"Shortly after we left the highway and started walking this way,

Wren was bit by a big rattlesnake high on her right calf. She was able to go for about a mile, but I swear, by that time it was already swelled up to twice its normal size. She was slowing us down. Quan Lee was going to kill her, but he called his brother first, and he said to leave her and let her die. He said "it would be a more painful and slower death that way than a bullet." So, we left her. She was in a lot of pain. I'm guessing that was a little more than an hour ago."

"Do you have any idea where that happened?" I asked.

"No, I don't... somewhere out there." She stated as she swung her arm back to the east. "I do know that we were walking almost directly west because the North Star was on our right, but this country looks the same and even more so in the dark."

She had barely got the words out of her mouth when I heard the muffled sounds of gunfire being discharged through suppressors. While a suppressor does silent the muzzle blast of a discharged firearm, they are not completely silent, and on a clear, calm, night like this night was, the sounds were quite audible.

Taking the night vision goggles from the dead man at our feet and his rifle and several magazines of ammunition I found in the pockets of his coat, along with the 9mm pistol which I tucked into the front of my jeans, I peered down into the coulee. Shots from Lee's men were being fired, but Weaver's men were not returning fire.

"What should I do, Judy?" I asked as I quickly explained the situation and how the plan was supposed to play out. "Mark is down there trying to get word to Weaver to call Mitchell and tell him to send the missile now because these men have got Weaver surrounded. Will is over near Clovis. I am sure that he has either managed to slip that phone back into Tihn Lee's camp or he's dead by now. I can't stay here. I've either got to help them or go find Wren. Tell me what to do." I pleaded.

"Go rescue your brothers, Ross. I'll head back and see if I can find Wren. Bring them all back, Ross. Bring my Clovis back to me and let's go home." Judy kissed me gently on the cheek and then cupped my face in the palms of her hands and kissed me on the forehead. "Listen Ross, it's in God's hands now. He'll give you the strength you need to be his instrument." She stated with a kind of faith that I have yet to learn.

"Ok. I'll do my best." I replied as I quickly stepped to the rim of the coulee and looked below. Pausing for a moment, I glared into the coulee. I could only see one of Weaver's men from my position, but a short moment later as I was watching him, I saw him take a bullet that quickly ended his life.

To my left I noticed the bright orange from the muzzle blast that had fired the shot. Quickly, sitting down, I found the man positioned across a small rock cropping, lying prostrate and looking for more targets. Removing my own head gear, I raised the AK-47 to my face and braced my elbows on my knees. The night vision scope found him quickly. Thumbing the safety into the firing position, I settled the cross-hairs on his head, took a deep breath, let it out slowly and squeezed the trigger. I knew at the squeeze that the shot was good. "Two down!" I confidently stated to myself.

Judy had already left to see if she could locate Wren. Easing along the rim of the coulee I moved quietly and slowly. I realized that at this moment Lee's men could not possibly know that danger was encroaching upon them from their own position on the hillside. I had to use this to my advantage as much as possible. I sure was hoping that Mark had not caught one of their bullets.

Another shot, confirmed from the visual recognition of the muzzle flash, gave me a clear indication of another shooter. It took me a moment, but once again I was able to locate the assailant through the night vision goggles. This time, I rested the forearm of the AK-47 in the crotch of a juniper tree and settled the cross-hairs on the man's chest. He was in a sitting position, just as I had been only a few minutes earlier. I could not tell, but it appeared he was wearing a bullet-proof vest, so I moved the cross hairs to the bottom of his chin, hoping to shoot just high enough above the vest to take him out. Once again, the shot was true. "Three down." I softly whispered to myself, wondering if perhaps Judy's comment about the Lord Almighty providing me with the strength I needed might actually be true. I had never been much of a religious man, although it was apparent that the faith of the Belden family was as strong as any I had ever witnessed. Perhaps, God was more active in the lives of those who entrusted their faith in him more so than those like me who really only acknowledged his existence. Somehow the thought of their faith gave me more confidence. I was trying to remember. I believe that Mitchell told me there were four men and Quan Lee, making it a total of 5 men. That meant that Quan Lee had only one more man with him, assuming that one of the two that I had killed with the rifle was not him. Tihn Lee still had three men with him. We had narrowed it down to six. I had a long way to go.

I had just started to move when a blast of flame blazed from a muzzle again to my left. This was not more than 75 yards from my present position. The bullet smashed one of the limbs in the crotch of the juniper where I had just positioned my rifle, scattering bark harshly into the side of my face. I jumped quickly into denser cover to conceal my presence. Obviously, they were on to me. I was going to have to be even more careful.

It occurred to me that the man that had been holding Judy did not have a walkie-talkie or any other communication device. I wondered if anyone other than Quan did. If they did not, they would not be able to tell one another that I was in among them. I felt sure that the man who fired at me assumed that I was one of Weaver's men. Still, among all of the shots that had been fired, I had not heard the report of gunfire from below. Were they holding their fire because they simply could not see the enemy? Surely, not all of Weaver's men had been killed already.

I felt pretty secure in my current position, and visibility was as good here as any other place I might find.

I worried for my brothers. The fear spawned of uncertainty has always been a very real struggle with me. In our youth, Will brought on a lot of those kinds of worries to our family. I would be hard pressed to say how many times we would go fishing down on the river, and Dad would give specific instructions to be back to the truck by dark. Everyone would show up except for Will. We would wait awhile, and if he didn't return, we would grab the flashlights, walking and stumbling in the dark, calling out his name, just knowing that he was hurt or had fallen in the river and drowned. Then, out of nowhere, he would appear, carrying his fish and wondering what the big fuss was all about. He finally grew out of it, or perhaps I should say, he learned his lesson. On one fine Montana summer evening, Mark, Will, Joe, Dad, and I all decided to leave the hayfields, and we grabbed our fly rods and headed down to the Yellowstone. As usual, Dad gave specific orders to make sure we were all back by dark. However, Dad had privately told Mark, Joe and me that he was purposely going to stay until way after dark, but not to let Will know. So, when all of us boys returned to the truck and Dad wasn't there, we decided we had better go look for him. Mark and Joe went upstream while Will and I went down stream. Yelling and calling out for Dad, Will was in frenzy. Will was nearly to the point of tears when suddenly Dad stepped out from behind a large cottonwood tree and clearly stated, "It's not a good feeling is it, Will?" At the moment, I think Will was so happy to see Dad that he didn't catch the meaning, but on our way back to the truck, where Mark and Joe were waiting, Will commented, "I promise I won't ever do that to you guys again." He never did. It was a hard lesson, but Dad was not opposed to teaching us a hard lesson now and then if he knew it would stick.

Right now, I was worried. Suddenly, a flash of flame streaked across the sky. I knew it had to be the missile that was destined to kill Tihn Lee. I was not in a location that allowed me to see the results of the fired missile, but I learned later how the situation unwound.

Mark had managed to slip down the hill into the bottom of the coulee and make it to Colonel Weaver without getting shot. As he was revealing the fact that Quan Lee and his men were quickly approaching their position and that they needed to be prepared to fight at any minute, the words had no sooner left his mouth when a bullet smashed into Colonel Weaver's chest. Mark quickly grabbed Weaver and dragged him into the thick sagebrush for better concealment, but in the process of doing so, Mark caught a bullet in his left hip while trying to save Weaver. Weaver was still alive, but it was obvious to Mark that he wouldn't be for long. Mustering all of his strength to endure the pain, knowing that his death was inevitable, Colonel Weaver pointed at his radio, and stated through his dying breath, "Contact my men. Tell them that hell is about to come raining down. Hold fire unless they have a clear shot." Weaver watched Mark through glassy eyes as he made the call. "Men, this is Mark Tyler. Your commanding officer, Colonel Weaver has been shot. Lee's men have you surrounded. Colonel says not to fire unless you have a clear shot." Obviously, Weaver knew that the report of gunshots would be heard by Tihn Lee and that might cause him just to kill Clovis and Russ's brother and come a running to save his little brother Quan.

"Grab that satellite phone off my hip, Son." Colonel Weaver ordered Mark. Frothy blood was spilling forth from the corners of his lips, an indication that the bullet had taken him through the lungs. Mark took the phone. "Make the call to Mitchell, Son." Weaver barked as his labored breathing produced a deep hoarse cough. Mark pressed the call button.

"Director Mitchell, this is Mark Tyler. Colonel Weaver has been hit."

"How bad is it?" Mitchell asked.

"He won't make it, Sir." Mark answered, aware that Weaver could hear what he was saying.

"Weaver says, fire the missile." Mark repeated.

President Watson could be heard in the background. "Make the call to Tihn Lee and fire the missile, Mitchell. Do it now." He ordered.

According to Will, when Mitchell made the call, Tihn Lee walked over and picked up the phone, able to locate it because of the ring. As soon as he answered the phone, Mitchell launched the missile.

"Mr. Lee, this is Director Mitchell of the FBI. I am here with the President of the United States on speaker phone. We know that you did not leave the United States, and we know that you have the Belden family hostage. I assure you that if any harm comes to them, you will be prosecuted here in the States to the full penalty of the Law."

Mitchell was just making conversation, providing time for the missile to make impact. The missile had launched successfully and was honed in on the satellite phone that Tihn Lee held to his ear. Lee however, was facing almost directly southwest and saw the flaming streak across the sky headed directly for him. In less than a second, he pitched the phone to his side where it landed at the base of a juniper tree while he leaped in the opposite direction. The missile followed the signal of the phone and literally tore the tree into pieces.

Lee jumped up from the dusty ground as mad as a wet hornet. Pulling his knife from its sheath he walked straight over to Clovis, who now had been suspended between two trees for several hours. His body was weak; the blood on his chest was caked and dried. Tihn Lee grabbed him by the beard as he had done earlier and yanked his jaw upward.

Nose to nose he stood in front of Clovis' face. Nothing but hatred gleamed from his eyes. Clovis stood still as a rock appearing annoyed at the defiant scum that stood in front of him now, which I am certain only augmented the disdain and contempt that Lee held for Belden. If Clovis was afraid, Will, who was hiding in the brush, only ten yards behind Clovis, could not really tell.

Tihn Lee didn't say anything for a long moment. His anger seethed inside of him and seemed to kindle so deeply that words just failed to come. Perhaps he was contemplating the words of Mitchell. It was obvious that he was now well aware that the U.S. government was knowledgeable of his presence and his motive. He also knew that he could never return to his homeland. Such a betrayal of peace agreements on his part would mean execution for sure. The fact still remained, however, that although he was guilty of kidnapping and bringing harm to Russ and to Clovis, he had not yet killed anyone. Surely, the punishment for his crimes would be far less if he if let Clovis go and just turned himself in.

I have no way of knowing if those thoughts ever crossed his mind. If they did, I guess he decided against them. Still face to face with Clovis, he finally stated with a hissing sound, "How do you want to die, Clovis Belden? Would you like for me to start here and gut you like an animal? He asked as he lowered the long bladed knife to Clovis' waist. "Or, would you just prefer that I slice your throat like you did my father?"

Clovis never took his eyes from Tihn Lee. "Do you not see the red dot of a laser beam on your body right now?" Clovis asked. "There's a shooter over there in the brush that is about to pull the trigger on you at this very moment." There was no shooter. Clovis was bluffing, just hoping that Tihn Lee would step back just far enough for Will to take a shot. Clovis had known Will was there, concealed in the brush all along. Evidently, Tihn Lee fell for the bluff and believed Clovis. Stepping back, he glanced down the torso of his body to see if he could see the revealing gleam of a red laser dot anywhere fixed on his body. Not seeing it, he yelled, "You liar," and started to step toward Clovis again, knife in hand, ready to kill him.

Tihn Lee was too late. His first step forward was stopped short when an arrow from Clovis' bow, shot by Will, pierced clear through his chest and passed through out the other side. For an instant, Tihn Lee was stunned, not sure what had happened and looked again at his torso. The blood was quickly soaking his shirt. Clovis just smiled with a casual smirk, "I told you there was a red dot." Still standing, realizing what had just happened, Tihn Lee started for Clovis again, but the second arrow from Will struck him in almost the exact same place. Tihn Lee crumbled to the ground.

Interestingly, Tihn Lee's men had disappeared. They were nowhere to be found. Will stepped out of the brush and quickly cut the ropes that had held Clovis bound. Helping him to stabilize as the pressure was released, Will moved Clovis over to the fire and set him down on the ground placing a jacket over his shoulders. He then did the same for Ronnie and Roy.

187

Quickly, Will gathered up water containers and some food that Tihn Lee and his men had with them and gave it to the three men. Two AK- 47's still lay at the ground near the men that Clovis had killed with his bow and arrow earlier that afternoon. Taking a rifle himself and handing the other to Clovis, Will stated, "Clovis, you know and I know that you're in no shape to help. Please stay here and care for these two men. I gave my word to their brother, Russ that I'd do my best to take care of them. I'm leaving that job to you."

At the mention of Russ' name, Ronnie and Roy jerked their heads up. "You mean Russ is still alive?" Roy asked. It had not occurred to Will that Roy and Ronnie had believed that Russ was dead.

"Oh yea, he's still alive." Will answered. "He took a slug through the shoulder, but it was a complete pass through, and I don't think it even hit a bone." Suddenly, the abuse and the hardship that Roy and Ronnie had just endured were forgotten. It never ceases to amaze me how good, wonderful news can transform the entire demeanor of a man's soul. I am not sure that the joy these two brothers were feeling at the moment can be measured. For certain, words are far too inadequate and feeble to even remotely describe it. I've known that joy myself.

Will turned to Clovis as they met each other eye to eye. Clovis looked beaten down, but his thoughts were not focused on the weariness he was feeling. Rather, he was concerned for his wife Judy and his daughter Wren, but he also had enough good sense to know that he would only slow Will down if he tried to go with him.

"You be careful, Will." Clovis pressed.

"Yes, Sir, I will." Will answered. As he turned to leave he took one last look at Tihn Lee's body lying twisted in the dusty soil.

"That was some good shooting, Will." Clovis complimented.

"I had a good bow." Will responded with a smile that grinned from ear to ear.

"Thank you, Son." Clovis softly whispered as he realized just how close he had come to meeting his Maker.

"Anytime, Clovis, anytime." Will replied. As he turned to leave, he stopped and turned back to Clovis.

"Clovis, how did you know I was behind you?" Will asked. Clovis smiled. "I smelled you."

Will just chuckled to himself and then vanished into the brush and disappeared into the darkness of night.

Of course, I was completely unaware of the events that had transpired in Tihn Lee's camp. There was no way for me to know that Tihn Lee was dead or if Will or Clovis were alive. That would have been information that would have brought a little peace and hope to my own situation at the time, but again, the uncertainty brought on a gloomy feeling of despair. I had been fortunate so far and had taken out three of Quan Lee's men. I wasn't certain how long my good fortune would remain. I really felt as if the odds were stacked against me and such thinking was making me move with cautious stealth.

Wren continued to cloud my thoughts, obscuring my mental focus on my present situation. I worried for her, not knowing if she was still alive. I could not allow myself to think the worse. I found my lips uttering prayers to God that she would be all right, but inwardly, I felt helpless. I could not desert my brother, Mark, to go aimlessly wandering in the dark looking for Wren, not having a clue where she might be, or if she was still alive or not. I could lose them both. I hoped with all my heart that Judy would find her and somehow be able to save her, although I wasn't sure what she could do about a rattlesnake bite that had already taken its toll on Wren's leg. Although I have been in perilous situations before, I believe this was the first time that I had ever prayed so fervently, knowing that I was completely powerless and that all things were beyond my control. Perhaps, it is in times like these that men are more prone to discover a deeper faith in their Creator than they have ever known before. For certain, I had no choice.

As I neared the bottom of the coulee, the brush was thicker, and it became obvious why Weaver and his men were unable to

189

see or locate the enemy. The sage brush was higher as were the junipers, and trying to look up on the hillside where Quan Lee and his men had positioned themselves proved impossible. I felt a little responsible for that because it was Mark and I who had placed the transmitter down at the bottom of the coulee, but we had done so on the premise that Quan Lee would follow the signal down and find it difficult to retreat, especially under the gunfire of Weaver's task force. As it turned out, it worked the exact opposite of what we had hoped or expected and neither Weaver nor his men fired a single round.

To the best that I could determine, there were two shooters of Quan Lee's men left. One cat-like footstep at a time I descended further into the bottom. The camouflage clothing I wore was made of fleece, and it was practically silent as I moved through the course sagebrush. My eyes scanned the area, cautious to detect any movement or something that looked out of the ordinary surroundings of the landscape. Seeing how the moon was almost directly overhead, full and bright, I removed the night vision goggles and placed them into the pocket of my jacket and allowed my vision to adjust to the night. While the goggles gave me a clearer view they also hindered my peripheral vision.

Taking a step, I stopped suddenly. Something I had heard or sensed brought my senses to full alert. I paused, listening closely, bending my ear closer to a faint sound that I felt sure I was hearing. I turned my complete attention toward the direction. At first I could not identify the sound and then the recognition hit me like the proverbial freight train. The sound I was hearing was someone breathing and the sound was close. On high alert, my ears strained to locate the source of the sound. Was the sound coming from one of Weaver's men or was it made by an enemy? I could not be sure.

Realizing that if I could hear the breathing of another man then the possibility remained that he might hear my breathing as well. I took short breaths and exhaled slowly. I wondered if the person I could hear was aware of my presence. Was he lying in wait for me, ready to ambush me at just the right moment? Ever so slowly, I turned toward the source of the sound, raising the muzzle of the AK-47 to waist level, quietly tripping the safety lever to be ready to fire. My mouth was dry, and my heart was beating at a pace that caused me to fear that whoever the individual might be would surely hear it pounding in my chest. Sweat beaded upon my forehead, and I could feel it also on the palm of my hand that tightly gripped the rifle. Still trying to locate the source of the sound, my eyes caught the glimmer of a vapor as it escaped from the maker's mouth into the cool moonlit night.

"Ross, is that you?" Mark whispered. Every taut muscle in my body immediately relaxed at the recognition of my brother's voice.

"Yes." I whispered in reply. "I'm right here." Mark stated.

Moving toward the sound of Mark's voice, I found him lying near the base of a large juniper tree. Immediately, in the glimmer of the moonlight, I could see the shine of wet blood upon the side of his coat.

Kneeling down, I looked Mark in the eyes. "Mark, are you all right Brother?'

"Yes, I'm fine. I tried to pull Weaver back into the brush. He had me make the call to send the missile, and I no sooner got the words out back to Mitchell when a bullet caught me in the ribs. One of them is broken, I can feel it, but it's really just a flesh wound. I've been thrown by broncs that caused more damage than this. I had to get out of there, but I dropped the phone in the process."

"Let me look at that wound." I stated. I knew that Mark would not always let on about how bad he was really hurt. He had always been that way.

"I'll be all right, Ross. I'll be all right."

Ignoring Mark, I unzipped his jacket and tried to examine the wound.

It was not easy to determine the extent of the injury in the low light condition, so I softly pressed my fingertips to his side. Mark winced a little, but didn't say anything. I could feel the jagged, broken end of a rib protruding through the skin, but there was not an extreme amount of bleeding. I felt sure that it hurt more than Mark was letting on, but I went on his call. "Well, you're right. You've got a broken rib, but you'll be all right."

"What are we going to do from here?" Mark asked as he carefully buttoned up his coat.

"I don't know, Brother. I've killed three of Quan Lee's men. That means there are two more around here somewhere. I'm not sure if Quan Lee was one of them or not."

"Have you heard from Will?" Mark asked.

"I'm right here!" Will stated as Mark and I both jerked our heads toward Will who had managed to slip up behind us.

"Dang it!" Mark exclaimed. "Will, don't you know that's a good way to get killed? I hate it when you do that."

"How did you find us and slip upon us like that?" I asked as I hugged his neck. I was much too happy to see him alive and well to be very angry with him.

"I told you, Ross," Mark stated, "Will, here learned a lot about vigilance and stealth hunting those whitetails and turkeys back in Tennessee. He used to do the same thing to me when we were hunting together."

Almost afraid to ask for fear of hearing an answer I didn't want to hear, I asked anyway, "Will, what about Clovis?"

Will revealed what had happened to Tihn Lee and shared the good news that Clovis and Ronnie and Roy were all alive and waiting back in the camp. "They're alive, but they are in no shape to fight or travel for that matter. Tihn Lee's other men took off when the missile hit."

"So, in other words there are still five of them we've got to contend with?" I asked.

"It looks that way."

"I'm open to suggestions about what to do next." I stated. "Did you get the phone, Will?" Mark asked.

"Yup, got it right here." Will answered.

"Let's call Mitchell. I can't see that it would hurt anything at this point. Tihn Lee's dead as are most of his men. Clovis, Russ and his brothers and Mark here need medical attention, and Judy and Wren are out there somewhere," Mark stated as he pointed his finger toward the endless miles of sagebrush and broken terrain.

"All right, let's do it." I whispered.

CHAPTER 20

Will handed the phone to me, and I immediately dialed the number. It was picked up on the other end before the first ring was finished. "Director Mitchell, please." I stated.

"This is he."

"Director Mitchell, this is Ross Tyler. We need help. As you know, Weaver is dead as are most of his men, if not all of them. The three he sent to Tihn Lee's camp may still be alive, but I do not know that for sure. Tihn Lee is dead. I do not know about Quan Lee, but we believe there are at least still five armed men. Clovis is alive as are the three men that Tihn Lee had captured and tortured assuming they were us Tyler Boys. They all need medical attention along with my brother Mark. At the moment, none of their injuries are life threatening, but they are not in the condition to travel, let alone to fight. Wren has been bitten by a rattlesnake, and Judy is looking for her, but God only knows where. Perhaps east of here toward the highway from which we came. We are out-manned and definitely out-gunned." I could feel the tension in my chest build as I revealed our situation to Mitchell, realizing that we were still in a very desperate situation.

President Watson cut in over Mitchell, "Ross, we are preparing armed helicopters with paratroopers and medics right now at Malmstrom. They should be in your location in an hour."

"Mr. President, please advise what we should do until they get here." I pleaded, not really sure what to do, but not wanting to just sit on my butt and wait either.

"I advise that you stay put. We've got your coordinates from that phone." Mitchell stated, cutting in over the President.

"I can't do that, Sir. I am going to move Mark and Will up the hill to sit with Russ. They can all take care of each other there. I will leave the phone with them so you can track them. You already know where Clovis, Roy and Ronnie are located. Please hurry and pick them up." "Where are you going?" Mitchell asked. I could tell that he didn't

like the idea of his orders being rejected.

"I am going to see if I can find Judy and Wren." I answered matter-of-factly.

Mitchell started to object, but Watson butted in, "Let him go, Mitchell. I would do the same thing if I were in his shoes. He's got to try and right now, time is not on his side."

I handed the phone to Will. "Mark, are you up to walking?" I asked. "You bet. Like I said, I've been thrown from broncs that hurt worse than this."

I knew he was hurting more than he was letting on, and yes, all of us had been thrown by broncs before, but I didn't recall ever having a rib protruding outside of the skin before on any of us. Extending my arm, Will and I helped Mark to his feet. The sudden rise made him a little shaky and off balanced.

"Ok, Mark, I assume you remember where we left Russ. You two make your way up the hill and be careful. I still don't know where Lee's men are."

"We'll be ok. Watch your top-knot!" Will exclaimed.

"Yup, watch yourn." I answered as we all chuckled to ourselves. The two lines were taken from the movie *Jeremiah Johnson*. We had all watched the movie so many times that we knew every single line by memory. Little Joe had used these particular lines all the time, especially when we had been talking to each other on the phone and it was time to hang up. It had become common place for us to say it, but this time, 'watching our top-knot' was serious business.

Turning east, I took off in a dead run. I had to find Wren.

Zigzagging through the sagebrush, moving like a ghost, it seemed as if my feet were barely touching the course sandy soil so prevalent in the Missouri Breaks. All of my senses were on high alert, alert for trouble and danger and alert for the slightest clue that might lead me to Wren.

"Oh God, please let her still be alive." I whispered repeatedly as Iran.

Stopping for a moment at the top of a rise, I looked across the vast ocean of sagebrush. The silver colored gray leaves created a hue across the landscape that made the night eerie, forlorn, and foreboding. It was a mood that I could not shake. Somewhere in the distance, two bull elk bugled their challenging calls to one another and nearby a coyote yipped, speaking a language that I did not understand. The thought occurred to me, and I pondered its meaning for a short moment as I stood there in the night which had grown much colder. How is it that, in spite of all the danger that lurched upon the land at that present moment, does nature still continue to go about its business as usual? The wildlife continued to do what they have been doing since the day of Creation and the disruption that we had brought to their habitat this night was merely an inconvenience and barely more than a disturbance. It dawned on me that their lives are lived in constant danger and surviving the danger means, not only learning to adapt, but either fighting to protect themselves or to get out of the way when it comes. It's the law of nature and those who violate the law usually die. For me, stepping aside and getting out of the way was not an option. I had to fight, not only to protect and defend myself, but those whom I loved.

Having briefly rested and catching my breath, I started running again, first down the hill from where I had stood and then back up the other side. I had no earthly idea where to look for Wren. My only guess was that she had to be somewhere between where I had been and the highway, but locating her was going to be harder than trying to find a needle in a haystack.

The moon had shifted now and the bright yellow light that had filled the land and the night was not as bright upon its surface as it had been earlier, but it appeared that the stars made up for it. As I topped the next hill, my breathing was a little more labored. Although the adrenaline was still coursing through my veins, I was fatigued. Momentarily catching my wind again, I took a couple of steps and then stopped dead in my tracks.

My eyes immediately turned to what had caught my attention. Footprints in the dusty soil quickly aroused my curiosity. Stooping to examine them more closely, I pulled my flashlight and held it near the ground where I could see more clearly, and the beam of the light would be less likely to be noticed from afar.

The tracks had obviously been made by Quan Lee and his men as they had earlier moved toward the signal of the transmitter. Judy's tracks were easy to identify as they were made by her cowboy boots and were much smaller. Wren's tracks were nowhere to be found, which meant that she had to be further beyond this point. All I needed to do was back-track the footprints, and they should lead me to Wren.

"What are the odds?" I asked myself. "What are the odds that I would stumble upon their tracks in the hundreds of square miles of this vast empty wasteland?" Somehow, deep in my heart I knew that it was more than just a lucky coincidence. Had I not been praying? Did God really hear my prayer? If not, what other explanation could I give for it? Although it had been awhile since I had attended church, I remembered our preacher reading from the Bible, "Oh ye of little faith." Boy, did that shoe ever fit? In fact, as I recalled, it had not been all that long since I had heard these words from Clovis.

Staying low to the ground with light in hand, the tracks were easy to follow. Following tracks of wild animals or a missing cow or horse was second nature to me. It was a skill that I had developed throughout my youth and even in the dark, these tracks were easy to follow in the dusty, sandy soil. Surely, they would lead me to Wren.

Whether it was gut instinct or something I was subconsciously reading in the tracks, I came to a place where I felt certain she was close. "Wren, Wren!!!" I cried. "Wren, where are you?" There was no reply. Panic began to swell up in my throat and my heart pounded in my chest. "Wren!"

Keeping with the tracks, I finally found Wren's track. She was wearing her hiking shoes and the track was much smaller than the others and did not press into the soil as deep as the heavier men. She was dragging her right leg. Finding her track, however, meant that I had missed locating her. Somehow, I must have walked by her.

"Wren, where are you?" I desperately asked again. "Wren!!!" I yelled frantically. Hearing the sound of anxiety in my own voice startled me a bit. So intent and so determined on finding Wren, I had not even noticed the tears in my eyes causing blurry vision until I felt one of them roll down my dust covered cheek. Wiping the tears away with the sleeve of my fleece jacket, I called again, "Wren, talk to me baby. Tell me where you are."

On my hands and knees, following Wren's track, it was obvious from the sign, that the others had left her, just as Judy had told me. I had no way of knowing the extent of the bite or how much poison had entered Wren's body. I only knew that, based upon the trail left in the soil from dragging her useless leg that she must be in a lot of pain and time was not on her side.

The sagebrush was thick and difficult to traverse. It appeared that she was headed east, trying, I suppose, to make it to the highway, but then her tracks began to move in a circle. I figured she was either unable to grasp her bearings on the direction she needed to go, or she was delirious from the poison and was wandering in circles. Certainly, she had to be close. "Wren, where are you Baby? Where are you?"

A soft whimper gave me pause. Was I hearing things? I held my breath and listened intently. I heard it again. The sound came from my left although her tracks led to my right. She must have circled back.

Still crawling on my hands and knees, this time toward the

direction I was sure the sound had come, I shined my flashlight ahead of me. "Wren, talk to me Honey, tell me where you are." Movement, further to my left, caught my attention. There she lay, propped up against a clump of sagebrush. Scrambling to her as fast as I could, I leaned the AK-47 against the sagebrush and knelt on my knees beside her.

"Wren, Wren, can you hear me?" I pleaded as I cupped her face in my hands and brushed the hair back from her eyes. Her cheeks were swollen and her tongue slightly protruded just beyond her lips. Taking the hose loose from the snap on my hydration pack, I put the end to her lips, which were cracked and split, and I dribbled a few drops of water on her tongue.

"Wren, you're going to be ok. I'm here. Help is on its way." I stated with uncertainty as I continued to place a few more drops of water on her lips. Removing my bandana from around my neck, I saturated it with water and began to gently wash her face and pressed the cool rag to her mouth and squeeze. This time she coughed and choked, but it was the first reaction I had received from her, and I was glad to see it.

"Wren, Baby, can you hear me?" I asked as I slowly moved her chin in my direction. She didn't speak, but gently moved her head up and down to confirm that she could understand what I was saying.

"Listen, I need to look at this leg. You're in no condition to travel.

Just sit here as still as possible."

There are not many things that cause me to become nauseated when I look upon them. I've witnessed some pretty nasty sights, but when I looked at Wren's leg, I instantly felt like puking. Her leg had swollen to the degree that her faded Wrangler blue jeans had started to split. In comparison, it was nearly three times the size of her other leg. As I shined the light on the tan, grotesque leg, I could also see small splits in the skin caused by the swelling. I located the sign of the bite, but the two puncture wounds caused by the rattlesnake's fangs had nearly sealed shut, also caused by the intense swelling.

Although sweat was profusely flowing down her face, she was beginning to shake and shiver. She had the chills, which I was sure were caused from a high fever. I removed my jacket and tucked it around her. Holding her right hand in mine, I brought her fingers to my lips and kissed them. She smiled softly, but it labored her to do so. Her fingers were cold, and I held them to my chest, placing them on the inside of my shirt for warmth. Her eyes never left me.

"I love you, Ross." She hoarsely whispered.

"Oh, Baby, I love you too. Please hold on. Everything's going to be all right." I repeated again.

Leaning forward, I kissed her softly on the forehead and smiled. Still holding her hand to my chest, I slid it further down on my stomach for deeper warmth. Her hand resting on the butt of the 9mm pistol, she smiled again. Looking deep in her eyes, there was a softness and gentleness there that held me captive and caused my heart to skip a beat.

As I caressed her face and stroked her long, dust-covered brunette hair, a loud audible click from directly behind me, broke the stillness of the pre-morning dawn. I didn't have to be told what made the sound. Slowly, I felt Wren's hand wrap around the butt of the 9mm as she gentle pulled it free from my jeans.

"So, I see you found your girlfriend, Mr. Tyler." Quan Lee's voice arrogantly chided. "Would you like me to shoot her and put her out of her misery and spare her from any more pain and suffering?"

Still looking into Wren's eyes, I hoped that she had the strength to fire the pistol accurately if I could somehow provide her with the opportunity. There are times when words are not necessary. I could read it in her eyes. She knew what she needed to do.

"No, I don't think that will be necessary. She's almost gone anyhow." I answered as I winked at Wren who slightly smiled in response sealing our unspoken understanding.

"Put your hands behind your head. Slowly stand up and turn around." Quan ordered.

Doing as ordered, I came to my feet, never taking my eyes from Wren's as I slowly turned around. Quan Lee was not a big man by any means. Just guessing, I would say he stood about five foot, 4 inches tall and might have weighed 150 lbs. Size didn't matter a whole lot, I decided. It only took about 4-5 pounds of pressure to fire the handgun he had pointed at me.

Looking briefly to the east, the morning sun was just beginning to cast a light hazy hue across the eastern skyline. I wondered if I would live long enough to see it crest the horizon. Quan Lee's eyes never left me. In fact, they seldom even blinked. It was vividly clear that his eyes revealed no compassion, no mercy, no grace, only pure, unsolicited hatred.

"So, Mr. Tyler, it appears that we finally meet at last. I was hoping that we would."

"The pleasure's all mine." I stated sarcastically. I must admit it's hard to be brave when you're staring down the muzzle of death.

"I was expecting to kill Clovis Belden and his family. I guess getting the opportunity to kill you just makes it that much more special."

"I guess you haven't heard. Clovis is still alive. Your brother is dead." I stated savagely.

I could tell that the news slightly stunned Quan Lee. It was obvious that he did not know what had happened to his brother Tihn. Perhaps, in all his arrogance he didn't believe that their mission could possibly fail, and yet there was something in his reaction that suggested it might be true.

"You're a liar, Mr. Tyler. No one can kill Tihn." Quan Lee snarled.

"Do you really think I'm lying?" I asked. "The truth is, my brother Will killed your brother, shooting an arrow through his chest."

"Shut up." Quan Lee commanded. "I don't have time to listen to such ludicrous stories. They're absurd."

In the distant far west, I could hear the drumming of helicopters as they moved across the early morning sky. Their lights were barely visible.

"It looks like your ride is on its way." I tauntingly commented.

Quan Lee's eyes were full of fire and hate. "They will never catch me. You Americans are all the same. You think you are better than everyone else, but you are not. Even if they do catch me, you won't live to see it. Now, get down on your knees." Quan Lee's orders were clear and explicit, and there was no doubt in my mind that his intentions were to execute me right there on the spot. Purposely, I glared at his eyes, making him lock his full attention on my own eyes so his concentration would not be diverted toward Wren. I slowly let my knees buckle to the ground.

Taking a step forward with his pistol held steady, pointed only inches from my forehead and ready to pull the trigger. "Good bye, Mr. Tyler." He said.

The sound of a gun blast exploded in my ears directly behind me. Quan Lee dropped like a rock, hitting the ground hard with a thud. Looking into what was left of his face, there was no doubt he was dead. The bullet had caught him straight in the mouth, leaving an exit wound the size of my fist out the back side of his skull. No doubt, it is what I would have looked like if Wren's shot had failed.

I turned and looked back at Wren who had already lowered the 9mm to her side. I crawled to her side as quickly as I could and looked into her beautiful brown eyes. She tried to smile.

"Thank you, Baby. Thank you. Stay with me now. I hear help is on its way. Live long enough to let me repay you." I stated as tears rushed down my face. I was doing all I knew to do and saying what I could to keep her from dying.

Quickly, I moved to a patch of sagebrush that was not encroached too tightly to others. I didn't want to start a prairie fire. Drawing my lighter from my pack, pushing up some dry debris, I quickly got a flame blazing that only took a few seconds to engulf the entire bush in flames. Surely, the helicopters would see the flame in the little remaining darkness. Within seconds, one of the choppers diverted from its path and was headed our way.

In only a matter of moments, the chopper was hovering overhead and paramedics were rappelling down their ropes to the ground. Next, they lowered a basket gurney. I stepped aside as I pointed to Wren letting the medics do what they were trained to do.

Injecting her with anti-venom fluid and inserting an IV into her arm, and putting her on oxygen, they were quick and methodical. Carefully, they lifted her into the gurney and strapped her in as the chopper moved directly overhead and hoisted her up into the chopper.

"Is she going to make it?" I asked, almost choking on the question. One of the older paramedics, the one I believe who was in charge,

looked at me. There was not a lot of hope in his eyes. "Son, truthfully, I'm surprised that she's still alive right now. I've never seen a snake bite that bad. All you can do now is pray." He stated as he and the other two paramedics hooked their carabineers to their harnesses.

"Can I ride with you?" I asked, surprised that the offer had not been extended.

"We don't have the room. I'll call one of the other choppers to come over here and pick you up. It won't be long. They've got others to take to the hospital as well."

"Which hospital are you going to?" I asked as the paramedics were being hoisted upward from the ground.

"Billings Regional." He shouted from the air over the sound of the chopper.

I stood and watched as the chopper sped across the sky, south towards Billings. Turning back toward where Wren had lay, I grabbed the AK-47 and picked up the 9mm and stuffed it back in my belt. Falling to my knees, totally exhausted, I prayed. "Oh God, I don't know what to say. I just haven't talked to you very much before. Please forgive me for that. I guess I've never really placed a whole lot of faith in you before, but Lord, I am convinced as never before that after all that has happened today, surely your hand has protected us. I don't mean to be asking for more than I should. You've already done more than I deserve, but if you've got it in you, oh God, please do me one more favor. Please, oh Lord, I beg you with every fiber that is in my heart and soul that you let my dearest Wren live."

A noise from behind startled me. I turned quickly, only to see one of Quan Lee's men leading Judy out of the sagebrush with a pistol held to her head.

"Drop your weapons." He ordered.

Slowly I slid the sling of the AK-47 from my shoulder and tossed it to the ground.

"Now, the pistol." He commanded, never taking the muzzle of his own pistol from the temple of Judy's head.

I slowly withdrew the 9mm from my waist with my fingertips and tossed it to the ground.

"Move over there, away from the guns." He directed with his chin.

Looking down at the distorted face of Quan Lee, the man then shifted his focus back to me.

"Not only was Quan Lee a good man, he was my uncle." The apparent remorse for his uncle's death was distinctly noticeable in the tone of his voice.

"Your Uncle was a murdering, woman-beating, scum-sucking coward. He got what he deserved." I viciously rebutted. What he didn't know was that my eyes caught the gleam of the rising sun bouncing off what I believed to be a rifle scope from a small rise about 300 yards out to the southwest. All I wanted was for him to lower his pistol from Judy's head long enough for the would-be sniper to take him out. I knew the comment might stimulate immediate anger and retaliation, and I stood the risk of being shot quickly, but for Judy's life, it was a risk I was willing to take.

I glued my eyes on Judy's. Deep in her soul, I knew she must be frightened, but outwardly, she gave no indication that she was at all. In fact, she stood brave, ready to face whatever happened next. Her eyes held my stare. Could she understand that I had a motive and a purpose for making a statement that would bring nothing but anger to her assailant? Every indication from her expression implicated trust in my judgment, even though she did not understand.

As I had hoped, the man pushed her aside, throwing her to the ground, and raised his pistol toward me and started to speak. The words never left his mouth as a bullet scattered his brains across a clump of sagebrush.

Judy jumped to her feet and came running to me and threw her arms around me. This time, she let go of her emotions and sobbed deeply upon my shirt.

"Where did that helicopter go?" She asked.

Realizing that she had no earthly idea of what had taken place, I told her. "Judy, that chopper is taking Wren to the Billings Regional Hospital. She's alive, but it's not good. The medics are doing everything they can. Clovis is alive as well, and so are my brothers." I stated, knowing the good news would be welcome to her ears.

Looking up into my face, I could see the worry in her eyes for Wren. Wren was her only child, but she smiled slightly at the news of Clovis. "I don't doubt that Clovis survived." She stated. "I quit underestimating that man a long time ago."

"That's because no other man in the world has as much to live for as I do, Baby." Clovis chuckled as he stepped out from behind a large patch of sagebrush.

Judy turned and saw Clovis. As unkempt as he appeared, he was still a sight for sore eyes, even for me.

"Clovis, are you the one who made that shot?" I asked.

"Yup. Wasn't no way I was going to let someone kill my girl." Clovis winked at me and smiled as he tightened his arms around Judy and pulled her close. Grabbing the satellite phone from his waist, given to him by one of the men from the other choppers that had picked them up, he hit the button and spoke, "We're ready to be picked up."

"Ten-four," came the answer.

"Ross, your brothers are fine. Will rode with Mark on the

chopper to the hospital and Russ, Roy and Ronnie are with them. We're going to head that way too, as soon as the chopper gets here.

It was just a matter of seconds when we heard the sound of the chopper coming our way and was soon hovering overhead. Landing in the clearest spot they could find we were greeted with assistance from the military men on board as they helped us board the chopper. I recognized three of them as part of Weaver's task force. These were the three men that Weaver had sent to Tihn Lee's camp.

"What happened to the three men who were with Tihn Lee?" I asked.

They sort of looked me over like I was asking a question that I wasn't supposed to ask. Finally, one of them spoke up. "Oh, we intercepted them as they tried to run away. They tried to surrender. Even threw down their weapons, but we wouldn't let them."

"Excuse me?" I asked. "Are you saying they tried to surrender and you killed them?" I asked.

"We had our orders, straight from the President." One of the men replied. "We were to take no prisoners."

I pondered the reply for a moment. "Works for me."

CHAPTER 21

As the helicopter lifted from the ground, and we leveled out for the short flight to Billings, I noticed the military men who kept looking at Clovis, and it occurred to me that not only were they in the presence of a national hero who had been honored and recognized by President Watson for his valor and courage and loyalty for preventing the President's death more than three years ago, but they were looking at a man who had fought bravely in the Vietnam War and considered to be one of our nation's finest decorated soldiers. Too, his moral fiber and character were undeniably above reproach. Would it not be, I wondered, the desire of every soldier to be half the man that Clovis had lived to be? I had those feelings myself.

Judy sat next to me on my left, and Clovis was in a seat straight across from her. They both leaned forward toward each other, holding their hands together. Clovis broke the silence, "Men, my wife and I are going to take a moment in prayer. You are welcome to join us if you are so inclined." Each man removed his helmet and reverently bowed their head, leaning closer to Clovis so they could hear more clearly as Clovis prayed. "Oh, my Lord, how excellent is your name in all of the earth, who from before the beginning of time to even now have been, are, and forever will be my God. In these past couple of days, you have showered your grace and protective hand upon me and my family and upon the Tyler Boys. I am lost for words to express my gratitude for your graciousness. For certain, I am not worthy. Oh Lord, it seems that

I have asked so much of you throughout the years and especially in these last days. I am almost ashamed to ask you for more, but oh God, it is only because I know that you can do abundantly above more than I could ever possibly ask or think. So it is that my wife and I petition you at this very moment with all that is within us to place your healing hand upon our precious daughter Kelly Wren and heal her from the poison that flows through her body at this moment. Please, I pray, oh Lord, spare her life, and if today a life from my family must be taken, then let it be mine. This is my most humble plea and prayer that I offer to you this day by and through the name of your Son and my redeemer, Jesus Christ. Amen."

As we all lifted our heads at the conclusion of the prayer, I looked toward Clovis who was looking into the eyes of his wife Judy. Tears were flowing down his cheeks. His complete attention was focused on the message returned through her eyes. He had no shame or remorse for emptying his soul in the presence of his wife. If I had ever witnessed a love so strong before in all of my life, I could not recall. I wondered how a man could be such a vicious and brutal adversary when defending what he believed to be right and yet love with the deepest compassion and mercy of anyone I had ever known. Even to this day, I have never known a more distinctive contrast to exist in any human I have ever met.

When we arrived at the Billings Regional Hospital, we discovered that Wren had slipped into a coma during her transport to the hospital and was in ICU undergoing the finest medical treatment that could be provided. Dr. Durham, the lead doctor overseeing Wren's medical treatment met us at the door. "I'm not going to lie to you. It's not pretty. Whether she lives or not will only be determined by her will to live or the grace of God, probably both and that's assuming she comes out of the coma. Even then, I'm afraid that she might lose her leg. If she doesn't show improvement in the next 24 hours, the leg will have to be removed. Hearing the news caused Judy to gasp and break down in tears. I saw Clovis bite his lip, as he pulled Judy to his side where she buried her head into his chest, but there was very little else to indicate how the news affected him. Personally, I felt gut-shot, and I had to leave for a few moments to collect my senses.

For the first time in my life I was truly in love, and Wren was the girl I wanted to marry and yet, here I was, uncertain that she would ever live long enough for me to ask her for her hand. The idea of her not in my life created an unfathomable void. It was like it was impossible to imagine, and yet I could not understand how that could possibly be. As mentioned before, I had only known her for a little more than three months.

"Ross, why don't you come down and visit Mark?" Will asked as he walked up from behind me. The truth be known, I was so consumed with Wren and her condition that I had totally forgot about everyone else, including my mother, who must have been worried sick.

"Have you called home?" I asked.

"Yes, Mom and Dad are on their way." Will replied.

"How's mama doing?" I asked

"Not very well." Will replied. "I'm afraid that her poor heart has endured about all it can take."

As Will and I walked to Mark's room, it occurred to me that Clovis had said nothing regarding his own wounds. Judy had not mentioned them either. Perhaps their immediate concern for Wren was far more important at the time.

When Will and I got to Mark's room, the doctor had already reset Mark's rib and stitched up the wound where the rib had punctured through the skin. The doctor had given him a sedative that had knocked him out, and he was sleeping like a baby. His wife and boys were there along with Will's wife and family and our parents. Will had taken the initiative to call home while he was in transit on the chopper. The whole family 'come-a-runnin,' as we say here in Montana. Everyone seemed to be in a cheerful spirit. Even Mom had managed to lay aside the depression and grief she battled continuously after losing Little Joe. We were all thankful to be alive and as well off as we were. Of course, everyone's primary concern was for the life of Wren. In such a short time she had blended in and had become as much a part of my family as anyone. All we could hold on to was prayer, and I believe it was the first time that I had ever really witnessed our family commune in prayer so fervently, but pray we did, and we prayed often.

The slice across Clovis' chest and belly took more than a hundred stitches and a dozen staples to repair. He was certainly going to carry a nasty looking scar, but he said it was just another one to add to his collection and didn't give it a whole lot of thought.

Kyle Sooner from CNN showed up later that afternoon. President Watson had requested that he cover the story as he had a few months earlier when Clovis had revealed the truth of the assassination of Vice President Peterson. After Will and I shared the events that had transpired in the Missouri Breaks and the deaths of the men who had stood guard at the Belden Ranch, Kyle took a few moments to put his story together so he could present it live on CNN for the world.

"Good Afternoon, Americans. This is Kyle Sooner, reporting live from the Billings Regional Hospital in Billings, Montana. Not more than just a few hours ago, Clovis Belden, whom the world knows so well, was transported from the Missouri Breaks region of Montana where he and the Tyler Boys were enjoying an elk hunting trip..."

Kyle explained in detail the history of Clovis and the relationship of Tihn and Quan Lee to their father, Ho Lee, a general in Vietnam that Clovis had assassinated as one part of his military assignments. "The Lee Brothers had waited many years for their opportunity to avenge their father's death. Fortunately, they were unsuccessful. President Watson will address the nation this evening and provide further information regarding homeland security and our current relationship with North Vietnam..."

Wren remained at the hospital for two weeks. On the fourth day after her admission, she came out of her coma. The doctor had made many small incisions in the skin of her leg to relieve the pressure and swelling and drain the fluid. After the second day he felt confident that she was not going to lose it after all.

I stayed with her constantly as did Clovis and Judy. I was fortunate enough to be awake with her in her room when she came out of her coma in the very early morning. Clasping her hand in mine and running the palm of my other hand over her brow and through her hair she managed to find enough strength to smile. I couldn't restrain the tears of joy that poured down my cheeks or the sobbing that gripped at my throat. My prayers had been answered, and even to this day I cannot remember a moment in my life where I felt such deep, profound gratitude.

During the two weeks of recovery, I continued to stay with Wren. Mark had gone home to recover there. Dad and Will had called a wrecker to retrieve my truck from the Missouri Breaks and took the liberty of taking it to a body shop to repair the damage it received during our attempt to escape. They also drove up to the Belden Ranch to attend to the chores. Clovis provided a list of things for them to look after and was very grateful that they were willing to do so.

The Montana National Guard took care of removing the men who had lost their lives during this brief conflict. North Vietnam denied any knowledge or involvement in the Lee Brothers conspiracy, and as far as they were concerned, they did not care what the United States did with their bodies or with the bodies of anyone who was directly connected to them in any way.

Although still not fully recovered, Wren was ready to go home after two weeks. The speed of recovery was unprecedented to the point of being miraculous. The doctors who provided for her care were astounded by her progress.

Clovis and Judy drove her back to their ranch. I told her that I would come up and visit in a few days, figuring that she needed more rest and time to recuperate. She didn't really like the idea very much, but she also knew that it was probably for the best, and I had some things I needed to tend to back on the ranch.

CHAPTER 22

Knowing that Wren would need a great deal of rest, I stayed home with Mom and Dad for the next week and a half. There were plenty of chores that I needed to finish before winter set in. Dad, Will and I worked together to get them finished. Mark spent most of his time trying to recover. While he was able to get around all right, his breathing was labored, and he struggled to exert himself. We managed to get along without him. Just a little more than a week from returning home, the weather and timing were perfect for mending fences. The three of us were riding fence and making sure that there were no breaks, and everything was ready to move the cattle further down out of the high country for the winter. As I rode Bella, my Appaloosa mare, along the fence line, we crested a small knoll where I pulled her up short to an abrupt halt.

Staring down into the dusty soil, a portion of an old cattle trail, I noticed a fresh boot print. Letting my eyes scan the naked grassy plains that surrounded me, I could not see anyone or anything that would arouse suspicion, and yet inwardly, that sixth sense that I have come to believe is real, kept telling me that someone was watching me, and perhaps danger was near. I could feel the hair standing up on the back of my neck.

Dismounting Bella, reins in hand, I knelt to examine the track with greater scrutiny. The track was fresh, crisp and clean along the edges with no sign of wind-blown dust. It was made by a hiking boot, size 6-7, so obviously made by a small man or perhaps a woman.

Looking for other clues to the maker of these tracks, I noticed a patch of dry, brown prairie grass matted down next to a rock. Walking over to the rock, I examined it too more closely. Someone had sat here, and it appeared that the person may have actually been here more than once. Sitting in the exact same place as the maker had sat, I tried to acquire the same view the trespasser would have. Immediately, it became obvious. The old homestead house that Dad had given to me was directly ahead about half a mile. A person with a good pair of binoculars or a spotting scope could easily sit here and watch everything down at the ranch house below. Shivers ran up my spine as I considered what this might mean.

"Who could it be?" I wondered. The only person I knew that really wanted me dead, Kirby's brother, was supposed to be in a maximum security prison and was not up for parole for nearly a year. Maybe it was just a hunter who had managed to trespass off of public property on to our ranch. I really did not know nor could I surmise a logical explanation.

Sitting there contemplating the meaning of the tracks, I noticed Bella lower her head next to my hip. At first, I thought that she was just demonstrating her impatience or wanting me to scratch her ears, but then I noticed that she was sniffing at something at the edge of the rock that I was leaning against.

Looking down I recognized the objects of her attention. Cigarette butts had been stuffed under the ledge of the rock. As I raked them out from under the rock, it was obvious that some of them were older than the others, meaning that my first assumption was correct. This place had been visited on more than one occasion. Someone had been sitting here observing the old homestead.

Still feeling as though someone was watching, I tried to let my eyes scan the area to see if I could locate anything remotely out of place, without giving off the appearance of being suspicious. Again, I could not. Still, the feeling of being watched haunted me and even seemed to intensify. Perhaps I was just being paranoid, but I didn't think so. Caution was in order. My gut feeling kept telling me that something was amiss, but I couldn't identify the reason. Bella showed no indication of noticing something out of place, so I really thought I was just letting my imagination get the best of me. Suddenly, it dawned on me that Dad and Will were just over the ridge mending fence. Perhaps it was they who were in danger rather than me.

Grabbing the horn, I swung into the saddle, laid my spurs into Bella's flank and charged out of there like the devil was after my soul. Bella sensed the urgency and practically seemed to float upon the wind as I pointed her toward Dad and Will.

"Go, go, go." I ordered Bella, whose ears twitched at the command of my voice, and her legs responded to a speed that I do not believe she had ever before demonstrated.

As we crested the top of the hill, I could see Dad and Will working on the fence about half a mile away straight in front of Bella and me. To my right, a person was lying in a prone position, rifle in hand, and pointed in their direction. I had no idea who it was, and it didn't matter. It was rather obvious that person was up to no good.

Wrapping the reins around the saddle horn, still in full flight, I reached for my lever action Winchester and pulled it from the scabbard and chambered a round, firing at the person as Bella and I charged forward.

Although the distance was too far for my rifle to make an accurate shot, the report of the muzzle blast from my rifle distracted and thwarted the person's plans to shoot Dad and Will. As the shooter rolled over and turned toward my direction, I immediately recognized that the individual was a woman. Without hesitation she raised the barrel of her rifle aiming directly at me. Still charging Bella straight toward the woman, I was working the old Winchester and firing as fast as I could, hoping to create enough fear in her to cause her to miss. Expecting to catch a bullet at any moment, Bella and I were quickly closing the distance between us.

Her rifle reported twice. I am uncertain what happened to the first shot, but the second clipped the left side of Bella's neck and burned across my left bicep. As I saw her working the action on her rifle, I knew that we were close enough now that she would not likely miss. Slamming Bella to a sudden stop, I raised my Winchester to my shoulder, perhaps a split-second before she brought her own rifle to bear again, and I fired.

The bullet slammed into her chest and rolled her into the sparse, brown prairie grass.

Pausing for a moment to determine if the threat of danger had been extinguished, I nudged Bella closer.

As she lay flat on her back, I could see the massive blood stain on the front of her camouflage jacket. She was still breathing. As she fought for her last breath, and life began to leave her body, she revealed her pallid face and her Vietnamese identity. Dismounting Bella, I slowly stepped forward, my Winchester in hand, ready for use if needed. Her rifle was out of reach as I slowly approached her. As I stood over her, her glassy eyes looked up into mine while frothy blood oozed from the corners of her lips.

"I am the last." She stated softly. "You have killed my family. I..." She never finished.

I would later learn that she was the youngest child of the Lee family and had been the venomous fang of hatred that urged her brothers to seek vengeance toward Clovis for the death of their father. She had tried to finish what her brothers could not. Why she started with my family instead of Clovis, I never have figured out.

As I stood there, I could not help but wonder again if marrying Wren would continue to expose the lives of my own family to danger and peril somewhere in the future. How many, I pondered, still desired to see Clovis dead. To my understanding, there was still a million-dollar bounty on his head. Would there be others who would try to collect? Even my own life had a claim staked on it by Kirby Nation's brother, Karl. I prayed he would never be released from prison.

Caught up in the trance of my own thoughts, I did not even hear

Dad or Will approaching.

"Ross, are you all right?" Dad asked.

Startled by the sound of his voice, I turned quickly, "Yes, I'm all right." Looking back at the dead woman lying on the ground, I stated, "I've never killed a woman before."

"Son, you saved the life of both Will and me. A woman can squeeze a trigger just as easily as a man."

"Who was she?" Will asked.

"I think she was the sister of the Lee Brothers." I answered. "She said that she was the last of the family," I stated, still not feeling comfortable with the fact that I had been forced to kill her. Even though I had no choice but to kill or be killed or allow her to kill my father or my brother, something still tore at my soul. It's not that I was cold or callous about killing before. The men that I had killed in the Breaks, in my estimation, received what was coming to them, and killing Kirby Nations has never brought the first ounce of remorse to my heart, but for some reason, killing this woman, although unavoidable, struck a nerve that pierced me through and through. In the years to come, after much contemplation, I finally concluded that the part that bothered me the most had nothing to do with the fact that she was a woman, but that I had completely brought to an end the bloodline of such a long heritage. I would learn for myself many years later a little of what that meant.

"Let me look at that arm." Dad proposed as he took my arm and rolled up my sleeve. There was a certain gentleness about the way he did it that I had never noticed before.

"Dad, how many times have you looked at someone's wounds or injuries?" I asked.

Dad chuckled, "I don't have a clue. There were many times during the war when I had to jump out of my helicopter and help a soldier inside or gather up a missing limb, or compress a wound to keep a man from bleeding to death. Why do you ask?"

"Oh, it just occurred to me that you have many times assisted me with a cut or injury in my life as I was growing up, but not until now did I ever realize just how good you are at it."

Dad removed the bandana from his neck and wiped off the blood from around the wound. "Yup, I know my way around emergency medical treatment." Looking at the wound one last time, he stated, "You'll be all right. We'll clean it up more when we get back to the house. Let's take a look at Bella."

Bella's wound was superficial and really not as severe as my own. We decided to head back to the old homestead and call the authorities to report the incident.

On the morning of October 23rd, I got in my truck just as the sun was starting to rise in the east. A light blanket of new snow covered the ranch. Dad stepped out from the ranch house, donning his jacket as he walked toward my truck.

"I'm guessing that this is the day?" He asked with a big smile on his face.

"Yes, Sir, today is the day." I answered. I was as proud as a peacock and as nervous as a cat on a hot tin roof all at the same time.

Dad chuckled, "Well, it's about time."

"Yes, Sir, I'd say you're right. I'll see you in a couple of days." I replied as I started to put the truck into gear.

"Ross, I'm proud of you Son. Good luck."

Clovis was feeding his cows when I pulled into the driveway nearly 4 hours later. The snow had already melted, and it looked like it was going to be a beautiful autumn day. I got out of the truck and helped Clovis finish up with his chores.

"So, this is the day, huh?" He asked. "The day for what?" I asked.

"Son, I wasn't born yesterday. You're walking around here like a man with a mission, and that smile on your face and bounce in your step pretty much tell me what you've got on your mind."

"So, it's that obvious?" I inquired.

Clovis just laughed. "How about a cup of coffee? I'll go wake up Kelly Wren."

Wren arrived at the table where I sat sipping coffee with Clovis

217

and Judy, and she pulled up a seat to join us after giving me a big squeeze and a wet soft kiss. She looked as pretty as the sparkling dew of an early morning Montana sunrise. The ten days we had been apart seemed like forever. Yes, today would be the day I would ask her to marry me.

"I was wondering if you were up for a ride. I thought we might pack a lunch and ride up to the Sun River and have a nice picnic there, if you are up to it?"

Wren's eyes sparkled. "That sounds wonderful. I'll go get ready."

Judy smiled at me and glanced over at Clovis. If what I had on my mind was so obvious to both of them, I wondered if Wren also knew? I guess it didn't matter.

"Ross, I'll help you saddle up a couple horses. I had to purchase some new stock since those guys killed my others." Clovis stated. "Does Judy need to put together a lunch for the two of you?"

"No, Sir, I've got it packed in my saddlebags. I'll grab them out of the truck."

I really don't know how long it took us to get to the river, but our ride together was fabulous. We laughed and talked and giggled and just had the best time either of us could remember. I was completely comfortable with Wren. It appeared that her strength had returned to her, and her spirits were high. That day continues to be one of my finest memories, although there would be many more to come.

Arriving at the river, I found a soft, sunny, grassy place, tucked up under the shade of a large ponderosa pine. Here we dismounted and put a blanket on the ground and got a fire going where I prepared rib eye steaks, baked potatoes, corn, beans and a bottle of huckleberry wine.

When our picnic lunch was over, we lay back on the blanket and enjoyed the afternoon sun. With my left arm under the back of Wren's neck as she lay by my side, we stared into the endless blue Montana sky. It was a beautiful day indeed. Subtly pulling the ring from out of my shirt pocket, I turned and looked into her eyes. "Wren, will you…" the sound of a heavy bullet striking flesh stopped my proposal in mid-sentence.

ABOUT THE AUTHOR

J. Allan Smith was raised in the Rocky Mountains of Colorado and Montana where he developed a passion for the mountains and their splendor. Now, he and his wife Vicky reside on a farm in Middle Tennessee and are both actively involved in education and the church. Together, they enjoy working on their farm and peaceful country living.

Look for
Clovis Belden's
Return in:

ALONE
ON
THE
SUN

Volume Three in the Series

Made in the USA
Columbia, SC
15 December 2017